SCENES FROM THE
LIFE OF
CLEOPATRA

SCENES FROM THE LIFE OF

CLEOPATRA

by

MARY BUTTS

THE ECCO PRESS

NEW YORK

TO

BETTY MONTGOMERY

Amicae delectissimae

CONTENTS

PART I

CONTENTS

PART III

PART I

I

In the year 332 B.C. a short line of galleys might have been seen, sailing in-shore from mouth to mouth across the Delta of the Nile. Sailing from East to West, from the port of Naucratis, hugging the coast; and at the poop of the leading ship a group of young men stared at the shore. From time to time they scratched its appearance on their tablets, and leaning upon one another's shoulders, compared results. More than once one whom they called Nearchos, the only one who wore his young beard cut short like a seaman, put off in a dinghy and trudged the beaches; or, mounting the ledge of rock which divided the sand from the true earth, stared across the country at his feet.

This went on for days. A wind from the north-east, pure and strong, filled their sails. A watcher on the bare, bright, palm-fringed shore would have seen, as in lovely miniature down the wrong end of a glass, that this was some sort of a Coming.

When human life breaks in upon the unhindered patterns of Nature, when things are about to happen that have never happened before, at the Turn of the Event, not one pair of eyes in a million has the luck to know what is up. Only this time the watcher—a man setting nets for fish round the shore of Lake Mareotis, would have seen in detail, so sharp, so staged

3

that it must have carried significance, that here was a Coming of men who were to make something happen that had never happened before: that has never ceased to happen since: adding enormously and incalculably to the Instrument with which men play upon nature and upon themselves. On the empty african shore, on the spur of rock between Lake Mareotis and the sea, western man, in one of his spells of incomparable activity, was about to break in. The galleys were part of the macedonian-greek fleet, commanded by Nearchos for the young Alexander; straight from the siege of Tyre and welcomed in Egypt not as conquerors but as deliverers, by a kingdom which, though in weakness and subjection, knew itself imperishable, the giver of sanctities, the most ancient throne on earth.

To the oar-thresh and the light thunder in the cordage, life was tuning in. The watcher said: "There go lords-at-sea"; and staring at the first ship under its hollow purple sail, saw on the poop a bare-headed young man in gold armour, unhelmeted, his tawny hair unbound. Also that they who were with him were also very young.

When the dinghy pulled in, he hid himself in the reeds. More from shyness than from fear, for he had heard what was happening; how the Hellenes, or some people next door to them, had turned the Persians neck and crop out of Egypt; the Persians who for more than a century had made the land a satrapy. Under Cambyses, a hell. They had not forgotten. The Hellenes were a familiar folk and welcome once they had learned

4

not to steal the holy cats. The Pharaohs in days gone
by had thought nothing of calling them in to do some
extra fighting. Now there was no Pharaoh, no Glitter-
ing Sparrow-Hawk, Divine-by-His-Diadems, to whom a
man could pray; and the Hellenes had come back without being asked. Fun to see the Persians skip. The
Priests had been telling this Alexander, this man from
Macedonia, that the God Amen was pleased with
him, had accepted him for His Son. And there were
rumours flying that said the young men had told him to
cut it out; and another that Alexander had gone one
better and said he was the God himself. Anyhow there
are times in the life of a man or a nation when things
have gone so badly that no change can be for the worse.

The sun set between Lake Mareotis and the sea.
The galleys sailed on into the flood-light, not the slow
decline, the shimmerings, the cloud-firings of the
Atlantic, but into a blare and a clap of sunset and the
instant leaping-out of the stars. Overhead the uncount-
able fire-points shook their spears. Already the galleys
were invisible, swallowed instantly by the night and the
sea. Not for long. Soon the watcher made out, not
in the least like stars, rolling a little with the sea-pulse,
their riding-lights.

.   .   .   .   .

Sixty years later, the watcher and the solitary setter
of fish-traps had founded a family of happy market-
gardeners, suppliers of fruit and fresh vegetables to the
young, the gay, the inconceivably glorious City that had

5

begun to rise within a year of the passing of those galleys, on and behind the spur of rock between the lake and the sea. From the East to the West, from dawn to dark, from the beginning to the end ran the spine of the City, from the Gate of the Sun to the Gate of the Moon, the Canopic Way.

Most cities are content with one main street, as though it were a stream and its buildings the trees standing along the banks. But Alexandria sprang new-born from Alexander's brain and Dinocrates', his architect, in the shape of a cross. From the north to the south, from the Royal Harbour to the Lake, ran the street of the Soma. Street of his body; and where it divided the Canopic Way, there was his body also. Under marble; under gold; under glass. Under the body-mask of his armour, and over his face, a skin-mask of gold. He had come back to be buried there. There were other kings buried round him, but the place of the cross roads was called Soma, the Body; and up and down the Cross flowed, and still flows, the life of Alexandria. The life in those days of the Mediterranean Sea, of the known earth, of the first city in the world.

'*This is my body*' he might have said. His body perhaps, or his mind, but hardly his spirit, 'in the heroic chaos of whose heart contended all things that can and that cannot be.'

The concern of Alexandria, at least down to that era we date as the beginning of our own, was most definitely with what man can actually be. There all the delights that keep our feet planted in the earth

6

flourished under kings equally amiable, ferocious and intelligent, above all as representative of their mixed people, as it is given kings to be. Not perhaps at first. For during the first three reigns, reigns of the Ptolemaic Pharaohs, last Pharaohs of all the Pharaohs of Egypt, it is possible to hear another pulse beating. Pulse of an earlier world, with a dawn-light still on it, and a touch of mist distilled from an earlier dew. Dew that had last fallen on Alexander's head, then dried up off the earth. Left us the earth we know. The earth of the Roman Empire. The earth of gradually accumulating knowledge; an earth where the worth of the individual had dwindled—until chaos came again. So on through all the centuries; vigorous mornings, long afternoons, exquisite evenings, terrible nights. Every hour of historic weather—with particularly fine sunset effects. Only no dawn. Inspiring sunrises, but somehow dawn left out. *'The dew of thy birth is from the womb of the morning.'* Nothing like the birth of Hellas again.

While in the year 56 B.C., two hundred and sixty-seven years since that young man went on the little yachting-cruise with the Companions of his Body, the weather, a strong north-westerly wind, was blowing up from Rome.

II

GNÆUS POMPEIUS MAGNUS sat in his study on the Esquiline Hill, beating a tattoo with his paper-weight, a small sphinx very finely carved out of green stone. The tattoo, light and rhythmic, kept time to a meditation which finally broke out with the words: 'Blast those bloody Egyptians!' Coarser expression than he usually allowed himself, whose vanity as well as his inclination kept up the old Roman *gravitas* in an age when, except for ceremonial parade, men had forgotten what it had once meant.

He sat back, a superb, beautiful old tom-cat of a man, Pompey, the Great, one of those beings over whom the Muse of History has wept. Because he was a man who at the final throw, lost the game he played with life, because he was not quite great enough for what Destiny had up its sleeve; and also because it seemed necessary there should be a foil for such a man as Cæsar. Necessary too that he should be a man only a little less great, and in some ways a better man; in simplicity, in love of country and singleness of mind. Only a man who looks as though he had been put where he was to give another man his chance. Yet Destiny gave Gnæus Pompeius a long run. It is only the miserable end, on a

8

strip of egyptian beach, that reminds us what life has up its sleeve—even for its darlings, for the men glory has crowned and calamity passed by.

Many successful soldiers are supposed to find matters outside their experience hard to understand. (Though this is no more than can be said for any other profession on earth.) But Gnæus Pompeius Magnus seems to have understood only a little less acutely than his rival and his colleague—young Caius Julius—not yet Cæsar—that they had come to a turning-point in the destinies of Rome. The high world-politics which were to bring him to his memorable end were by no means outside his grasp. If he favoured the aristocratic past, the land-owner and the countryman as against the city mob, he was not necessarily mistaken. His City had given birth to a generation of men, superb as we have learned to recog-nise certain essential forms of splendour, incomparable in statesmanship and war. Among whom there were none greater than Pompey—excepting one, and he was unique. While even Cæsar's murder is not like his murder. A certain innocence of mind not incompatible with high culture, personal luxury and devoted public service helped Pompey to his ruin; and when it came it was as though a piece of Rome had fallen off. At Cæsar's death as though the heavens had fallen. Yet at that moment he and Cæsar and Crassus the banker bestrode the earth, and its kings peeped out between their legs. While by every rickety throne the situation was pretty well understood; and equally that there was nothing on earth to be done about it.

9

Like a wave falling back a few feet to regather, Rome and her Empire were determining their final form. The Punic Wars were over, the unpoliced sea swept clean again, and this by the man tapping on the table with his egyptian toy. All Western Europe Rome was securing for herself, as a man takes something hitherto unused to fit it for his use, and eventually for its own use. In Italy she was established like a man in a fair inner room of his house. If Rome came as a wave, she remained as a wall; now she was turning to the East, and what thrones remained there were whispering, whispering and whimpering; and if brave, it was with despair; and if afraid, often with intelligence. On the whole, intelligent despair—despair of their survival as independent powers—filled the complex of kingdoms that lay away east of the Mediterranean. All the ancient principalities that ruled the islands and the lands north of the Bosphorus, beyond the Euxine, overlapping one another into Hither Asia, on the line of Alexander's arrow-flight, to the mountains where that arrow had turned, swung its way half-way home and into the Archer's breast. That would do for a frontier. Like a great beast with the head of a God, the Roman Genius stared out over Asia, determining what its kingdom, its power and its glory should be.

It had taken the pattern from a Greek, as it had taken and was to take many things. Now its mind was moving to execute its last turn, its final accomplishment. As far as the mountains and the sea that enclose India, the earth had been sealed with the delicate and lovely device of the Hellene. A stamp struck upon barbarism and culture alike. Now Rome's seal was raised to un-stamp that pattern—for the earth to become one place, under one law and one city; as a Greek had thought; as the Roman could execute. Let the little hellenised kings whimper and chatter! That some of them at least were weeping would have made Rome laugh, if she had trained herself to hear tears. When it was over, like a wise nurse, she would give them back their toys. Suppose the toys had been broken? Man is quick to make himself new things to play with. Suppose the roman signet not so lovely in device as the greek? Grant it, so that the blood-mixed wax sets clear.

Gnæus Pompeius Magnus was thinking out his version of those things. A flawless, exercised body lay back easily in its roman chair, the greying hair sprung off the wide skull like a vigorous plant in twist and spring and spiral, tipped by a light silver crest. His meditation led him to Egypt.

The old Flute-Player was at his tricks again. Tricks that made Pompey laugh with the rest of Rome, but what a creature to have in power over a land! The oldest land: the richest land: the land Rome had her eye on next.

They were waiting for the water to run out of the clock, the float to lie stranded in the glass of a nation. To be filled again from the roman fountain, whose waters should not cease to drip till the sun rose no more.

Which meant in effect keeping an eye on the Flute-Player, on Ptolemy, Pharaoh of Egypt, Ptolemy XIII,

Ptolemy Neos Dionysos, called by his exasperated subjects Aulêtês, the Piper. Born in doubtful legitimacy,
he had stuck on his throne somehow for a generation.
Yet he was the perfect type of the monarch who goes
too far: who is a little bit more than the most abject
or the most tolerant of his subjects can endure; who, if
he is not murdered and hangs on by sheer shamelessness
and sheer wits, brings a dynasty to an end. Yet, it must
be admitted, that better than any virtuous monarch, the
Flute-Player's eccentricities served Rome's turn. His
cruelties, his debts, his extravagances, his religious
peculiarities—idle, silly, acute, insane, yet not quite
unattractive—played into her hands; whose concern was
less with him than with the whole land of Egypt,
granary of half Europe, whose crown was Alexandria,
still the first city on earth, and Rome, in comparison,
a provincial capital, a little out of the way, and her
future a dark horse whose colour was just about to be
discerned. Or rather that there were riding out of her
three horses, a white, a black and a red.

In policy the Senate finessed. They were not quite
ready yet for Egypt. So when the Alexandrians kicked
the Flute-Player out, they put him back. Holding in
reserve what his predecessor had made—a will, leaving
the kingdom to the Senate and the Roman People. Given
them the will and changed his mind and asked for it
back, and made another will. (In the stir of those trans-
actions the original document got lost, could not finally
be produced when it was most wanted—at least not in a
valid form.) Meanwhile, when Aulêtês seized the throne,

they had made him buy his recognition to the tune of a million or so, replacing him after the rebellion; even leaving him a legion, which, left to amuse itself in Alexandria, turned into something completely unlike a roman legion and later was to give trouble alike to Romans and to Greeks.

Pompey grinned. Really, the whole business reminded him of the old nurse who had brought up the children of his family, the tumble of boys and girls, half-brothers and half-sisters, whom the roman quick-divorce laws brought together in one household; where the new baby might be by the Domina's last husband but one, and the one after it be born in another man's house. And it was often convenient for the most domestic-minded woman of the series to take the lot. Old Luba was a ruler in her own right: and what were her nursery-politics but a re-hearsal for great affairs? He could hear her—kind, crafty, experienced old thing, managing a spoilt child for its good, the peace of the household and her own conveni-ence. 'Now, Master Ptolemy, if you behave yourself you shall have it back. Nurse isn't angry, she's sorry you should tell so many lies. No, Nurse doesn't want to keep it. We've others to think of as well as ourselves. When you've learned that you'll have a better time, and stop giving people the fidgets. You can make me a nice present now, just to teach you to think of others, and later on we'll find out what's best to do.

'What do you want me to do *now*? Look after your rabbits when you've gone? That's a nice thing to ask of poor overworked Nannie. No, I don't say I won't,

13

but really, Master Ptolemy, what a lot of work you do make, to be sure. There, then, I will. I don't suppose the poor little things would get much to eat if I didn't. Little pets! You can see from their pretty eyes they're glad I'm here. *They* know what's good for them, with their mother gone and all, till they're old enough to look after themselves. Of course, if they were some rabbits I could mention, the bigger ones would eat the little ones up. Still, I don't suppose that sort of thing happens in *your* family——

'No, I won't have them about once they're grown, leaving their rabbit pills all over the place; and let's hope they'll have better manners than some people I could mention. Well, they say it's early training as does it. Now if you'd been my little boy, Master Ptolemy, from the start——'

The rabbits in question were Aulêtês's four children, heirs to the Upper and the Lower Land, the Blue Nile and the White. On the belly of the earth, the navel had shifted its place, slid down from Delphi past Athens to where the oldest of Rivers poured itself into the sea. The Sea—not the haunted plains of Ocean, but the sea a man can handle like a lover, perish in like a lover, master like a lover, cross and recross, handle as a man does a beloved body. There on the spur of rock between Lake Mareotis and the sea he had raised his city, last physical creation of the Hellene, last challenge, symbol, instrument, act of faith and will. Bulwark against the witless flow of blind being, the planless politics of the barbarian or of eastern man.

14

So, above all, the Flute-Player's children were heirs to this, to the Pharos and the Library, the Serapeum, Canopus and the Park of Pan; to the island palace called Antirhodes. To the Palace itself, to all the Canopic Way between the Gates of the Sun and Moon. Then —under stone and crystal and gold and spice-brittle flesh—heirs to the Soma, the Body. For in Alexandria he still lived, Alexander, but as though in antithesis. For its tough, witty, intelligent peoples, light-minded, with their feet never off the earth and their tongues never still in their heads, seem to have little to do with him. Those were not the people he would have thought of to inherit the city of Alexander-made-God. Yet, with their wit and their laughter, their thrift and their wealth, their tolerance and their hatreds, their learning and their delicate sensuality, more than any people or place on earth they kept some part of his work alive.

Now a Power which was a version of his concept of Power had its eye on the place. A Power nearer to him and less near.

Ptolemy Aulêtês, with more care and more sense than was expected of him, had left his four children to the guardianship of the Roman Senate, and particularly in the charge of Gnæus Pompeius Magnus, announcing the news to him by an embassy, with gifts. One of which was the little sphinx, very old, made of green stone, and now growing warm inside his powerful, confident fist.

It was just the kind of business that he foresaw might lead to endless trouble. The Piper was not likely to last much longer after the life he had led, and there would remain four brats. All his stock, all bad stock, each bent on poisoning the other. It was not like a private wardship. There would have to be some pretence, at least, at legality and the succession. Unless, of course, the Alexandrians got finally sick of the business and massacred the lot. Now that would settle things. Two boys and two girls. All still in the nursery. It might be possible to marry the girls off—to husbands who would stand no nonsense. Pompey had heard all about Ptolemaic queens. He knew about female ferocity when their men have grown soft and taken to art in palaces. Art was enough and a palace was enough, but palace-art—together they put an end to thrones. For the boys a training with the Legions would do no harm. They'd need it if they were to hold Egypt—he struck his thigh with the sphinx. He'd forgotten. In Egypt they married their sisters. The Lagidæ were no Egyptians—proud as Hades of their greek-macedonian fairness and their barbarian accent which had long become an elegance. All the same, they'd taken to brother and sister marriages. To the Roman that smelt a bit. Besides, who'd want to? Why, it made for bad morals to start a lad off like that. Horses though—. And he'd heard Julius say that if you wanted a marriage more binding than the *confarreatio*, he couldn't think of a better than to be handfasted to your own sister because you were a pair of gods; and you couldn't breed rightly, not for the kingdom, the power and the glory, by anyone else.

Those were the kind of thoughts he had, Caius Julius,

still away in Gaul. The Gods alone knew what he was about; a man, if you judged him in the field, the most roman of them all. If you judged him at board, or, as men said, in bed, the most greek Roman there had ever been.

Pompey was born too late to question the greek influence in roman national life. It was a generation and more too late to do anything about it; yet by now it was clear that it had its disadvantages. Scipio Africanus had begun it. No better man, but what had old Cato said—that Carthage must be done away with? There were moments when it was possible to wonder what would have happened if he had been able to say '*Athenae delendae sunt*'. Anyhow he'd been right about Carthage. Who in the world was a penny the worse that Carthage no longer existed, now Pompey had dealt with the pirates as a farmer deals in his garden with a wasp-year? He knew this—that the world with the Greeks out of it would be an easier thing for a Roman to handle. What had Julius said to that—and he wasn't drunk? Temperate man, like all these men-and-womanisers—that it would not be worth while to be a Roman and rule an earth with no Greeks in it? That he was tired of fighting in the West among barbarians; and that Pompey had had the best of it, flying the eagles at civilised human beings.

Caius Julius—Pompey's mind was far from Egypt now, turned on his colleague, rival, the most mysterious of all roman men. Mighty men Rome had bred in handfuls and was to breed, shrewd and honourable

17

men, fierce and cruel and power-hunting men, hardy
and brutal men; utterly devoted and God-and-City-
fearing men. But never before or after did she breed
anything greater than herself. Her sons were all aspects
of their Mother; what it was that Pompey suspected
in Julius was the secret of the double mind. Not the
common double mind which made men prefer first the
City to themselves, then themselves to the City; chop
and change, hunt with hare and hounds, sit on the fence,
and ultimately turn traitor either to City or to self. Until
the City turned on them, settled their hash. Pompey
knew that no such crude antitheses explained his friend.
Twy-minded—until his fortieth year no more than the
most affected, most elegant, most amiably-insolent of
aristocrats. Now with the tribes of Western Europe eating out of his hand. Able—O dear Gods—able, but what
lay behind it all? The sphinx in Pompey's hand might
be an image of the man, if you can imagine a sphinx as
anxious to answer questions as to ask them. A sphinx with
its talons filed and gilt, dressed in the finest linen, the
whitest wool. Clean as a cat, and like a cat in and out
of salons, and the beds of Senators, listening to what
women had to say. Being very tender about them.
Speaking Greek, as one of them had said, "rather better
than an Athenian." An amateur of all their ways. What
business had such a man to be another Scipio, another
Marius? Another Gnæus Pompeius? The ancient
question nagged at the great Roman—what did it mean
for a man to straddle opposing qualities as easily as he
sat a horse? Here was no mere eclecticism or dilettant-

18

ism, a delicate picking and choosing, or swaying from one side to the other as though under dual control. Why, the man lived his infernal contradictions, easily, generously, in his stride. He had told Pompey: "Any fool can take one side or another. It takes a whole man to take both——" This with his smile they all knew, at the same time thin-lipped and tender.

What followed Pompey understood enough to sense, if he could not state. What has happened to the man who rides the double horse of the soul, and in two directions at once? If only once, for an instant, he has had an experience beyond what is common to men. He also has become that which separates him from other men. Life is shown to us, projected, in pairs, contradictions. It is all choice between this and that, twin-opposites. A man who has resolved even one opposite has gone outside life as it is presented to us, with its before and after, its true and false, its dark and light, its acceptance and refusal, its here and there. Such men usually go about merrily, their secret a source of fear and distrust to others, sometimes of awe and love; and incidentally accounting for some of the great tragic crimes and deaths, executions and assassinations of history.

Caius Julius—it was by reason of this that he made his colleagues uneasy, his friends and his opponents in the great race for power. Already the group was forming that by some law of attraction shapes against such men; and the questions were being asked and not yet answered: "What is he?" "What has been done to him?" "What has he seen?" "What will he do to

19

us?" For such men can rarely explain themselves, at least in terms of men who have not seen what they have seen. For that answer must come out in an indirection. Such an indirection as the Oracle at Delphi had understood once, when the Pythian spoke in ambiguities, and the Kings of the East and West got answers that were more than they bargained for. Before hellenic genius had shot its bolt.

Caius Julius, if he knew what had happened to him, did not tell. The level eyes looked out and through men's skulls as though they were not there. Drew in their glance on whomsoever was speaking with ready sympathy, exquisite attention, polished wit. Then there were his armies, the Legions he played with as though upon an instrument, throwing their units about like a god at ball. Not, it seemed, with the solid calculation, the hurl and crash of Pompey's line of battle, but, as certain men who had followed his campaigns said, as though the body of each legionary were a note in the song of war; to be sung in part, in unison, but always in tune. That was why he found fighting barbarians in the West, with their tactics of charge, massacre, loot, flight, a bore. While his interest in those he had conquered bored his colleagues; his dream of a roman future on the plains of Gaul.

Caius Julius—to return with Pompey to what Rome wanted to know. When he returned again, what had he in his mind? What was he about to do, to the Senate and the Roman People? To Gnæus Pompeius Magnus, in whom, in a perfectly fatal combination, were mixed admiration of him with annoyance, contempt, affection, fear, a touch of worship, and more than a touch of mistrust; and his own matchless good sense and self-confidence for once a little misplaced.

He thrust back his splendid hair. (Caius Julius was growing bald; that light hair, fine as a child's, wears badly.) He could manage the Flute-Player. The old scoundrel was on his last legs, and he didn't suppose his brats had one between them to stand on. With all that inbreeding it stood to sense. Then the egyptian business would settle itself, and without the cost of one roman life. . . .

First Governor-General of Egypt—He'd take the job in his old age for the sake of the climate; and it would make a good setting for Cornelia to play the Governor's lady. With that library she'd have all the books she wanted, and their mathematicians could come and talk to her—the young wife he was so proud of. Whom the whole City was proud of. Not the one he'd had before, Julius' sister and darling, Julia. You don't get that sort of thing twice, and better not think of it when it's gone. Besides, he'd not done so badly this time even, in young Cornelia with her learning and her loyalty to him.

III

IN THE PALACE (I)

AT the same time, in Alexandria, in an upper room of the Palace, on the ledge of a window looking out across the Royal Harbour to the Pharos, a girl fourteen years old sat with her feet folded under her, an arm round one of the delicate pillars dividing the long windows, and looked out to sea.

She was small and rather fair, meagrely thin in her adolescence, her bare elbows pointed, her little knees showing sharp through her tunic's tight-drawn pleats. But the bones were exquisite; centuries of selective breeding had worked them into a small but perfect statement of what the human frame can be. There was promise too of strength, the blood-stream running almost visibly in the transparent body, as perfect as its proportions. Promise too of vigour, and later of a just perceptible rounding-out that would sweeten the whole without over-softening it. Promise too of an intelligence, insolent and witty, in the eyes that held already more than the candour of innocence. That candour was there—it was the lashes cancelled it, brushing the hollow under the eyes that a violet had brushed first. A girl to remind one of de Maupassant's 'Who first made one wonder if she had ever been a maid, and a moment

22

later if she would ever be anything else.'

Not all of Beauty's points were there. The lips' pure scarlet set a very little off the planes of the cheek. Such mouths get kissed and kiss again, but are those that count the kisses, keep them in a box for future reference. Nor had it been kissed yet, or the girl yet given a snap of her fingers for a kiss.

Her kisses, officially, would be those given in marriage to her younger brother, elder of the two boys, when on the Flute-Player's death they would be crowned together, Ptolemy XIV and Cleopatra VI; and the children he would get by her would inherit the land. That was how it was always done in their family, since they had ceased to be clan-chiefs, centuries before, up in Macedonia. Then, if anything happened to the boy, it would all have to be done again with the next brother, to a baby. And if anything happened to her, she would be replaced by Arsinoë, her sister; and everyone knew the kind of holy cat she was.

She pulled up a cushion, of blue leather stitched with silver masks, an old plaything in the Palace's nursery wing. Masks she had thought of as a baby to be old Lagid faces, grinning or frowning at you, Aunt Berenice and Grandfather Ptolemy-Lathyrus, fat silver heads of hair with horns twisting out, and silver teeth-studs grinning as though he had you in his mouth. Now she sat on it comfortably, her cheek against the cool moulding of the window-frame. Nurse had begun to lacquer her toe-nails, a clear jade-green, and she had on royal sandals, a little silver wing rising on each side of the foot, arched like wind-running Hermes, white as the foam of Aphrodite's bath. A court poet had just written some verses about them—verses that took on paper the shape of the goddess' sandals. Difficult to do, but the words had been rather stupid. Nurse too had been more reasonable lately, pinning up her hair at the back in close curls. Out of the way, and not down like a maid's before she gives her dolls to Artemis, or in Athens goes up to the Acropolis in a saffron robe, pretending to be a bear. A light circlet kept it in order, an alexandrian goldsmith's version of the Double Crown; motif of wing and dirk and serpent worked low across the brow and flat over the ears. Nurse still went on insisting: *always* to be dressed like a well-bred greek girl, not like those egyptian women, rings to the armpits and the other half of them showing. A silver cord held up the pleated lawn tunic under the tiny breasts; no wigs or rings or ribbons or earrings like those sunbaked hussies from up the River—strips of embroidery four inches wide from knee to navel called an apron; and the rest of them in a glass shift. She would have to dress like that once, though, when she was crowned: wear a great wig reeking with spices and a dress of the stuff you could see through, called 'woven air.' Carry magic: do magics. Be magic. Nurse would be in a fury, dressing her for that. Nurse said that Lagid brother and sister married because they were so holy that they could not have children except by one another. Cleopatra happened to know that that was not true. Besides, how could it be true? Men are only a kind of beast and there

24

are no holy beasts. Not holy in men's ways, anyhow. Only the image of a sanctity, or a carrier of it, whatever the Egyptians said. They couldn't make the Apis Bull make love like a man. Or not make love at all. A Greek wouldn't try. To a Greek her marriage would be unholy, evil magic, and lately it hadn't brought the Lagidæ much good. Only the priests, the egyptian priests from up Nile, from holy Thebes, said it was because her family had done it wrong—not treating themselves as though they *were* animals, and every other generation crossing out as the breeders do with beasts for stud; not observing the right abstinences and times for conjugation; just having one another till they were bored, and then going off with whomsoever they fancied next. Nor had queens lately come to much good in Alexandria. If queens there were going to stay queens, they must find some new way. Find what? The girl had not the least idea. Only that it was she who must find what had to be found. What good was Arsinoë with her catty piety——?

At that moment there came down the long gallery two young women. Of the same age as Cleopatra, playfellows of her childhood and now just promoted to be her women of honour, Charmian and Iras. Charmian, the child of an ancient egyptian house. Iras a Greek, daughter of a General whose family had a kind of hereditary attachment to the Lagidæ; and king in, king out, served them and the intricate policies of their house. While the family of Charmian hoped the girl would grow up into a sort of spy for native interests at court, a hope that the future was to treat as roughly as many parental hopes.

Meanwhile they both presented a perfect image of the double nature of the kingdom and the civilisation over which she was to rule, as they stood before her, the Egyptian and the Greek. Both in greek dress, at that court which before all things stressed its hellenic culture; and yet by some magic of policy or personality made itself, if not representative, at least tolerable to Egypt—Egypt, after its stupendous past, now going rapidly downhill. There had been native risings against the Lagidæ, ferociously suppressed or amiably adjusted as the occasion or the character of the ruler had determined. Until, centuries later, under Christianity, the question of egyptian nationalism was to come up again.

The two girls settled themselves on the floor at their mistress' feet, their chins on the low ledge of the window, their eyes like hers turned out to sea.

Dark blue roughened water, travelling with a strong wind, lifted itself at the foot of the Pharos in spray. *'The north wind that blows from Thrace.'* Below them the Royal Harbour lay unstirred. On the Pharos the bronze tritons shouted back at the sea through their horns. Below them again, moored to the Palace quay, the Royal barge floated, its gilt woodwork and its metal star-winking in the sun. Away to the west, divided from the Royal Harbour by the marble bar of the Heptastadion, the masts of the Western Harbour showed half the shipping of the earth standing out and in; loading and unloading; the fruits of the earth pouring out of the land and into it again.

Behind docks and harbours the City lay, colonnaded white, and drawn together at the Soma in a crown of bronze and gold. If, centuries later, speaking of Alexandria, now become a provincial city like a lady with a past, an arab poet said that he had worn there 'a garment of perfect pleasure,' what must it have been like in the last days of its earthly royalty? A Jocunda rather than a Melancholia 'to transcend all wit'; its hour already passed as Mistress of pure science, its hour of majesty passing and the spiritual City yet to build, still destiny saw to it that at the hour of change, of passing, of temporal defeat there should be a queen for that city and a city for that queen.

．　　　．　　　．　　　．　　　．

> "—*Think of me*
> *Upon your knee*
> *The boy for you*
> *The girl for me—*
> *Just me for you and you for me—*"

Iras whistled the contemporary version of that lyric. The three young ladies settled down to gossip; until Charmian, gravely observant, saw that Cleopatra had something on her mind.

"What is it?" she said. Then Iras: "Now we're your women of honour, is it rude to ask? D'you want us to be tactful and respectful? I shall want practice if you do——"

"No," said the girl. "I want you to listen, not because

I am your mistress, but because we have always spoken
of everything that is in our minds. Have neither of you
noticed what's happened? That I am now all but Queen.
Father can't last much longer. After that last party of
his in honour of the God, when he danced naked, and
fell down with more running down him than wine or
sweat. There was blood flowing. No, Ptolemy the
Piper is really turning into a God." (The esteem in
which her father was held was perfectly indicated in
her most pleasant voice, pure in enunciation, flexible
for cajolery or command; and one day to be tuned in
for passion; but now naïve and with the decision of a
child trained for power.) There was coming upon her
adolescence one of those moments when the human
organism assembles a multitude of its past experiences,
and finds them suddenly forced into significance; and
the child or man—for such moments need not become
fewer—advances a year's growth in an hour. So the life
of the imagination quickened in the being of the royal
child, leapt in her nerves, and broke through her lips
into speech.

She did not look at her women as she began, her
eyes still out to sea, where air-spun water beat on
marble, on the Pharos, the Eighth Wonder of the World.
The young voice spoke coldly:

"A long time ago we came down from the north and
made this place. (We did not think of it, but we made
it. I know who thought of it, but mine were the
people who made it come true.) Iras, your house helped
mine; and yours, Charmian, found us deliverers from

that age's world-bully, the Persians. Very glad the Egyptians were when we came and gave them to live in peace in their cities; and, though the last of their Pharaohs were dead, they soon found an Apis-bull to say that our house was from the Gods."

"Are you practising," said Iras, "for the rhetoric-master?" "Be quiet," said Charmian, "we are listening, Cleopatra. I know it is important. Go on." More and more she turned away from them, speaking to herself, to an audience of ghost-Lagidæ, from their palace-window to the earth. Small shoulder to small shoulder spanned light column to light column of coloured stone.

"My lord and ancestor, the first Ptolemy, made this City, at the will of his friend, the Hero, Alexander; he who not by birth only, but by his deeds on earth, was numbered, living, among the Gods." It still sounded rather like a lesson. Iras said:

"I don't believe you believe about the snake in Olympias' bed." Charmian looked grave.

"It wouldn't have happened *like* that." Cleopatra nodded at them.

"I know. Only the divine gets born somehow, and old Ptolemy's will was part of Alexander's will, which was part of the will of the gods. They called him Sotêr and this land's saviour, and his son's wife got her hair in the stars."

"Which bit of you," said Iras, "would you like to see there?" Cleopatra turned up the toes of her winged feet.

"The print of my sandal, I think. With little stars

29

at the edges to point the wings——" Then suddenly she cried out:

"It won't do any longer to think like that. They're no more than court-compliments now. The Lagidæ have to get their feet hard down on the earth again." Like a litany the tremendous names of her ancestors rolled off her tongue. "Sotêr, Philadelphus, Euergêtês, Philopator, Berenice, Epiphanes—. Think what we were when the Masters of Nature stood beside our throne, measuring the Earth and the orders of being, and raised for us the Pharos to light all ships, and made the Dioscuri to be praised of men——"

This was not the rhetoric-master. The two girls were silent.

—"What have we been doing since? The time came when my fathers started to booze in their palaces, swear and booze and play the king with a toy-box. While it was our mothers' turn to play Epiphanes, the God-made-Manifest, when the war-elephants ran screaming, and Arsinoë rode before the phalanx at Raphia with her hair for standard, and restored our frontier to Coelê-Syria and the Orontes.

—"Death came to her the same way as life, when the wall of fire walked in—the curtains, Agathocles and his wife soaked in pitch. She met the fire-wind as she met the wind in battle, and they went down roaring together in this very house."

Charmian said, "Tell us the rest again."

"Then the people took Epiphanes, her little son, on a horse, and led him all the Canopic Way to a throne in the Agora. They asked him what they should do to the man and the woman who had murdered his mother, and he cried. 'Shall we kill them?' they said. 'O please kill them,' he sobbed. And they took them and set them up naked and cut them in pieces. He was the first of us to take the blood-walk to the throne.

—"And ever since then our men have stayed snivelling in the Palace, snivelling and playing-off the kings of the earth as they played with dolls."

It was a not-unfair account of the lives of the later Ptolemies, who had discovered, and ceased to enjoy, the fact that life is full of uncertainties; not enough money, and too much: duties of state and possibilities of parties: mornings after banquets and risks of poison: that the world would not stay put, and even sex got a bore. Which led to revolted wives. They had begun to orientalise themselves, a process their City, unchangeably hellenised, resented. An impulse their queens resisted vehemently, occupying themselves with affairs of state: while egyptian custom put much of the authority into their hands. Egypt that was always trying to be Egypt again, never quite a full oriental monarchy on the lines of Persia or of India. Egypt for a thousand years examined by and examining the West. Egypt, because of its religion, particularly attached to the divine, every act of life being so many threads attaching men to the unseen. Yet with the Ptolemies a silence had fallen on Egypt proper, a silence behind which it was possible that a menace lay.

There was silence again as the girl still stared from

31

the window. It was evening. Soon the Pharos would be sending out its tower of fire, a signal to ships thirty miles out to sea. In her husky voice Charmian asked:

"O my lady, when one moon has wasted to a thread, another is born. What is your will for your House and your Double Crown?"

"My will? What use is it for me to talk about my will? When Ptolemy, my royal father, *bought* his throne and his title back from Rome. Bought it with a year's revenue. The king of Cyprus stabbed himself first. That is not the way either, but don't you understand? I shall reign—rule I dare hardly say—by their grace—grace of those boors and fighting farmers and promoted peasants no one outside Italy would ever have heard of if Carthage had known her business. They asked their loutish gods to please be so kind as to show them how to build ships, and once aboard hung over their gunwales, sick as cats; and now the world is to be properly grateful because the Carthage triremes no longer ride the seas, and some pirates are smoked out like wasps or hung up on crosses as if they were lions; when every ship that runs aground on Pharos belongs to us by right. Carthage kept the waters sweet enough. She had to for her own business.

—"See here, Charmian and Iras. What good is my father, with his debts and his music and his sprees he calls being one with Dionysos? One with the seamen on leave and Apollo Hermaphroditus is more like it! He's cadged all he can and cheated all he can; bought his title, which is *my* title. The earth is tired of him, the

32

earth has had her last laugh out of the Piper, who never paid for his fun. Instead, it is we who pay, his people and his children—pay for the royal comedian's free entertainment—with the slow roman farmer's grin for the last laugh. A grin I'll have off their faces if I die for it. And what am I? The last of the Lagidæ; and in me I know, by some trick of breeding the ancient blood runs pure. What have I? One brother, and he hates me. A second brother, and they should have sat on his face at birth. A sister who hates me, and whom I hate. If one of the two were good enough, I would bear him children to our House. For I think—and the world thinks—that we have only to wait. Those Romans began to rot when they left their farms and started to gorge on the good things they had not learned to enjoy. That we learned to enjoy when the first Lagos helped loot Persepolis. They have not spoiled us—oh, I see, you mean you think they have? But not all of us. They have not rotted me, nor the people who make up Alexandria. They only spoiled a few men the gods were tired of. What harm have they done me, the Treasures of our race? The rare, the elegant, the exquisite things only the great of soul know how to use, the gifts of Isis the Bride and gold-playing Aphrodite.

—"Let the Romans gorge themselves a few more years, till their bellies swell up and they fall into weariness and into childlessness. If we can fool them a little longer——"

"Which way," said Iras, "will the greek cat jump?"

"At least she is watching the same hole as Egypt's

holy cat," said her mistress sweetly, "for the roman rat to crawl out, dragging his belly. You wait—and I shall find what it is I have to do?"

Charmian and Iras sat on the floor, trying to judge the question, each in her separate way. Iras said nothing. It was Charmian who spoke at last.

"We will find out what this waiting means. We will make it come true," and leaning over, she kissed the sandal wing on her mistress' light foot.

IV

Iт is a long way from Larissa, it seemed to Pompey, from
the plains of horse-taming Thessaly. A long way to
Africa. To where a slow, immortal, most holy river
crawls through a waste of crocodile-haunted marshes to
the sea. There is almost peace—if you can call it peace,
emptiness and quiet—when you have lost the toss, come
down on the wrong side of the fence, backed the wrong
horse. When your heart's choice has turned—not so
much into a stone, as into a hollow nut, with a dry
worm in its dust.

'*The dice of God are always loaded.* You have been
wrong all the time, all your life: the splendid edifice of
your life was not a tower to stand fast for ever, but
one of those moveable things of wicker for sieges, pushed
along for cover for men creeping up behind it. Caius
Julius was not your fellow; you could never share
the earth between you, nor wear the Roman Genius for
star on both your foreheads. He was never your friend.
He had been waiting for this, working you, leaving you
to work yourself into the right position—for him to
destroy you. Butter the floor, wedge the sword-blade,
at just the right angle—so. The fellow will slip up
and spit himself. That was what he had been after, all

the time. Clever lot, the Julian Gens. I came from
no such house. None of their magic about me. I never
thought it would matter, but it's told in the end. Now
that little fellow's got the earth to himself.

—'Funny places things happen in. Who'd have thought
that those fields, outside Larissa, among the horses—
Pharsalia they call it—would see the end of Pompey the
Great? The soothsayers never spotted it. Not till we'd
fought did I know what a fight it had been, a fight that
wasn't a fight, and half my men running across to shake
his hand. The first time I'd ever fought *him*. I was
never a Roman to fight by choice with a Roman, but
when our comic battle joined, I tell you that I felt *him*
through it all, and what was in his mind. What he's
out for, and I was an old dog he was sorry he had to
kick.

—'But he'd kick as hard as he'd need to, all the same.
I wonder what he'll be up to now; what he thinks he'll
get out of it. How far he thinks Rome's weeping to
have *him* for master. Half the Senate would knife him
and the other half lend the knife. How much longer
will he last? He's got some great game up his sleeve,
something we're too weak-minded to hear about. Something he'd say has got to be done, and he the only man
on earth to do it. The Cæsar-touch. So, by your leave,
he'd better be getting on with it, since nobody else
will; and we'll all be so much better when it's done
that the Senate and the Roman People won't know
what to call themselves. They won't . . .

—'Give himself to Rome for a king, I'd say if anyone

36

were to ask me. No one will ask you for your opinion again, Gnæus. You be sure of that.

—'No, there's nothing inside me now, only a squeal like a leak in a trumpet; but I wish it hadn't happened for Cornelia's sake. She won't have it that I'm done. Not old enough to know when a man's finished or not. Got us all on board after the battle and every ship she could lay her hands on, and the cash and my papers and her jewels. Had me laid on a mattress—feels like the lid of my tomb—and sat beside me on deck and played her little lyre. Old songs about the ups and downs of heroes.

—'If I told Julius he was as big a fool as me, he'd only smile and say that wasn't the answer, not the part of the answer that mattered; and that what mattered was a secret between Rome's Genius and himself. And I'd agree. Be ready with a tear for him when his time comes. I haven't many for myself.

—'Steady, this north wind. Blowing us straight on Alexandria. Bubbles in our wake streaming away behind us, and the wind hurrying us as if we were racing the last of the stars. But we're not. They'll be down in Ocean, down in the sand or wheresoever it is they go, before ever we sight Pharos.

—'Cornelia didn't want us to make for Alexandria. Said there was no faith in the Flute-Player's son or in Achillas or Pothinos or any of that crowd. The ship-master over-talked her and I wish he hadn't. There was no strength left in Pompey to back up his own wife. Besides I've always done my best for Aulêtês' cubs; but-

37

toned 'em into their royal robes, shoved the elder pair on to their throne. We're not ready to eat Egypt yet; and the funny thing was the Flute-Player thought the world of his kids—loved their mother or some such thing. Made me swear by all the gods of Rome and Egypt and his own pet Dionysus that I'd stand by them. Not that I ever wanted to do anything else.

—'Rome'll be different when I'm gone and Cæsar has it all his own way. Though what he calls it is Nature having her way with him. There'll be some surprises though for the men who helped him there. He'd say he sharpened his ears and heard Nature telling secrets. I can't have done that, or I wouldn't be running for my life to see if a tuppence-ha'penny fifteen-year-old Pharaoh I smacked as a lad would be civil to me. If he isn't, I suppose we'd better make for Antioch. What about Herod? Cornelia could put him in her pocket.

—'I've been a fair husband to the best maid in Rome. Sweet and wise she's been, with her music and her philosophy and her delicate ways. She'd have done for my son, but she's been a dear comrade to me. A roman wife. There's something in that.

—'Glad though that it isn't my Julia—*his* sister, but that sort of thing doesn't happen twice to a man. She died, and a bit of even *his* heart was buried with her. Along with most of mine.

—'Mustn't maunder. It's near dawn; and it's to-day I must meet those people: remind the boy that I helped him to his crown and persuade him that the old dog still has a tooth left in his head. Forget I haven't a leg

38

to stand on; that I'm their natural enemy.

—'Not take Cornelia ashore, whatever she says. She'll be all right if she keeps clear at the start. If everything's lost, she'll save something, cash, papers, honour —my name perhaps. One of the people you can't take away from. *Anima naturaliter*—what is it? We haven't a name for it yet.

'What's that man at the mast-head crying?—"Pharos fire!" Dawn in an hour and I can feel it getting up. We'll soon put ashore and find out what's doing. Let's hope they won't be thinking of Hannibal. By Jove! It's much the same touch. We pressed *him* pretty hard. Let's hope they won't look at it in that way.

—'Wake up, sweetheart. Are you warm? Come in under your old husband's cloak. That's better. . . .

—'So I have to get shaved, do I? To meet those smart Egyptians. D'you mean to say you've got me a clean shirt? All right. I'll change. I believe we'd find you housekeeping in the middle of a battle—running round both sides with bandages and hot wine.

—'So Corax raced ahead, did he, from the start, and they know already we're here? They'll be coming along soon to say if they want us. Now I'll land first. I'll never have the face to tell the lies I must if you were there. And if I tell 'em right, we'll be sleeping in the Palace. I wanted it for you as its Governor's lady. We may have it yet.

—'Stop that nonsense, saying you brought me bad luck. D'you suppose I can't manage Achillas and Pothinos and Theodotus of Chios—a gippo general, a eunuch

39

and a court reciter? The boy's off somewhere, scrapping with his sister—the baggage my boy had an eye on once—leaving these gentry in charge. Bad luck again! Let's hear less about luck. Pompeius Magnus, his wife by his side, the noblest lass in Rome. . . .

—'So it's Pelusium we'll strike first, not Alexandria. Corax says the court's shifted there since the row began. Suppose he knows best, but I'd sooner have made straight for Pharos. . . . Not so far off, though. We'll be there to-night.

—'Not making much of a show about our arrival, are they? It's early yet, but I thought they'd send a brace of state elephants at least. One for you and one for me. In Egypt too, where the lasses have the same rights as the men. A few horsemen, and what might be a crowd, leaving the City. That must be Achillas in the fancy armour. Rides well. . . .

—'So, as the king's away, he's come to do the civil with a few of the guard. The regular procession is due in about an hour's time, when they've sobered up the elephant-keeper and found out where the royal coachman spent the night.

—'Right. So I'll be off first and get the most I can out of them. They're great boot-lickers, you know—with an extra tongue sometimes they keep in their cheek.

—'Child! Remember whom you're married to! What are these gips to me? What are you saying? *"No man's a free man in a tyrant's house?"* Cut out your friend Sophocles. Courage, I tell you. In an hour, Sweet!'

.   .   .   .   .

40

Cornelia stepped back from the bulwarks now he was gone, feeling her way backwards without looking, until her back touched the mast, looking at the shore and at the men gathered there, steadying herself an instant, her arms flung out. Sitting in the stern of the dinghy, his eyes also on the shore, his hands on the tiller ropes, her husband could not see her; who saw nothing but the shore and the men who were waiting for him there. She could only see the tall back in its creased tunic and the curled thatch of hair stirring in the wind. He was sitting a little bent and she knew he was reading over from the tablet on his knees the greek speech he had composed for young Ptolemy's benefit. She had made up most of it for him, and got it flattering and elegant. He was remembering her alterations, to the kind of compliment a boy likes; trying to get it right, and telling himself that a roman boy wouldn't have swallowed such stuff.

It was the last thing he would ever do. The last thing she would see him do. The last thing she would do for him. All but one thing. She had not brought him luck. She had not brought her young first husband luck. One she had loved terribly and one loyally. She had only brought herself luck. Why was that?

'Will it be made equal for me because I am to stand here and watch him die? Here I must stand and not move, knowing—until he is dead. He thought he had a grain of chance; but I knew. Then I must do only exactly what is proper for me to do.

—'Because I am a roman woman. I would rather be

41

that than any other sort of woman. Rather be that
than the wild young queen there with her mystery
and her passion. I've wanted sometimes to be like her,
like her and her brother, wheeling over one another
like two hawks. They said too she understands mathematics, which is what I care for, and the things of the
mind.

—'I have to see to what must be done: have to see we
get away safe and no more Romans are lost. Pay for my
luck. *After one Roman has been offered up.'*

Thinking had made her almost blind. When she
looked again it was still the back of Pompey that she
saw, as the small boat drew in. A group of men stood
on the beach. Some way off others could be seen arriving
from the town. She saw a riderless horse held by a
groom for Achillas who had dismounted. Of their own
convoy, the ship she was on stood nearest in-shore, with
the rest strung out behind, merchant-men and war
galleys, half-manned; all they had been able to get together, fretting like horses at the bridle to catch the
changed wind, now beginning to blow off the desert;
the rowers holding them steady. She saw the crews
hanging about, waiting to spring at the cordage and
hoist sail; knew the rowers, their hands already on the
oars.

'Quite right,' said her mind, and then that how most
of them were ready to cut and run now, before the
alexandrian fleet had the advantage of them. Pitch her
into the sea after Pompey, for that matter. No, not
quite yet. As much as hers their eyes were on the shore,

on the company gathering on the beach. On what was about to happen there. The dinghy had drawn in now by a rock at the shore's edge.

She saw him standing up. She could see a little group of them with Pompey between. He was on shore standing in Africa. She could see the men's legs dragging a little as they waded in the sand. That man Achillas had on gilt boots with high heels. He was coming to meet them. Voices travelled over the dancing dawn-pale sea. No words.

Cries too, of a crowd arriving, and something grey and moving which might be the state elephants. Perhaps it was all right, and in a few hours' time he and she would be riding on them into Alexandria. She had never ridden an elephant. Pompey had told her you could be elephant-sick. How awful to be ill on a state-entry. The awful songs the Alexandrians would make up about the roman matron who was sick on her elephant in the Canopic Way.

That must mean it was all right, those people; and a troop of horseback ahead of them with a standard. By midday they would be together again, remembering who they were. So much she would have to do for him. She would have to talk to the eunuch Pothinos, because they *must* be civil and Pompey could not stand eunuchs.

Alexandria. At last. She'd seen so little of the world. There would be the Library. And all the books in the world. That manuscript there was no copy of in Rome. She would ask Pothinos to get it——

43

Stop. Stop. Stop. It was happening. It was happening. They didn't mean the elephants. A groan rattled in her throat. Sweat drawn out of her by nothing in the dry breeze flooded the sockets of her eyes. She had seen a man go down on his knees and Pompey stoop forward to raise him. As he bent, another man had leaned across and stuck a sword into his back. Two more men had swords out. Tiny men doing small things very hard, like toys on strings, on an enormous beach that ran on round the earth. Toy men and only one man there who was not like a toy with something sticking out of his back. Achillas was sidling up on a cat-step in his gold boots, holding a sword too. Like a dancer. That is how you kill people.

'Ah, my husband, is that what you do when you are killed? You draw yourself up. You are very upright. Your back is like a tower. You are drawing up your mantle across your face, which is what a Roman Senator wears.

—'You are standing up. Because you are held upright by their swords. Propped up on cold iron sticks that cross inside your hot body and meet, and grind on one another. They have drawn them out, and still you stand, your back to me and to Rome. You have covered your face from the men with the red swords.

—'The blood is coming out now. There is red on your back. Red on the tower. It is all so quiet. Little waves slip-slapping; and a long way off I can hear a procession with drums and flutes.'

She looked about the ship. The men's hands were

44

stealing to the ropes. She nodded. The captain shouted an order, his voice choked.

The Tower. The Tower. It was swaying—it was falling—it was lying. Face down on the sand, a fallen tower and red.

The convoy turned on its course. The hot wind off Africa swung the ship over. Cornelia left the mast-head and reaching the stern, sat there. In mercy to her the captain would have led her away. "Not my mercy," she said slowly, "I must see what I have to see." She saw the three men with swords, as it were disputing with other men in the wordless play that needed no words. Men from the City, just come up. Last of all she could see that something was being done to the tower where it lay, something small and round taken off it and held up for everyone to see. 'Only that it is not the inward parts. It is not like after a sacrifice.' Then she saw that lying along at the edge of the sea-wash, the tower no longer looked so tall. Indeed it looked no longer like a tower, but like a red naked body, asprawl, and shorter by a head. A head? That was the round thing, capped with silver and running scarlet, that Pothinos the Eunuch had in his hands.

V

U P - R I V E R (I)

UP-RIVER, far up the Nile, a very different group of men were watching which way the cat and the wolf would jump. The Holy Cat of Egypt, the highly secular Cat of Alexandria, and the Roman Wolf. In holy Thebes, Thebes the Hundred-Gated, where for millennia in and out the sands of Egypt had been poured, as into a great glass whose grains were now running out.

For three hundred years now a store of hatred had been distilled there, distilled slowly, implacably, served out by the great priestly houses to the common people of Egypt, drop by drop, cup by cup. Distilled hatred of the Lagidæ, those foreigners, those half-Greeks, with their false Gods and their synthetic God and their light strangle-hold on the ancient land, which had known no such dominion since the days of the Hyskos, the Shepherd Kings.

Hatred served out with policy, and after a good crop of well-exploited grievances, with enough of it to make the common man drunk; and account for the native risings, each entirely unsuccessful, which disturbed many reigns of the Lagidæ.

A hatred which took the way of such hatreds: no

46

account of the Persians' insolent misgovernment the
Lagidæ had ended, nor that they had given Egypt a
line of Pharaohs and crowned women who had raised
Egypt to be a world power again; had given them at
the start at least three kings who had made her glorious—
and with a kind of glory unique in her history. A
hatred that took no account of anything, and least of all
of what was likely to replace them. Indifferent to services
rendered, to agriculture and to irrigation, to temple-
building and service and adornment; an effort at least
to placate, and even to understand and please. A common hate, taking the course of such hates, as impervious
to the claims of necessity as to affection, to common
gratitude as to common sense. With for slogan rage
at the Lagidæ's god-making, Serapis or Zeus-Osiris-
Aesculapius, with a touch of Dionysos, whose gigantic
figure had risen in the Serapeum, his alexandrian
house; and whose strange synthesis had managed to
become a god and a loved one; who had caught-on
as a new saint catches, a figure towards whom the
Alexandrian could direct his supplications, and to men
far off prove a friend.

A hatred that took the course of such hatred: indifferent that it could produce no native government
to replace the alien. A hate whose business was its hate.

It is said that you cannot go on hating all the time.
That is certainly true of most men. Nor would the
fellahin of Egypt have troubled much either way, so
long as there was *a* Pharaoh, and no magic happened
to interfere with *his* magic, the rising of the Nile. This

47

hate was grown and pressed out and served from a very
private vineyard, among huge pillars and in cool secret
rooms, at very private altars, at Thebes, among the
Priests of the Sun.

We know very little actually about this Priesthood,
surely one of the most amazing fusions of the spiritual
and temporal powers the world has ever seen. Before
history begins, they are; and once, a thousand years before, when their young king had entered so closely into
the divine presence as to tell them they were no longer
needed, they showed themselves stronger than their
king—stronger than God. Amenophis IV did not long
survive, but they did; and the funeral arrangements of
his successor show how far they were prepared to go on
behalf of the man who agreed with their notions about
God. As they smelt the earth before each Lagid's greek-
shod feet, they thought about the little wine-press of
their hate, whose product drop by drop should destroy
them. Destroy its distillers with it. It was that sort of hate.
With the Lagidæ went Egypt's last temporal greatness;
and only Alexandria built itself a spiritual city, realised
again that there are factors in the human soul above
the possession of power by Roman and Egyptian and
Greek.

Yet the hatred went on hating, until, from one point
of view, the very Gods of Egypt perished that it might
be preserved. And since early Orthodox Christianity
did not supply it with sufficient food, the Monophysite
heresy, working in with the tax-collector, ended roman
rule in North Africa; under mask of a movement of the

common people, betraying it to the Goths. Until finally Alexandria fell into arab hands; and with the city went the destruction of the Pharos and the house of the soul that under Plotinus and the early Fathers had been raised there. With Egypt lost to Rome, an arch was thrown down in the structure of civilisation, the western earth given back to the powers of chaos and old night. Then, for more than a thousand years, she is heard of no more. With the Nile valley for ditch, cracked voices singing to cracked lutes—the price of a hate?

Hatred—at Karnak, from a temple-palace of incomparable splendour. Hatred of a woman, of Cleopatra Philapator, Cleopatra VI, now queen, and at that instant exiled in Syria; chased out of Alexandria, as Pompey had learned, by her brother; and reacting to the treatment as might be expected in a woman of her house.

.   .   .   .   .

In isolation, in antiquity, with ceremonies reckoned by the moon; in privacy, in stillness, at a hidden shrine; before a God, secret to the priests, whose name was a secret from them—was evoked the destruction of her house.

With ceremonies like those of exorcism, ridding and avoidance, with stench for incense and spur-valerian burned, with invocation to the God on the hither side of his nature, and evocation of him in a shape of horror, ran the prayers.

Prayers that were spells, taking the powers of evil

49

determination in man's soul like a stone out of a box. A cold stone that must be warmed between the breasts till it split, and a cold worm drop to the navel and coil there.

Told before an altar locked and sealed three hundred years. Three hundred years, when a Persian had been shut out and a Lagid shut in.

Opened seven hundred years before to destroy a holy king, Amenophis IV in his chariot, his mouth on the lips of his queen.

Stone shut up on an altar, under a stone; cut with the word that is written on the other side of the moon.

The floor of the room, sealed three hundred years, written with scrolls, the intolerable words of the dust.

As at the altar a priest plucked out, sound by sound, the unspeakable Words of Power, plucking on a single string.

Singing while the oil of her consecration was wet, the undoing of the sacring of Cleopatra Lagos and her brother, the desecration of a Pharaoh, of the Brother and Sister, Body of Osiris, Body of Isis, who are two Gods and one.

Done by drumming, done by droning; sounds that unset, that unmake, that unlock, loosening the soul from the body, separating the will from the execution, the purpose from the desire.

'In the name of Sebek; by the ache of the bone-break in the neck of the Beast: Cleopatra Lagos, be uncrowned.

'By the chastity of Pasht: by the slashed breast: Cleopatra Lagos, be uncrowned!

'By the wings of Horus; by the drill of fire in the eye of the Blind Hawk, fly shrieking down the sky! Cleopatra Lagos, be uncrowned!

'By the sex of Isis and Osiris' lost sex, go seek for what cannot be got, unsandalled on the desert sand.

'Sand breed stones, stones breed crabs, crabs wax hot, as the bronze that upholds in Alexandria the pillar of your insolence. Crabs eat the flesh of your feet. Cleopatra Lagos, be uncrowned!

'Husband, lead her in chains—

'Lover, cut off her hair—

'Son, cut off her breasts——

'By the flick of the snake's whip and the prick of its pin—Cleopatra Lagos, be uncrowned!'

So it went, on the lips of men, who later were to take from the words of Christ the honey and the dew.

'. . . We have opened what was shut. We have warmed what was cold.

—'We have torn the red heart out of our living breast.

—'Cleopatra Lagos, be uncrowned!'

VI

OFF PHAROS

'DEAR me,' said Julius on his yacht, with a few war-galleys behind him, making brisk time for Pharos, 'I wonder what they are up to this time. Pompey getting me up a reception, no doubt. Have to quiet him down—tell him Pharsalia was an accident. Really, O Gods, when you start to help, your aid is sometimes more than one bargained for. Bargaining, yes. That's what we call religion mostly. I don't want "to pursue him with the furies of my resentment," as the actors say. Quite the contrary. Any final breach between us—let alone anything like private animosity, would go down very badly indeed at home—very badly indeed. Rome's two chief men "locked in fratricidal embrace"—dear me, no. I've got what I want, and for once policy goes hand in hand with inclination. I must shut us both up inside a metaphysical temple of Janus and hold hands.

—'Let's see, though—if it should come to fighting here at the start, how much money have I got with me? And whom shall we have to meet? Achillas the gippo—and that old legion that got left here in the Piper's day, Gabrinus' lot. Gone to seed, I've heard; but they'll stiffen the Alexandrians——

—'So the boy's off, fighting the girl. I suppose I had

52

better pop them both back on the throne and tell them not to do it again. Depends on what line Pompey's taking. Send in the bill for our expenses, anyhow. . . .

—'Mustn't plan too much. Don't know where I am yet. Can't know till I find Pompey. He comes first. I've got him where I want him. Now I must see his seat is well-cushioned——

—'O Rome, Rome—you are flying the eagles East, as a bird at the sun where his nest is. And I—I am a man before whom stood another man, between him and his mirror. Pompey hid me from the image of myself. Now there is nothing between me and my own image. What do I see there?—"Cæsar," as you call yourself now, you're getting on. They laugh at you for wearing your laurels to hide your bald top. But it's not for vanity. It's for swank. To show I've cheated Nature with the right to grow fresh green leaves each day. Not many bald-pates grow laurel instead.

—'And don't I need a holiday! Peace with old Pompey and then a rest. Just not clever enough or cynic enough to trust me straight away after that fool of a battle.

—'There is the whole earth, and just a little handful of men to tell it what to do. All those millions in Gaul, and Vercingetorix and me. After a bit there wasn't even Vercingetorix. Only me. And in Rome there were Pompey and Crassus and me. And again there is only me. And here there is a brother and a sister, and it looks as though there was still going to be a brother and a sister. And—perhaps incidentally—me. Looks as though I spent my time eliminating, and I'm a most affectionate

man. Friends by the score, but it's women who get
something of what it's all about. A nice young new
mistress is what I want, someone with a life before her.
Someone to show the ropes to, and get the best that there
is out of me.

—'I won't have it that we're in the grip of something
that has the last laugh at us. Not laugh. At least I
hold that they meant something when certain of the
Hellenes claimed an invisible Friend. . . .

—'Better not turn up in armour. Too like a victor.
Tact. Tact. Fair altarless Goddess, will a time ever
come when I need you no more? Not in your life,
Caius. Side-lights on history: *"Balbus, having rented the
fishing on the Rubicon, gently but firmly insists that
Julius Cæsar cross further down."* And I did. When I
don't, will men be savage enough to be brave enough
to murder me? There's a part of me resents it still. This
getting round of men—for their good and my good and
the good of the Senate and the Roman People. That's
to say, I suppose, for the good of mankind. . . .

—'I *am* on a holiday! Leaving my mind to play as
though I were a dolphin following in the wake of my
own ship. Look-out man, what's that? Pharos? (I see
myself spending the next few years, running to and fro
from here to Ostia and back.)

—'Straight for the Royal Harbour, captain. We can
land from there and deal with the town.

—'Coming out to meet me, are they? Looks unfriendly,
To your stations! Give the word.

—'And perhaps I'd better slip on some armour. Hades!

54

where's my batman? *Still* seasick? Caius Julius, they are not going to be nice to us. Pompey must have told them things.

—'Hullo, heralds, after all. That's a smart ship. That dandy Achillas and his crew of fancy-boys. They work her nicely. Now do I stand on the poop and yell and ask them their intentions? Or do I try and look as roman as possible and wait till I'm told? Depends if Pompey's on board. No, I don't see him. If he is, I shall lie on my back and wave my legs for joy. No, he's not——

—'They're drawing alongside us pretty close. Shouting's not the style. It's Achillas all right. Dear Gods. What a good-looking man. My type? I think so. . . .

—'Yes—I see what we must do. I don't think they've quite made up their minds and I'll have to do it for them. There's something they're not certain about—or —or—there's a surprise waiting for us.

—'*We* take the strong line. As usual. Land at the Western Harbour and tramp the Canopic Way, very firmly to the Palace. How often have we had to do this sort of thing?

—'Not in Gaul this time. Fate divides men's work unequally. My fighting done against savages, and for loot a barbarian's arm-rings. When the fighting was over, Pompey dined at the palace among ravishing girls and boys he didn't want; scents he couldn't smell, and women he'd no use for; who only loved my girl, Julia. Poor lass, how she'd have hated it—that this war should be between us. It was too hard for her, the life we're leading just now on earth. Suits me or I've made it

55

suit. It was out of pure gentle-heartedness she died, the little goose. I only knew what she meant once, when I saw the pirates crucified. She couldn't stand it, not so much the killing in hot blood, but the things we have to do to make what must be happen. Not the kind of thing I'm usually patient with, but she was mine. The closest kin I had.

—'No God of Reconciliation in Rome for her to pray to, she said. I can't say that I see quite what she meant by that. Something that wasn't Necessity, something of the Divine to include us all—her father and her husband, and Curio and Crassus, Dolabella and old Cato and young Clodius; Cicero and Catiline even. I suppose politics are not enough to divide men for ever. Or to unite them.

—'It's for her sake I'll do more—more than make it easy for the old man. I'll make it glorious. He can go back to Rome with all his honours. Antony'll keep him out of mischief.

—'Good gracious me—where have I been wandering? Keep your thoughts, Caius Julius, on what's ahead of you. You didn't leave Rome to run aground on alexandrian rocks. Rome—Rome——

—'Rome—I ought to be there, not here. "Consolidating my victory," as they say. Rome. I've had enough of you for a bit. Wolf-mother, I'll lead my own sort of life awhile. If I don't, I shan't be able to finish what I've begun. Antony must see to things there. The one man I can trust and it'll teach him.

—'I'm for Alexandria—a boy and girl tumbling one

56

another on and off a throne. Alexandria—new Gods, new faces, new sports, new vices, new thoughts. Alexandria—where Serapis holds the scales between the West and the East. Alexandria, on whose strings you can hear if you listen the last notes of the song of Hellas—not in Athens, pedantic little hole——

—'Alexandria—oh the ivory and the gold—*"Mistress that loves the heights of Golgi and Idalium and the high peak of Eryx, Aphrodite-who-plays-with-gold,"* give once again to Caius Julius, your servant, a measure of your favour and your delights.

—'Here we are and here we land. Official reception at the Western Harbour. State entry to the Palace from the Gate of the Moon.

—'So he wouldn't come out to meet me? Not a word about them till I've heard about him. Show how we Romans hang together.'

.   .   .   .   .

Pothinos the eunuch— (everything known about him sounds too like a eunuch to be true)—stood outside Cæsar's tent. On one hand a signet ring, of heavy gold; under his arm something the size of a melon, rolled in a stained and stinking cloth. Inside the tent a secretary was explaining that, in the young king's absence, he and Achillas, representing the government of Egypt, welcomed under conditions Caius Julius, the Roman, under his new titles of Cæsar and Imperator, and asked for an immediate audience.

The fat man moved swiftly and gracefully into the

57

presence of the lean, slight man, seated at a camp-table, in state armour, his helmet by his side; and round his head, over his fine, thinning hair, the chaplet his barber kept fresh with the utmost difficulty, in relays of leaves across the seas.

The eunuch sank to the earth. Cæsar inclined his head. The East made a gesture at the West. It was the moment for drama, as Pothinos saw, and had served it up; the man usually and by necessity forced to go round about to his point, strike at an angle, take the oblique view.

For once there was no need for that. The man who has killed another man's enemy has power over that man. Has put him under an obligation, and next time he may do the same thing to him. That is not the whole story, but it was all that Pothinos saw—that this time the man who was not a man, had taken more than manhood, life itself, from a man whose whole nature and actions had been an expression of supreme manhood.

It seems that only in the last century has an important part of the human race realised that the man whose manhood has been taken away takes to himself a revenge, elaborate and costly and insatiable. For since nothing can be restored, there can be no satisfaction and no redress; and the nature of the *castrato* is free to develop into a monster, his ego still ravenous however gorged.

Something like this explains the great tragic *castrati* of history, those masters of indirection, of cruelty, and luxury and intrigue; who, robbed of one thing, would make all other men beggars for that theft.

Yes, it was a moment in Pothinos' life as he rose to his feet in the stuffy shadows of the tent. (This Cæsar would soon see how long a eunuch need kneel.) He drew off the ring, unwrapped what he carried under his arm—(Achillas had wanted him to pitch it in through the open flap, to roll under the table at the Roman's feet). Street-boy trick. That was not the way.

Show what you have—do not throw. Just place gently. Right way up, so that the wide dead eyes meet those narrowed slits of living jelly; so that the eyes of the living Cæsar meet the eyes of the dead Pompey, his greatest enemy, once his greatest friend.

Good nerves, this Roman. He has not started; hardly stirred even. Puts out his hand. Only for the ring. Turning, he has it to his lips. Now he is looking at the head. He is not pretending not to weep.

"Take it away," he is saying, "old Roman, old adversary, old friend. Old lord of this our state—take it away, Pothinos. You have not done what you think you have done to me."

Now he is weeping, his scarlet across his face.

"Take it away, Pothinos. Now you can see to it that you give it an honourable grave."

'He cannot see me now for tears. Even when he is blind I should be afraid to look at what that man sees.'

59

VII

'CHARMIAN! Iras! Stop crying, you wet hens! Do you suppose I am the first queen in Egypt to endure this?'

The sea ran up and down the steps of a small landing-stage in a bay of the coast, thirty miles east of Alexandria; on a rainy night, cloud-low, the wind pushed its way through unpleasantly.

By the quay-side stood a building, usually empty but for stacks of oars and sails and lines and crab-pots, boat and fish-tackle, now a little displaced by a few rugs and pots of the royal ware, and bits of riding gear and boxes of state-papers, and court-sandals thrown into corners, for feet now changed into the rope-soled sailors' shoes for shore and ship-work.

A building that housed temporarily, and with a sporting chance that it would provide an exit to their eternal home, the young queen, two of her women and a dozen or so faithful friends. Faithful at least to the point of disliking Achillas, Pothinos and their young king more than their queen. Relic of a considerable army which, when chased out of the city by young Ptolemy, she had managed to raise. And equally managed to lose, in a pitched battle, where her troops considered that they would feel the sun less if they joined the other side. So it was the queen who had to run. First in her chariot, from which she had hoped to imitate her ancestress at Raphia; then on horseback; on a camel, in a litter, on foot. Though disappointed in her battle, she had rather enjoyed herself. It was almost the first time she had left Alexandria, who had been reared in a palace complete in itself as a small city and ideally healthy. Now she had seen something at least of the coast and the desert, places of raw nature man had left alone; a certain amount of peasant hut squalor and crocodiles in their marshes. Nothing of Achillas or Pothinos, Ptolemy or her Nurse.

She was now seventeen, in whose veins ran not one drop of eastern blood, young enough for the delights of a perfectly healthy body in arduous use. Too young not to enjoy the scramble or to believe that life could go against her, or that out of a rough and tumble world would not come the heart's desire.

Very lovely too were the odds and ends of court properties they had snatched up and brought with them. A silk carpet like a magic parterre for bare sandy feet, a transparent scarf embroidered with shells, a box for jewels of lapis and silver and rough pearl. A cup and dish for the queen of rock crystal, that Artemidorus, a young officer of the guard, filled with harsh wine and handed to her, as though it were a cup at the Mysteries; a silver headdress, the disk of the full moon between the horns of the new. These lay about on fish-crates used for tables, and stacked sails on which they

61

slept. A broken boat for the queen's bed. Then sails hung on a rope divided the place in two, one part where there was a fire for the queen, and in the other, behind the curtain, Artemidorus kept guard. The rest were disposed of round about in similar stowage sheds. All but the queen, her women and Artemidorus grumbled furiously. Charmian, who would have passed the days sitting on her heels and staring out into the desert, into the fire, or across the sea, wondered at this. If they four were happy, why not the others who had less to lose?

The other side of the sail-curtain, standing with his sword drawn, Artemidorus prayed. To all the Gods and Goddesses: that they would keep his mistress, give her back her crown: avenge her: glorify her: keep her a maid—not of course for ever, but as long as possible. The other side he could hear them laughing, gossiping, scolding; translated it into kingly anger, royal courage, words of daring and divine wit. Daring it was, for the girl had her plan and was telling it to Charmian and Iras. Also the best way to tell it to Artemidorus, who would have to do half of it—here their voices fell to whispers—make him see that it was a piece of royal policy. And a lark. This to the two girls who loved her, Iras for what was similar, Charmian for what was dissimilar in their natures.

"Do you want me to start reciting a list of my ancestresses who've been in the same sort of hole as this? What you have to *do* is to get me into something fit to wear. Something out of the rags we have here that will look as decent as possible. When I roll out of the carpet at that man's feet, I shall be frightened, I shall be hot. And I must seem what I am. This body of mine is all I've got——" The harsh wind ran in through the windows, swept the fire of damp wood out on to the tiles, raised smoke for them to swallow. It was most miserable. When she had done coughing she added:

"The Queen, don't you see, will fall out at his feet as a woman. She must be all the woman she can be. The woman who will fall out at his feet is a queen, and must have something for a queen to show.

—"Don't you—won't you see that it's the only way? Only this man Cæsar can make me a queen again. I cannot live and not be a queen——" The rain spat on the wretched fire over which six small hands were now thrust out. The draught ran three times round the room, found a place it liked and blew from there. Outside the sea slapped on the steps. Charmian who understood one half of what Cleopatra said and Iras the other heard her say again:

"Some women can rule in more ways than one. Be great I mean in secret or in their minds. But after my sacring I can only be great in the way I have been made. I am either Queen of Egypt, Isis-on-Earth, or no more than a sailor's harlot, running the quays. Now this Roman has come, to give orders in Alexandria, in my City, pick up my little brother and spouse—not that he can even do that—as you pick up a puppy to have a look at it and send it off with a kick when it makes a mess. That man! Great roman beast, back from the world's end, filthy with barbarian blood. Trampling our ancient delicacies—maybe he'll give Pothinos' back-side a kick. No, he won't. Pothinos did his dirty work. Put a sword through Pompey, his old friend, our most virtuous guardian——

—"But he hasn't come just to pat Pothinos on the head.

—"And it is to this man I must go, as a queen, as a maid; as one who must be given something, but who has everything to give. Sit on his knees. Flatter him. It is for this I was made exquisite. The passion and mystery of our House into a bit for a Roman to squeeze——"

Charmian cried out:

"Then you shan't go. Send me. Let him defile me."

"Or me," said Iras grimly, "as you say, 'who's to tell him the difference?'" "Besides," added Charmian, "Artemidorus won't let you. If we tell him——" But Cleopatra was on her feet, beating at them with her hands till Iras caught hold of her wrists. Then suddenly she began to cry, and Charmian flung herself into her arms, and the three girls stood, locked together, in the manner of three young goddesses, Korai, only weeping. As the draught spun round them and the smoke, they stood, their heads touching, united, separate, and especially separate, from the other half of the race of men.

Until the queen put them away from her gently, and said steadily and with a laugh:

"Don't you see that it's got to be done? Don't you

64

see that I must become that man's mistress as soon as possible? Don't you see also why I have to make him out the worst possible kind of man? I dare not hope he will not be like that. I have to know the worst that can happen to me.

—"If you told Artemidorus, he'd expect me to fall on his sword. It may come to that, but not yet. If my maid's body can queen me again, let it. That must go sometime, and this is better than Ptolemy's bed. Only I dare not hope. Only I dare do what I must do, and this man once unpolicied may set me again among the lords of the world.

—"Now find me what I've left to wear, and it mustn't crush——"

They found her a tunic of dark blue lawn, ironed into stiff pleats, that with luck would shake out into place and give her slight body an untouched, hieratic look. The moon circlet would do also; its horns were flexible, would bend back into a shape to hold her hair and could be straightened out. They found also the pair of sandals with silver wings, and a breast-girdle clasped in front by a great onyx bee; her royal signet with which she was married to Egypt, the rest of her hands left bare. Antimony they had and powder and vermilion for the lips. These hidden in a box in the pocket of the mantle, also of blue and without ornament of any kind.

Artemidorus was summoned, and told no more than was good for him, persuaded.

So, in a little smack, with him for steersman and

a pair of local sailors for crew, in the comfortless dawn, down the weed-oiled steps into the bitter wind—out on to a sea barren as the winter Atlantic, they shipped her on board; along with the great bale of carpet out of which she was to be unrolled at Cæsar's feet.

VIII

IN THE PALACE (II)

In Alexandria, in the Palace, at night, Caius Julius sat thinking; while round him a 'savage little civil war' ran its silly dangerous course. Rather as though a small animal maddened by some drug or let loose in furious pain were dashing this way and that, with its wits gone, and as likely to destroy itself as anyone else. But equally dangerous to friend or foe. To an arbitrator, as he had thought himself, between the two parties, an entire nuisance; especially to a man who had come there for amusement, not for a situation which had nothing to do with him and which was getting on his nerves.

Besieged as he was in the Palace, with insufficient men and not enough ships, and no prospect of help save from his own sharp wits—in the middle of it all the Julian luck held and the Gods had sent him a present.

Sent him an actual goddess, Isis. Aphrodite-on-earth, not the 'divine Julius' as he had lately thought it politic to advertise himself in near-Asia, but born it. To her subjects a creature who was a physical incarnation of the Deity, Our Lady of Earth and Heaven, Mother of men and Gods. Not 'Herself,' of course, but Her representa-

67

tive, an idea of Her made flesh, a being endowed with Her mana; and for once something adequate as a form of physical statement, and with also a share of that element, not capricious as one would call it in a mortal, but incalculable as becomes a divine being.

Cæsar had heard of such divine—not in one sense holy—kings. For Rome it was a piece of mixed luck that when her greatness came she was a sort of *tabula rasa* on which her conquered could write what spiritual ideas they would. Cæsar was about to make himself one of these semi-divinities, on the late greek model, a sort of daimon or incarnation of his own fortune and genius. And he knew that among such beings the prestige of the Pharaoh of Egypt stood highest, who for un-counted ages had shown the world how man can be man and immortal man, god, priest and mortal ruler in one.

Now one of them had turned up in a bale of carpet at his feet. '*Like the sweet apple*'—not yet quite sweet; unpicked fruit with a tang to it. Her fierce, haughty, quite unpractised attempt at seduction he had nearly ruined by laughing; then felt something like pique. She thought of a Roman Senator as a kind of savage, did she? Then he saw what he was offered, responded gravely: saying that two divine beings, two rulers of more than half the earth, one a man practised in the technique of love, and one a maid: in a palace, hard-pressed by their enemies, in a tight corner in fact, might just as well delight themselves and generate mana for victory by having a romp in bed. If Her Magic of

68

Egypt would so far condescend, he was sure the result
would be propitious.

Five minutes later he had her laughing, a most lovely
laugh, he thought. Half an hour later they were lying
on the state Bed of Egypt, not in use since Berenice
her half-sister's day with Archelaus of Comana. A bed
that was really a room, with large gold statues round
it of all the Gods of Egypt and some special fancies of
the late Ptolemies. Including several highly unconven-
tional aspects of Dionysos and Aphrodite Pandemos.
They laughed. Then she whispered to him the highly
personal offering he must make. And then he found
that he had to undress her, who had never before undressed herself; and—since they were living in a place
under siege—more than once an orderly forgot and
thundered at the door.

She slept beside him, her transparent shift torn open
to her waist, flung down on her side like an exquisite
wild animal in a net. Cæsar watched. This was what
he had wanted. This the Gods had flung to him. Cæsar
and the Egyptians' Queen, two ephemera of eternity,
thrown down one to the other. A gift granted, an answer
to something like prayer. Casually granted, or was there
some purpose? His mouth hardened while his eyes grew
bright. 'Mine be the purpose, anyhow,' said his soul,
speaking suddenly, as it realised that, Gods or no Gods,
something could be made of this. This just-made
woman, this royal creature—he would have the training of her for more than vanity or ambition even or a
sop to passion. 'I believe I've done it again,' he said,

69

smiling, 'and Cæsar's last work shall be his last woman. And his best.'

—'After war, I make magic. What is such a coupling as ours but magic? If it is not, it is nothing. Cæsar and the Pharaoh of Egypt. Rome, Hellas and the East. Here is something begun that will have no common end.'

Thoughts of Cæsar in the night-watches. Round them stared the gold faces, yellow, smiling, equivocal masks. With Serapis, Dionysos, Aphrodite up to larks. When she shivered—the embroidered state bedclothes were scratchy and she lay outside them on the coverlid, her body upon the pale embroidered nakedness of Isis the Goddess—he took off his general's cloak and laid its scarlet over her.

．　　　．　　　．　　　．　　　．

It was morning. Profoundly rested, he watched her wake, the dew of sleep on her pure skin. She came back from the bathroom, damp; and he pulled her tunic on over her head, and she set on the little moon-crown to confine her hair. And when she thought he was not looking, it amused him to see her tear a strip from her shift and lay the scrap of white and scarlet-stained linen before the statue of Aphrodite, between her feet.

Not a woman in the place to attend her, Cæsar's last lover, the woman he would place on a throne as high as ever queen sat. Strange thing the contact of bodies. He now knew perfectly how to win this absurd little battle, with a handful of men beat the boy, her brother, and his army. Only yesterday he'd been quite worried what to do about it. Now the Gods had sent solace and solution in one. Meanwhile—send for the two girls who had stuck to her. Kill Pothinos—she had not insisted on it, but he'd a score of his own to settle with that meddler in the affairs of kings. Take Arsinoë, the bitch-sister, back for his triumph. That would please her——

'For the while,' he thought, 'I must be nurse, body-guard and bedfellow——' But the queen turned on him.

"Hide in the women's rooms while you are getting me back my kingdom? What's my second name?" Explaining that, if he fastened the buckles, she knew where to find a suit of her brother's armour.

"No parts of me to tie up with string. Won't young Ptolemy be surprised?"

There followed a gay morning. For a moment it seemed as though it might be difficult for them to leave the royal bed-chamber together. He glanced at her to whom such a consideration had never presented itself. Then he remembered that she was something a roman woman could never be.

For a moment he left her. Then returned. Threw open the carved and gilded doors and stood behind her, wrapped in his scarlet. The long corridor was lined with his men, in armour, with their officers, at strict attention; and as she walked out between them, the sound of sword on shield, the thunder of the full roman salute drowned the light unhurried steps of her winged feet.

71

IX

U P - R I V E R (ii)

Six months passed. Ptolemy, the king, the angry little brother, was dead. Disappeared in a hot bit of fighting; and beside Cæsar the girl reigned unquestioned, to be formally associated later with the child, Ptolemy XV, on the throne.

To ensure her safety and her child's, get her away from alexandrian excitements and complications, show her to her people, teach her the arts of government, satisfy his own curiosity and prolong his delight, he had insisted on a voyage up the Nile, a week-in, week-out gliding up the river in the barge of the kings of Egypt, first cousin to the boat that is called Millions-of-Years.

In ease, in elegance, in splendour, in quiet, in joy, even in peace they sailed. Passing through the land, from Lower to Upper Egypt, through gardens where it never rains, and the fruits of the earth are all and the River is the life. Past Memphis, the Gate, where the Gods take charge; Past Khu-Aton we call Tel-el-Amarna and Abu Simbel and Arsinoë and Abydos. Khu-Aton where the king whose Lord was his Shepherd played with his queen—Amenophis IV with Nefertiti in whose images is shown the lost beauty of holiness.

72

Until they came to Thebes, to the pillars of Karnak, and to Philæ, the Ptolemies' special care, who had built a temple on the island where the East and West meet with a kiss.

Long brilliant days, and nights when it seemed that a Goddess held up the dawn, when Julius Cæsar and the girl Cleopatra glided up the Nile, like Isis and Osiris before Horus was born.

A comparison that struck the High Priest of Amen at Thebes—in public—as apt.

The body of Cæsar rested and the mind, and his spirit, ten years cramped in armour and choked in the blood of battles, the bitter dust of politics, woke and plumed itself. Shed dead feathers and put on new, as he drew the girl to him, and their pulses, beating above the rowers' gentle strokes, seemed like the pulse of the earth's blood running; and it needed no priest to tell them that the growth of the child in her body was the putting-together of a hero, the immortal, the desire of nations, the life-awaited child.

'To watch, to encourage, to restrain the royal young creature by his side'—a long way from the plains of Gaul, the dark green rain-wash of Britain. To enjoy himself, to await his first-born son; to observe, not without concern, the intricate shadow-dance of intrigue behind the splendour of their official reception in Thebes. Entirely *sub rosa*—what else could they do, the shaved and anointed men, but kneel in public and pray, while Cæsar stood behind, his hands on the shoulders of their mistress? For their training and their ritual

73

taught them that this was a Gamos, a Sacred Marriage, of two beings who were themselves the Source of Law; and to arrange for Cæsar's association with Cleopatra as the father of her son, half officially, but in such a way that later it could be made wholly official, if, in the future——?

They drifted. They played. One day Cleopatra appeared in public in her state rôle as Isis of the Egyptians. Not the hellenised Isis-Aphrodite, but the primeval Virgin Mother, Sister and Spouse. Our Lady of Compassion, of all beasts, of lovers and of plants and stones and trees. It did not become her. She was not ready for it. It sat badly on the European, the cosmopolitan, the Greek. And despite a hardly-hidden tongue in her cheek, she looked pathetic in her ritual dress.

Afterwards Cæsar scolded her; that was not the way to rule. Then she spoke of the alexandrian version she knew well how to play:

"I will do it there," she said, "the way I know, a better version and with a better cast. Then you shall see the goddess——"

'O Dea certe,' he answered, wondering what was the ultimate truth of this.

For her part, she was content. For the brute of her and most of her world's imagination there was instead this man, in whom wisdom and sensibility, power and wit seemed mixed equally; whose ancestry even was as illustrious as her own. (In those days before the Colleges of Heralds it is hard for us to determine how

far men truly believed themselves to be descended from
Troy. Were there documents? Was it an act of reason?
Of pure faith? How critical were they? Though it is
possible to notice a period in the lives of successful men
when they found it convenient to stress an ancestry.
At least the whole world had been lately reminded of
the descent from Anchises of the Julian Gens.) Nor
did her maternity dismay her, who was to bear three
more children; and Cæsar no poor alternative to mating
with a brother who was still a child.

They had the Chief Priest to dinner, with his wife,
a little woman like a black wasp; and then Cæsar
learned that the queen had in her a most royal faculty
to please; 'a conversation full, not only of humour, but
of elegance and wit . . . an unerring social sense and
the delicacy of personal perception.' Also that, to the
ancient ecclesiastic seated beside her, whose fruits she
chose, placing them before him on his plate, it meant
nothing. Rather that it was a cause of offence, filling
him with some secret loathing, fanning his wife too into
a fury which would have shown itself in some insolence
had any other man but Cæsar sat at the queen's left
hand.

So, all through the meal, he watched that bitter
process, fine qualities evoking their opposites in men's
hearts. Saw them cried down, misinterpreted, denied;
saw grace, youth, goodwill, solitary grandeur and
approaching motherhood a target for men who were
about to work an evil miracle—by defaming to trans-
form, at very least make inoperative, those lovely things.

75

Understanding how Cleopatra by her very nature would be thwarted, defeated. Made unfortunate. Made to suffer. Brought to shame by force of traduction.

Until she became in some measure a reflection of the thoughts that slandered her. And here Cæsar was impotent—impotent as a slave; and what did it profit to be Cæsar to sit still and see such dreadful things in action? And Cæsar goes on being Cæsar, and the Gods go on being the Gods—'Until the day comes when I'm caught in it too. I'm already caught. Even now the things—the thoughts, at least—are in motion, that must destroy Cæsar. And Cleopatra and Greece and Egypt. And Rome? But——'

Thus momentarily he shivered at the old man's courtesies, and at the woman's chatter which did not dare be anything but civil. Civil and obsequious and deadly—how well he knew that trinity. And that day they had taken part, for luck, in a service of the rejoicing of Isis at Horus' birth.

X

THREE months later. Night; and this time Cæsar alone, by a ledge of the Palace window, in a high gallery. Looking out at the Pharos, sending out its thirty-mile beam across the floor of the sea. A night without wind, a night of the moon. Night, when the sea is an open scroll, pencilled with the moon's patterns, and the stars are half-out, and earth and sea lie open under the white flood light. But in Alexandria the night had two rulers, the moon and the Pharos fire, two light-paths, one climbing the heavens indifferently, one illustrating a sea-road, from point to point where the buoys swing, from the curve of the earth to the harbour, where it seems as though the earth held out her arms to receive ships.

Behind him he could feel the City, all glimmering, all marble. In comparison, stone-built Rome, tumbling its seven hills with its arms round the Capitol's neck, seemed no more than a cluster of peasant huts.

Older than Alexandria by several centuries, Rome had staggered up, fulfilling needs as they came along, here a splendour to commemorate some triumph, there a huddle of tenements; and round every corner some pocket 'of the unanalysable past.'

While, so he felt, minds similar to his own had de-

77

signed this place; it was all plan, all reasoned proportion and loveliness; all man getting the most out of a superb situation; and when it was inadequate, supplying what was lacking by sheer technique.

Thoughts of Cæsar in the night watches. 'Cold-blooded, am I? How can I help that? These are the kind of thoughts I have the moment I'm left in peace.' A servant approached him, prostrated himself, sniffing his sandals with quickened breath.

"What is it?" he said, looking down on the bare polished back, unscarred by any whip. It was one of a family of servants who served the Lagidæ, generation in and out, with nurses, confidential valets, gardeners, grooms, washing-women; who were wholly trusted; whose pride it was never to rise to any position but of affection and trust. A far-off heritage from Macedonia. Also there was between them and the Lagidæ an inviolable pledge that they should never be made eunuchs; and the Lagidæ, so Cleopatra had told him, believed it would mark some dreadful end if one of them were to suffer this.

Ceremony over, he stood up, and Cæsar saw him face to face, his eyes shining past his, as a man face to face with an epiphany, recognising it, adoring it, sharing it. Speaking as a man saying what his ancestors have said:

"The Queen gives birth." And Cæsar heard himself answering as men answer:

"Already. It *is* to-night?" The man was smiling at him now. He smiled back.

78

—"I was uneasy, but I did not know." ('Now what do I give him? She has made him her messenger. I know better how to reward the man who brings me news in battle.')

—"I will wait here. Come back each quarter of an hour. How does she?" In the man's face he read something of the fierce pain, the excitement, the laughter and wild cries that filled the room where Cleopatra was bringing Cæsarion into the world. The man turned and went out erect. Cæsar folded himself back on to the window-seat, his chin on his knees.

—'News of my son's birth—no, not money, a jewel's the thing. These old servants think cash rather an insult. Nothing on me. Shall I get it engraved? Have it stuck on the coins? Not yet. No, better do it at once. We don't want people to think that we think that they think—and all that. No secrecy.

—'Never had a son I could call my own. There's Brutus though. He must be mine. How often Servilia and I have worked out those dates. Son of a sister's son's the nearest I've got, and I don't know exactly what the gods meant when they sent that gift.

—'No need for alarm. She's strong as a tree-cat. Says she wants to nurse it herself so that no milk but hers shall nourish Cæsar's child. Quite the old roman touch I told her and she flew into a fury. I heard a lot about those cows of matrons from one greek-macedonian-alexandrian slip of a queen. It's true too in a way— one half of the earth still thinks us savages, getting up culture because we're essentially incapable of it.

79

—'So to-night's the night, is it? It is strange. I am not quite pretending when I say that these people and this place are having their way with me. I might easily put her to death and to-morrow proclaim this place a province. Men would say that I could not because of what is happening to her now. Yet I know a man who would, and he my kinsman—Octavian, my nephew. Yes—but—in an hour or so I may have a nearer kin.

—'And you, Caius. Surely to-night for once you can let your mind bring forth. Do what she is doing. Each of us according to our kind.

—'*I came. I saw. I conquered.* Neat little dispatch for the Senate to pick over and the roman mob to howl up. While here I've been the least little bit conquered myself. Never before, Caius, never before. Not by Clodius even or by Servilia. Not because you were afraid of it, but because there was literally no one about who could. It was the pirates who came nearest to it, hanging on their crosses. Queen, it's from that little adventure and that moment of submission that I trace my life. It is not all politics that I've stood for for the common people. Oh, I knew the future lay there, the *way* to the future as it must be. Accent on the *Populus* this time, with the Senate in the state it is. Pompey was wrong. His way lay ruin. Wanted the old roman *virtus* for passport because he had it himself. Couldn't see that he was the last of something that had had its turn; and Rome's destiny a greater thing than the rule over tired aristocrats in the East and virgin warriors in the West by a committee of pious farmers whose

80

homes happen to lie half-way between.

—'I am aware, O Powers, that there are flaws in this argument. Made, I assure you, only to strengthen my own will.

—'How goes it? Great pain but no danger? How long will it be? You can't tell yet? Give her my love. No, say I send her the greetings of one general in action to another.

— ('I won't go to her. I saw a hundred thousand men dead in a heap in Gaul, and I don't like seeing her hurt.)

—'You have your orders. I will await you here. . . .

—'. . . Rome, Rome. Do I love you as an Athenian loved his city, *"the violet crowned, the divine walls?"* No, I think not. Differently anyhow. Something not so lovely as that city gave you your birth. An idea man had in his mind of a world under a common direction, a common employment of the natural powers. Great works done and no waste. Our version of the good life for man.

Thoughts of Cæsar in the night-watches:—

—'Man's life too is changing, as though it were becoming longer, and we more tired and more patient of subjection. I am one of the men who have noticed this change, whatever it is. Made it plastic for myself. As I am one among the several men who want what the Greek Alexander wanted, and know how he wanted it and why. Yet, when he died, something died off the earth. He was an end. When they claim a Marius, a Scipio, a Pompey, a Caius Julius, for another Alexander,

81

it makes one laugh. We're not that. Whatever we are, we're not that.

—'Yet a little trickle of his will lived on here; and as things are, we are quite irreplaceable. So I must do what has to be done and call it me——

—'Well? What news? None yet. She says: "The Commander on the right wing has yet no need for reinforcements." Tell her I will hold back my men until we ride together into Persepolis.

—'That spirit of hers may carry her through yet—

> 'O thou, who plumed with strong desire
> Would float above the earth—as the poets say.
> A shadow tracks thy flight of fire——

Little she knows what winds she will meet. Her girls have their eye on me for making her endure this. What was I thinking? That something of that godlike will lived on here in Alexandria, and even among the Lagidæ, that in the end they begot her.

—'What we pray for secretly, what we whisper in our prayers, is for something to make us endure. This life, if it please you. To this have we come, since the greek hawk fell into the sun and was burnt up. That's why the Stoics were hatched—and the Epicureans, for that matter, and the Cynics and all the schools of Hellas. People would have laughed at them once, to whom all things seemed possible, and man's mind the law-giver over nature, and the great arts his play, and his end union with the Gods. We know better now—what we choose to call better; and if it wasn't for the common man's life-instinct and the great man's instinct for getting things done, we'd chuck up the sponge. Only, we Romans know at least that, as things are, we're indispensable. With a chance perhaps—so far as it is possible —to make flesh of other men's dreams. It won't be the same thing. No better than the way we copy their statues. Men with Rome's work to do weren't given the greek touch.

—'Light hands of the Hellenes, on the chisel and on the tiller, on the bridle and on the things of the mind. We've lost that touch. When I've finished——

—'Yes, I mean that. It is I who will give the Roman Genius its final direction on earth.

—'Or let's call it this. We will make the earth man's habitable house. Then something must come along to light a fire in it. Let's hope it won't burn the place down——

—'Was that her cry? So it was, man, from your face. Don't you know—it's for Adonis you weep, not Aphrodite? I don't mean me, but Goddesses don't die. I forgot. You're from the north and she's no Goddess to you, but the woman-child you first put on her horse.

—'Tell her, tell her—that all the spoils of Victory shall be hers, and hers for ever. What more can I promise?

—'. . . Pain about again. They are hanging on crosses at this moment, up and down the hills. In the skies there are birds watching, the vultures some men mistake for our eagles. When I rule, I'll see to it the eagles don't foul their own nests.

83

—'They are down in the Capitol pits, gone mad as they sent Jugurtha. Pain. In Rome we have good nerves for pain. From the blood and sawdust in the arena I've seen rising the ghost of it. Pain—that little boy Octavian likes pain. When I die he will see to it that the doctor who attended me and the slave who forgot to give me my medicine and the slave who sat up with me all night have pain.

—'I am a roman general, and I am aware of this as of one half of creation. That is not suitable for a Roman or a soldier. Some day I shall come to a bad end for knowing too much.

—'The Gods do not mind about Pain. It was those poor devils of pirates, and the queen, my young love, and Caius Julius when his wounds ache and when Julia died. We know about Pain.

—'If a God were to understand Pain, he would conquer the earth. Perhaps we'll get a God like that. It would teach that God something to know pain—not like that smiling white devil in the Bacchæ.

—'I said once to a boy I thought to kill: "Believe me, it is much less pleasant for me to say this than to do it." Because, candidly, I've had to keep myself like that. I'm a merciful man—I mean I'd be a merciful man if—what I mean is that there are possibilities in mercy we could allow for even if nature doesn't. A quality some of us would like to know how to insist on. Possibly a key to the nature of the divine.

—'In all my life I have found one man who has no use for pain. Mark Antony doesn't see the point of it,

84

for others or for himself. Says there's quite enough going about free. A man I like to see drunk, to observe him well-wish the earth, cancel death-sentences, give away anything from the table-service to one of our estates; try to make love to three women and a boy.

—'Marcus—he thinks our Octavian a bad joke. Octavian will make him laugh on the wrong side of his face if anything happens to me. While Octavian, he's able, dear gods, he's able. Has capacity—my capacity—for power; but if I were not there that easy mercy of Marcus' would be the death of him.

—'If anything happens to me, those two will have to fight it out. That won't do. My easy Hercules of a boy-friend's no match for that pretty weed our house has put forth. . . . Spotty as old Sulla's mulberry-mug.

—'Nice description I'm making of my possible successor. Caius, cheer up, it's not come to that yet. This night you have given yourself to your mind to lead. Where have they led you, my friend, these night-thoughts?'

For the fourth time he swung his legs off the window-sill and stood up, this time listening for steps. There were no steps. Yet something in his body more than in his ears registered that there was a stir in the Palace. More than the eternal stir, the pulse of any great building, something localised, yet hard to locate. Down the corridor to the queen's room all seemed quiet. Then in the recesses of his being a voice began to say: 'Let it be over. Let it be over. Time, time. Hurry, hurry. Open the doors and let it out. Let my son out; and

85

each time he stirred from his seat, it became harder for the other Cæsar to take charge again. A piece of grit had worked inside his sandal. He withdrew once more to the window and took it off and shook it out.

'Let us suppose. Let us suppose Rome were in Alexandria where grace is. Grace and knowledge, wealth and royalty. A king and a queen. Suppose Rome poised, the young eagle between West and East. Suppose a subtler will to direct our execution. Suppose again the Roman Genius with the right hand strong and the left hand light. Suppose the Latin Wolf and the Lamb of Egypt pasturing together by this stream. Suppose the Roman Empire a community of nature-ordained men from the Persians to my blue Britons. . . . Suppose Octavian different or dead. Suppose that what I have to do were done without cement of too much precious blood——

—'Suppose—suppose those are steps coming to tell Julius Cæsar that his son is born.—'

This time there were steps, striding swiftly; and behind them he knew there were doors opening and lights streaming and sounds that were cries of joy. He stood up, spare, slight, half-concealed in the shadow. His wreath fallen on the sill, unchapleted, the light gleamed on his skull.

"Caius Julius, Cleopatra our Queen has borne you a perfect man-child." "I know that," he answered; and at the ineffable smile, the old man whose business was with the help that love alone gives knew himself in the presence of another birth, pangs of a supreme mind;

86

that before him stood the father, the first man on earth, the Roman Cæsar, lost in Cæsar. The Queen was his wife and he a king, a first citizen of Rome, but king in Alexandria; and from Alexandria might be king over the world. His Roman Empire was more than Rome's Empire, it was the Community of the Lands of the Western Earth. On his left hand stood his captain, Mark Antony, on his right the Queen; and between his knees—blood of the Lagidæ and the Julian Gens—Cæsarion, the crowned child. Cæsar, whose will had never failed, saw this. Saw it, straight as the line of the roman road, how it lay and where it went. As God creating sees that it is good. Then, as the conception took its perfect shape, and he loved the form of it, in the rapture, his mounting intellect took one further step—into a state he had known before, feared and rejoiced in, when his being, dissociated from his body and from time, knew, first with ardour, then with cold, that the virtue of this conception was that it mattered everything and it mattered nothing. Everything and nothing: was all-important and non-existent: man's salvation and completely immaterial to it. At the same time, he was more Cæsar than Cæsar had ever been, nor was it necessary to be Cæsar any more. He could feel his body also, dry and hot, wet and cold, in glory and in extinction. Cæsar was overwhelmed in Cæsar, whose control of Cæsar had been the being of Cæsar. Cæsar was lost in Cæsar and reborn of Cæsar—self and not-self, subject and object whirling in some spiritual fusion, dissolved into their ultimate particles and set-

87

ting to partners like a system of planets; and it was the instant of death and the reassembling of a new Cæsar, new as the new-born man-offspring of his thin loins.

He fell—on the marble pavement *'bright with serpentine and syenite,'* a huddle of muscle and drawn skin and slight bones. A huddle of white clothes, barred with the crimson of the Roman Senator, but now black in the moonsquare travelling to floor. Falling sickness of the 'bawdy old adulterer,' or the mysterious collapse of the epileptic, reaction from its instant's contact with reality? The old servant let him be a moment, then lifted him, and laid him along a couch at ease, and waited until his faculties returned.

The two men were still alone. Cæsar sat up and shivered, and the servant wrapped him in a covering of furs.

"Tell her," he said, in the voice of a man speaking, though faintly, from a victorious field—"that all I have, all that is here, all that is in Rome and in Egypt shall be hers: shall be ours: shall be his. This I, Caius Julius, this I, Cæsar, this the Roman promises to Cleopatra the Queen. And to Cæsarion, her son and my son."

PART II

I

IRAS TO PHILO   (1)

*"Iras, first waiting-woman to the Queen of Egypt,
Cleopatra VI, Isis-Aphrodite-on-earth with whom is
associated on the throne* (it looks better to put this in)
*the Roman Senator, Caius Julius Cæsar, the Divine
Julius* (very lately divine, and this place isn't used yet
to that sort of thing—nor too pleased about it, let alone
us—I'd better begin again—)

*"Iras, the Queen's maid, to Philo, her dear brother,
Alexandrian. Greetings!*

"My dear,

"I have an infinite number—the Queen says there
are such things—to tell you and only you. To the rest
I will write what they will expect to hear. To you only
what is happening—and keep these letters from all other
eyes, a thing I would not be stupid enough to ask if I
had need to ask it.

"Listen. It is not going to be easy for us here. As
you warned me, when the others could only laugh at us
for our exile among barbarians. And I had better try
and make it clear to you what this place and these
people are like, for Cleopatra's sake and our own and
for the city's and goodness only knows what besides.

Including your own sake, sweetheart. No point, as again you said, in our all coming to shipwreck for want of a chart on the roman coast.

"No, I am too interested as yet to be homesick, like Charmian. She would be—from pure love of Egypt's yellow sands. Fierce little Egyptian that she is. She is so much better than I that she makes me cross. Her whole life is nothing but the Queen—for whom I would do *anything,* not *everything.* Does that make sense? I mean I'd not do *more* than everything—Take Everything in one great piece and count it nothing.

"Listen, my spirit. You want to know it all, and where am I to begin? Make sense of it as I go; for you know and I on what great business we are here, you and I only and Charmian and the Queen.

"Be sure of this, that arriving, we have not seen everything; let alone conquered. The roman women, the celebrated matrons are *cows.* Cows and first-class bitches crossed with cat, and their litters mostly monsters. Get it clear—with the older ones it's either virtue that simply isn't human (so how can it be proper virtue?) or else it's worldly and would-be-ultra-smart in a crude way that's rather terrifying. They don't mean to miss anything, now that Rome's got rich, with its arms elbow-deep in other people's treasures; and the nails they stain scarlet are sharp. Red and sharp and filed to points. Strong hands too, well-shaped but never fine —fine like your hands and mine. Hands of the Hellene, after all; and my nails blue and violet or pale green, the colours you told me to stick to.

"Of course, there are just a few darlings. Old ladies from the country, not a bit fashionable, but brought out to impress us with the old roman stuff. Then Cornelia, our Pompey's last wife. (She's young, but you can't say 'widow' here. Why, they change about, even when one is having a child by the last, and was married before to the new one's father.) Off she goes, after preposterous I-take-you-for-life-and-evermore-ceremonies, to the new one's house, who used to be her son-in-law, and has it. There is something brutal about it. At home we're more civil at least. Perhaps we're happier. Or have learned to be gentler with one another. Anyhow our adulteries are in better style. Yet these women are mistresses in their households; and, as I said, some of the country gentlewomen are all such women should be —the sort of loving head of a great family, where even the slaves are friends.

"But it's the great town ladies we have to deal with, and since the person I serve is a woman and a queen, they are going to count in her affairs. (Which are as truly mine as they are Charmian's—the same tune played on different instruments in different time. *Frater carissime*, do you understand?)

"You must not think from the way they are handed about that the women here are nothing but things to sleep with and breed from. It's not so simple as that. (How could it be, with women what they are?) They haven't the tradition of public life the women have in Egypt, but they're every bit as fierce and ambitious as the men. Not only for their men either. For them-

93

selves. And when they're magic, they're magic—like the Vestal Virgins. And if they are always being exchanged from husband to husband, I believe they *like* it. They've worked it somehow to suit them. (They can always meet at a pinch again and have an affair.) So they fall in with the men's plans and politics, and make everything they can out of virtuous submission and the good of the State. Peripatetic olive-branches between one faction and another. I'm a woman, and I know. The men swallow it. It suits *them* all right. It's a weapon too. 'Think how you tore me from Caius or Lucius'—or whoever the last one's arms were. Knowing that you can always get back on the quiet if you want to; and it's Isis knows who's the father of which. Take our Caius Julius. Everyone *knows* that Marcus Junius Brutus—my idea of a fool, but Charmian is inclined rather to sit at his feet—is his son, and by one of the most pious of the matrons. Everyone knows. Nobody cares. Which is after all very sensible. One might want 'a little more poetry about it' as our washer-woman used to say, but if you don't——. More about poetry later. As to Brutus. No need to cock your narrow eyebrows. He is no danger to the one, the whole, the only, the first, the last, the beginning and the end, the object, the subject, the whole six cases of the latin noun; the aim, the means, the reason and the passion of our existence here. That is to say he will not affect Cæsarion, the only son of my mistress and the master of this City— so master of half the earth, and so for the time being our master.

"(If Charmian were writing this, it would be all about the baby. I'll spare you. Take it that he grows, and that he rejoices us, who have all seen what wretched scraps have at times to pass muster for princes.)

"Let me repeat the situation you guessed so well. Under cover—well, under no particular cover—we are here to insure Cleopatra's marriage with Cæsar, according to roman law. True consort though he may be in Egypt, it does not count here. We have had to swallow that. (I should like to see old Nefer-Aten's face in Thebes when he hears that the Words of Association he said over them don't amount here to a row of beans.) And Cæsar has a wife, the last of a row of them. It is not that that's worrying us. Though it will not be easy, perhaps I dare not think how difficult, to get their marriage undone, and with that secure Cæsarion as our Cæsar's heir. For this reason: one roman matron can be exchanged easily for another, but we are foreigners. There *is* something provincial about this place, or what one might imagine in a village where all the farmers know exactly all there is to know about everyone else. You know the peasant of lineage. Think of some place up-Nile where the cultivators say: 'My forefathers were here in the time of Queen Hat-Shepsu, and bred for King Rameses his hunting cats.'

"While these Romans—how can their memories be as long even as Hellas, let alone Egypt? Of course they fake their pedigrees from Troy, and even our dear Caius must be descended from Anchises. 'Dear,' why yes. For he is our dear.

95

"Yes, Philo, even I find it easy to know that there is no greater man on earth. 'Heaven help the earth,' you say, and perhaps you're right. But I mean that in himself he *does* include every sort of greatness there is in the world, and builds it up into his own greatness. He is a tower and a rock, a great calm and a great mind. He is a tree. And inside him there is something that burns. A light that's cold and suave and rather terrible, more light perhaps than heat. Cleopatra says she does not love him with her body, not as that body would like to love, but with all of her, as though there were no difference of parts. She is more herself with him, she says, than ever she was before; and they talk politics and people, and how to be a king and sometimes about the arts. We supposed that Rome had no poets, but Caius talks about a man Catullus, and in rhetoric they are stupendous, because, as he said grimly, they have something to say and for every man on earth to attend to. I couldn't help thinking of those innocent great tall blue things in the island of the West, having to listen to it all. There's as far as he got, and he had to leave in a hurry. I suppose Rome's good for them, but if they don't want it to be good——?

"The Matrons—oh, yes, I must finish them off before I get on to the men. We are very polite to them; and yet, I fear, not polite enough. The truth is that no courtesy is sufficient when all are looking for offence.

"Listen again—you see we have to conciliate; please and conciliate, as well as take all the spirit out of them. When they are gaudy, be miraculously simple. Then outdo them by the quintessence of splendour. When they are coarse—and they can be—be witty; when they are cruel—they can be horrible to their slaves—be kind. When they are free, intelligent and amiable, like Cornelia, make friends with them and enjoy them.

"And yet in every hundred hours there is always one when a voice asks why I, your sister, a Hellene, why Charmian, of a priestly house before ever Troy was, why indeed Cleopatra, blood of the Lagidæ, Alexander's inheritor, Pharaoh of Egypt and its incarnate Goddess, should stoop to please these promoted peasants, not ten generations off the plough.

"Have I shown you then how we find them gross? Theirs is the kind of mind that wants what other people have, in this case the graces, the long sureness bred of our past, alexandrian; and seizing on them, pretends to despise them. (And snatching, gets them wrong. That *always* happens.) It is the same with dress and accomplishments, and all our civilities. I could tell you a thousand absurd things—of one lady who, for extravagance, poured out the perfume you use one drop at a time, neat, and took the skin off Cleopatra's hands. Going one better than our scented water (they dye theirs purple and a wicked deep green). While the woman's husband said something about waste and spat in his finger-bowl, saying it looked like blood. The son blushed with rage, and the daughter laughed.

"There! Multiply that story in a thousand manners and degrees. If you want to puzzle them, do what Cleopatra does, seek out the old, the unfashionable, the

97

unpretentious, the country gentry. There be at ease:
take a turn at the loom in the weaving-room of some
cool manor in their hills. Hills—hills and the sea—
I'm in love with them. Philo, I am learning trees. No
more dry palm-rattle, and things potted in tubs, all for
flowers and fruit and rarity and strangeness, but Trees.
Beech are their names and oak and chestnut, like
towers. Or pillars of a temple that planted itself, and
each pillar a person you can know. And to each tree
his Dryad, his invisible companion, who is the tree's
soul. Who dies when the tree dies, dies with her love—

> *'Dear tree of joy and bliss*
> *Where truest treasure is,*
> *I do adore thee——'*

Cleopatra and Charmian and I are in love with three
trees. They are growing a morning's ride out of the
city. We ride out early and under their branches pass
the midday heat. When we have eaten and rested, then
we say our prayers, and dance round them in a ring.
Throw ourselves against them and try and take them
in our arms, and kiss their sides and climb up and lie
in their arms. And our Caius Julius clapped his hands,
until Charmian almost liked him. (Nothing will move
her that these Romans have no more than the power
that is in the beasts without their wisdom. So she says,
and a lot more about the things on which they set their
hearts having no more permanence than the dew. It
doesn't look like that to me, but you can never tell

with Egyptians, who do their sums in nothing less than thousands of years.)

"But the trees make us feel less alone, as though we had found friends. We told Cæsar that and he smiled, said that trees were a safer lover than he was. Anyhow, they'd be here when he was gone—'when you too are gone, my children.'

"He is busy, often too busy for us, extending everywhere his authority and his power. Philo, I need not tell you again what depends on it. You have it clear? This marriage to Cæsar, which will make Cæsarion his heir, will make my mistress not only Queen of Egypt, but mistress of Rome as well. Will make our Cæsar not only Rome's master but Egypt's Pharaoh, and all that goes with it. While if it does not happen, we have no more than Egypt. And he no more than Rome; and the world will have to wait for its Master and its Mistress, its shape and its direction. (This he has carefully taught us, and I think I understand it now.)

"The difficulties I have told you. Also that there is a lad Octavian, who thinks himself his heir and who has powerful friends. Among them this man Cicero, I will explain later. Last and most of all, that in Rome even Cæsar is not utterly master; that he has his enemies, not only in the Senate, but among the people. Oh, I know his power rests within the people, and the lower the people, the louder they howl for him; and there is no need to tell an Alexandrian what a mob is. But this Cicero was here to-day—to borrow books, and the Queen is sending the yacht for them. (And with it, this

99

letter.) Do you think he is grateful? Forget it. As he
will, even to return them. In his mind it is he who does
us a favour, whose father was a small-town lawyer or
something like that. 'The books the Queen of Egypt
gave me,' he will say, leaving them about to be seen;
who came here to find nothing but faults, and that she
should so quickly do him a service only another cause
for offence. I remember one thing he said, quoting
a Greek, that though 'you must give the lion's cub a free
hand, it were better not to have reared him.' Cleopatra took him up: 'Surely it is part of Rome's strength
that she lets her lions roar?' Thinking, as she told us
later, of Marius, Sulla and the Scipios. He answered
with his thin smile: 'Rome knows well enough when
the skin of her greatest lion makes soft walking for the
Senate's feet.' He was thinking, Cæsar says, of the man
who made his name, Lucius Sergius Catilina, whom he
drove to death.

" (Listen to Cæsar and the rest of their orators, pointing my words and rounding my sentences. It is only
now and then that I babble as I used, when it delighted
you. Now all the time I hear words, weighted and
sharpened, carved into great sentences; and my ear
catches the sound; while my mind is being used—used,
I suppose, for kings' purposes. I shall not be a girl much
longer.)

"Then he went on to explain—Cicero, I mean—that
there is in the common people a natural hatred of
human greatness, that a wise statesman knows how to play
upon, to prevent such a man from coming to too much

power. 'Does the man in his greatness allow that?' we asked. He smiled primly: 'He must not be allowed to injure the State,' he said. Cleopatra said again: 'Must a great man always be judged by his enemies?' 'It always is so,' he said, with that air of the withdrawn philosopher, which is one of the old man's masks. No one is greedier than he for honours or for fame.

"Now have I said my lesson?

"Now do you see something of the dangers? But I can hear your light voice, asking the inevitable question: 'Will Cæsar then make himself their king?' It is the question of questions; and the answer, I think, is 'yes,' and that he must never be called it. 'Rex' is their word for king, and the sound of it makes every Roman like an animal on the look-out. 'We are undone,' they seem to cry, and 'Treachery! Treachery to the State!' It is strange. Say the word, as I did the other day, barked it out behind a senator's broad back and folded gown, and round he jumped: 'What's that?' I excused my bad Latin, asked if it was not the translation of Pharaoh or the greek 'Basileus.' He looked nastily at me: ' "Tyrannos" is more like it,' he said, 'a word not in roman use.' I was meek, I was baby-puzzled; wrote it all down on my tablets and asked him some more words. He breathed over me, stale with wine, too close, as they do. It was my fault. . . .

"Now you will ask me this, I know. You will say: 'Is it worth it? Could we not let it all go by, Rome, Egypt, royal state? With a Queen's great private fortune, lay down the crown to the people who are collecting them? Take one of the islands and build a palace on it—a city even—and live there? Vanquish them in another way—gather the men round us who care nothing for what the Romans want? Who care for the things of the mind and the eye and the ear, and the fair things made with hands. Lead these Romans, conquered to another tune, our tune, not theirs, the grinding of swords, and roar of burning cities, the rumbling walls? Their music, not ours. You could have all the power you want, and be remembered for ever for the things you kept alive and the delight you gave.' People can do those things and they do not do them, and you, my brother, can't see why. You tell us to leave the danger, not through fear or we'd be running all our lives, but because we have found another way to do what we have to do, and win a victory that leaves no bitter taste in the mouth. Leave this world and its scramble for power, that ends up heart-broken when it's got it, on a throne or a cross or a sword. You said something like that before we sailed, and I asked Charmian, who wants really to be a priestess. Asked Cleopatra, and she made a good answer, if there is an answer—that queens and their girls must pay like other people; and the Lagidæ have to be born again; that you've got to do, as magnificently as possible, what's been put upon you by the Gods. Choose—the '*pure things for a prince to endure.*' Only so far as I can see, they're not pure. Nor am I a prince. Cleopatra asked what Lagid had ever bargained to keep his hands as clean as all that. . . ?"

II

"So now I have begun to tell you the politics, the ins and outs of the parties that make up their state, and you can guess how Cæsar has the people, and where that shoe pinches. Yet I do not suppose that since Alexander's day any one man has enjoyed such triumphs. There was only Pompey to compare with him—in our day at least—for the particular roman greatness—and Pompey we killed off for him in Egypt; meanly, but we did it. And he is great enough to be ungrateful to us.

"Listen again—oh yes, and I submit in part to your scolding—when you say that we are not wise to be too strange, too remote; that it would be better to step down, meet these people on their own ground, not shame them by playing the exquisite. That Cleopatra must forget that she is a Goddess. That last is true, but how can the rest be possible? I cannot have our Lady smeared. Keep out of faction, yes, and so we have; but to hide the truth about ourselves and what we are, and what they are? When it is so amusing not to pretend. After all, how is their good opinion possible? When have men *not* slandered a woman who is young and alone and a Queen?

"Now for the men who concern us most. First there

103

is Octavian, and I did not know it was possible to detest a schoolboy so much. If we were the kind of persons men suppose us to be, we'd give him something to insure our baby's inheritance. Philo, there are moments when I feel I might—that I could—that I should. Telling no one—my fear being that Cæsar would guess. He is not a man whose hand you can force. Think and advise me. Shall I do it? Can I find a way by which it is impossible that Cleopatra should know? Or, I suppose, Charmian? Do it in such a way that the blame, if any and that unlikely, falls on me? Of the people about her, I have the clearest head. If you approve, if you think of a plan, let me hear it.

"Why am I so sure that a schoolboy should be got rid of? I do not know, yet I am quite sure. There is something abominable in the nature of him. Already he hates us—well taught by Cicero—and, I suspect, by this Brutus. Which is bad luck for Cæsar, seeing that he is his son.

"Yet, strangely enough, Brutus has no desire to replace Octavian as Cæsar's heir. He is not that kind of enemy, but rather one who must draw his excuses from philosophy or from the Gods.

"One piece of good luck—though I know even it will be twisted and turned against us—little Ptolemy is sick. We had to bring him with us, for his safety and for ours; Pharaoh he is in some sort and a future consort to my Mistress. A little gilt stick of etiquette and diplomatic excuses for us to tap the Romans on the cheek. Not really important; and privately a nuisance, being every-

thing that Cæsarion is not; and he never had any wits
and whines all the time, asking for Arsinoë, the only one
of us that he ever loved.

" (We have had trouble with her—the kind of trouble
you are so sure is coming that to watch it is no more
than watching a scene in a play. Since we came, she
has lived in the country; and one day arrived here,
unasked, and screamed at Cleopatra, saying that she
would rather have walked in Cæsar's triumph than
stayed behind and born his bastard; and when Cleopatra told her she spoke from jealousy and want of
enterprise, she flew at her with a knife. We pulled her
off, and then Charmian surprised us. Woke up for once
and drew herself up, shining like a priestess, and spoke
to her the most terrible egyptian words. Putting the
curse on her, who had lain hands upon the Anointed
of Egypt, and the even more awful curse of the fratri-
cide; and you must believe me when I say that it
worked, for I saw Arsinoë's knees double under her,
and she fell down, and when we got her up, rushed out
of the house—Cæsar's lovely house across the Tiber—and
she'd brought no escort, and the Furies know how she
got back; and all we hear now is that she spends her
nights and days creeping about a shrine of Artemis;
and Cleopatra wrote a letter and told her the kind
of Iphigenia she was.)

"You can't do anything with people like that. So we
don't. But that hateful little Ptolemy mopes; and she's
had time to teach him a filthy set of words about Cleopatra, which are all he'll say now, except that he's a God

and she isn't any more because of Cæsarion. Cleopatra
made him feel what the sole of her sandal felt like on
a God's sit-down; but when Arsinoë'd gone, we found
him squeezing the juice out of some poison berries he'd
found in the garden into Cæsarion's milk. Tried to
poison his dagger too and scratched him; and Charmian,
who never leaves the child, sucked it out and began a
curse for him too. But all he would do was yell: 'I'm
the Pharaoh, and you can't curse me!' 'Can't I?' she
said, 'when my ancestor did the sacring of Akhnaton.'
So she put something in his drink to make him feel that
if he wasn't cursed, he wasn't much like a Pharaoh.
After that he behaved better for a bit, talked less about
hating us. Instead he took to saying he hated everything
else, food, people, smells, colours, all the things you
can't change anyhow—and his pony, and any of the
servants he'd liked before, which did not make him any
easier to live with. Though we don't understand what
has happened to him, except that the fever which rises
from the lands round these seven hills has hold of him;
and now Charmian, for her kind of reasons, nurses him
night and day. Has an idea that he ought to say he's
sorry—perhaps to make it pleasanter for him in the boat
called Millions-of-Years.

"Let's hope anyhow it'll finish him—so long as they
don't say we did it.

"I must go. This evening we receive Senators and
their wives; and the Queen's not dressed and I'm not
dressed; and I must see to it that Charmian does not
wear egyptian clothes. It wouldn't be that to them, but

a girl undressed; and where we see a priestess, see only a slave or a courtesan.

.   .   .   .   .

"When they had gone, he died. Like a small lamp you've blown out. (And where is there an embalmer? We hadn't thought of that, and it must be done because of what people will say in Egypt.)

"When Cleopatra came, Charmian had him in her arms. He was just going and thought she was Isis come to fetch him, and said he was glad he hadn't to be a God any more and here was a real one. And the funny thing was, he *did* say he was sorry.

"Anyhow, he's dead, and it's as well. Only they are sure to say we poisoned him. I can hear old Cicero, spreading the glad news. I wonder if it is worth while *not* doing such things if people believe it of you anyhow. It must be a special kind of person who finds virtue enough to live on, and virtue alone.

"Last and strangest of all—Cleopatra bit her lip and ran her nails into her palms—you know the way she has. Said: 'Another Lagid gone. He'd have been one of the worst, another Physkon. It's *got* to be as well.' Then something about liking what you get if you can't get what you like; and went off, trying to whistle. What we call 'putting the Queen's face on it.' I am glad, if we can stop the poison-story. But Charmian *minded* about it. Ran after her and said: 'But he was sorry, after all.' Then they cried, both of them; hanging over Cæsarion's cradle.

"Outside our Egyptians have set up a tiny wailing, as at a small Pharaoh's death."

107

III

"I HAVE told you about the people who do not like us. Now about those who do, and it will not take me long.

"There are—to begin with and pretty well end—the men of Cæsar's set, and they out of loyalty to him. They come and pay their respects, and here above all Cleopatra must play the queen and nothing else; claiming his protection in all things, and being her own protection. Dull? Yes, it is, but after what you said before we sailed and in every letter since, it seems necessary that Charmian and I play the watch-dog, both of us, lest for an instant she should forget.

"The only one with whom it is possible to be at ease is Cæsar's right-hand man, second-in-command, publicity agent and general confidant, Mark Antony. Except for a feeling that we could rely on him at a pinch, we see little of him, and he's a glorious creature. To him, as to the rest, it is we who are pieces in Cæsar's game—men most of whom are just a lot of pushing soldiers, ready to follow the eagles to wherever they look like flying next. Over Egypt perhaps.

"One thing more I have to tell you—to be scolded in your next letter; but the rest of our friends, I swear, are the stiffest of the Matrons. We give little parties for

108

them and for the virgin daughters they take such care of,
and precious little they know about them; and *no* men
asked, and half the women country-dowagers at that.
But your scolding will be for Cytheris, and she's getting
old, the actress this Mark Antony used to love. A darling,
and if she had been known in Alexandria, the world
would call her by different names. She comes here
sometimes when the Matrons don't. All except one, the
widow of that Catiline Cicero helped to kill, Aurelia
Orestilla. Quite different from the rest, though married
into the stiffest of high families. Haven't you noticed
that it takes people like that to breed someone out-
rageously different? Too lovely and witty and exquisite
and badly behaved. And such a rest. Besides, Philo,
she is useful. Tells us everything, for she knows everyone, even if they won't know her; every scandal,
divorce, murder, marriage, bastard, abortion there has
ever been. Then her own story—how she has picked
her way through the official and the private killings,
the conspiracies and proscriptions—even the quite
frightful end of Catiline, the last one she actually
married. Always on the right side of some man, of
course. From her I learned her husband's side of the
story—that Cicero has seen shall not go down as history.
He would have lifted the debts and the mortgages
off the backs of the common people when he went for
the bankers. So as to give the old roman virtue a chance
to breathe again. He thought their State strong enough
to stand the upset, and perhaps it was and perhaps it
wasn't. Perhaps by the end he didn't care.

"While Aurelia O—so she is called in a song everyone sings, though it's years old—comes here a great deal, and tells us all about everything. After all, we are women of the world. Is your scolding on the boil? Remember how young we are and how she is completing our education. If you saw her, you'd adore her— you, who are always amused at Dowagers with a Past. She is still lovely.

"Oh, will a time ever come when we can forgo all this carefulness? Set up for ourselves, a crowned queen and her maids? I believe, Philo, we *are* too young for this. Too young to have no one—except you at a distance—to take care of us; too young to have to take such desperate care of ourselves. You might say; 'What's Cæsar for?' But you know too much for that. You know there is always a point where we can no longer trust Cæsar; when he would, kindly but absent-mindedly, like a God, put us aside. That's not to say he will, but he could; and the Queen knows it. It has changed her eyes. But this is being unhappy, and we're not. Not yet, you say? You are not to say that. The Anointed of Egypt: the express image of the Goddess: Hierophant of the Mysteries of Royalty and Beauty— I hear you say coolly: 'Dangerous things to be.' Would you have us be no more than a roman soldier's whim? It makes me remember when I was a child, lost in a desert temple at night, dashing myself blind against great blocks of stone.

"To-morrow we are going away. To stay in the hills, not far off. Distraction while they're embalming the boy. (Mark Antony found us an embalmer who knows the egyptian rites.)

"To call on the King of the Wood. Cæsar will not tell us who he is."

IV

"I HAVE not liked Nemi or the Goddess there, whom they call Diana and say she is Artemis. She is not Artemis nor any Maiden. Nor is Hippolytus king in that wood. It is a demon and a filthy one at that, an evil spirit doubled in the man and woman who are priest and priestess there.

"This we found at the end of our ride, with Cleopatra drawing ahead like a centaur, and Charmian as usual like a sack of apples, half-empty, on the nearest thing we could find to a bed. If only I had seen your profile beside me. Instead you must listen to what we found there, what was waiting for us at Nemi, in the woods.

"The place is in the mountains, a boat-shaped cup from hill to hill, and the water in it the profoundest blue. Blue of stone, blue of crystal, blue of petal. Blue. Not of sea or eyes or sky. Rock-blue. At one end a mountain crag is flung up, a place for eagles and that hero the Hellenes call Rhesus, son of Apollo and the Strymon-nymph. Half-way down a bow of water is drawn and broken over the rock's face and falls into the lake. We rode round the steep sides through vineyards. Then, as we came to the end and the foot of

112

the crag where the temple stands, there were trees. As
the Queen said: 'Each one a lover.' The tree called
'castanea', that holds its fruit packed tight in a green
spiked box, which splits on the branch and the nuts
pop out, polished like brown glass. (The same nuts we
boil in honey and cool to set in a sugar-skin.) All
round us the thorned boxes were splitting, pop and
crack and light tumble through the leaves, salt and
sweet together in the mouth, and sap-warm with the
sun.

"We were choosing three trees to be married to when
I saw Charmian, looking as she does when something
is happening before it begins. The Queen and I
looked at Cæsar, at his most disagreeable smile, dismounted silently and went with him on foot; trotted
after him, leaving the trees. The trees ended, and there
was the King's House, like a very old stone box, and the
pillars were of wood; and squatting near it, but not in
any line or relation to it, a living-house of sorts. They
didn't matter, because in an open space in front of the
Temple steps there was a Tree. A tree like a tower,
its branches raised to the pure sky, each leaf so brilliant
in the light that you might call it a tree of glass.
Also a horror-tree. For its trunk, Philo, was all naked
and smooth and bloody and hung with puppets. And
models of things, our sexes mostly, made in clay. And
skins too, the dried, flayed skins of beasts.

"There were a man and a woman sitting under the
Tree—I am telling you what we saw, not what we
feared. Not a mystery to which we would be initiate;

113

and a cruel demon in Cæsar told him to bring us there.

"The pair were all dressed up. Rings and chains, bits and pieces and charms all over them. Fat too and old and painted to look young. Old as Cæsar perhaps. Only stamped with vileness as he with greatness. Both their eyes darting about as though they had to look all ways at once, but hers had a wink that said: 'I'm on the right side.' Both of them looked all over us in an instant; and then she put her arm round his back and began to paw him as they got up.

"The man was the priest, the King of the Wood, and he stank of wine. Only he wore a sword, and his hands were always itching about the pommel; and he had a dagger too, and a shield lay beside him. (Where there was no grass, only trodden earth some fowls were scuffling in.)

"As I've said, he was painted and fat and breathed wine, and he was all hung about with charms and trinkets like the tree. But sewn on a mantle you could throw off in a flash; and underneath his priest's gown was hoisted up and looked as if it had armour underneath, next his skin, and a phallos of stripped leather stitched right up it. He had red eyes. Eyes of a man who never goes to sleep. Must not: dare not: cannot: never will again. At the same time, they were both like something at a fair, and she a showman of sorts—his showman. A showman who is part of the show.

"What *is* all this about, you ask? I'll tell you first what Cleopatra said: 'What are they afraid of?' 'Come along,' said Cæsar, 'I'll show you'—and led us up to them, saying:

" 'Well, Bimbo, how are you getting along? You've lasted a good time.' The man—you mustn't think he looked at us even for a second, all the time his eyes were everywhere, and the woman kept turning to look behind his back—drew himself up. Cæsar apologised.

" 'Your pardon. One forgets now you're a king. How d'you like it after stealing the spoons at Metellus Cimber's?' Cleopatra said that Cæsar's words were like drops that filled a cup of terror to overflowing. So she asked him: 'What is your royalty, sir? I did not know that I should ride out from Rome to see a king? You must leave your Golden Trees and come and eat with us under our common ones.' But he only said like one repeating an insolence by rote: 'The King of the Wood does not leave his Kingdom,' when 'dare not' was what he meant; and we saw he was mad, past any charm of hers. As she said after, we ought to have answered that then we would stay and eat there with him, only we felt that we could not eat in that tree's shadow: that though it was a temple precinct, it was unclean; and the naked light around it was full of shadows. So she said: 'If you will not join us, will you give me a branch of your Golden Tree?' As she said it, he came forward a pace, with his red lips drawn back to show long yellow teeth like a horse, and we heard Cæsar saying:

" 'Down, Bimbo, this young lady does not know what it means to be King of the Wood'; and the woman said: 'The noble Senator's quite right. If you don't

115

behave, Bimbo, I shall drop off too when you're having
your snooze; and then someone'll come along and you'll
have to fight like you did last month. I'm not saying
I'm not ready for a change, and you're a bit old anyhow to be King of a wood like this. A cross is more
your line.' Charmian had not heard this. She had
slipped off inside the temple, and came out then, drawn
up to what we call her priestess' size, as though she
might be as tall as she willed, thinned to a flame—to
the idea of a hierophant. This time she was very angry.
She came up to the man and said roughly: 'How do
you dare use Artemis' pure name, when you have in
there a devil? He is inside now, gnawing the head of the
dead child you had and she strangled——' The woman
began:

" 'But it's I who serve the Goddess, my noble lady,
and to be sure she doesn't like babies, as your virginity
knows as well as I; and as to thinking I'd so far dare
as to have one here——'

" 'What d'you know about it?' said Cæsar roughly;
but Charmian only drew in a long breath, standing as
though she were lifted up by what she had taken in to
herself, her head as it were high above Cæsar's head.
Then Cleopatra, although she is afraid to cross him,
slipped her arms through hers, saying: 'I don't think I
like this place. Let us go back to the trees.' They turned
and we followed; but I think the woman had guessed
who we all were, for she ran after us, saying:

" 'You mustn't mind us, my lord and ladies. It's a
hard time with him I have, who's never been the same

since last time that man who'd killed his mother nearly
got him; and he would have, only he was so dying for
a sleep, he didn't care, and I had to help him stick him.
And to-day the chickens wouldn't eat; and half the time
he says he'd sooner have spent three days on a cross
than hang about here, waiting for someone to pick his
bit of greenery; and next time whoever wants it can
have it and finish him; I'm about ready for a change.'
She stank so that the Queen walked further away. She
did not shrink or hurry. We did. Cæsar threw her
a coin, saying: 'Drink that.'

"At lunch while we ate Cleopatra was silent. Then
Cæsar began to explain that the Temple was a very old,
odd place, 'and I admit that the name of Diana, whom
you Greeks call Artemis, was not the first name used
there. That wretched King of the Wood (no one quite
knows how the rite started) has always to be a run-away
slave. Again I doubt if any Pontifex Maximus could
tell you why. I know I can't. But if he has done something to earn him the cross, if he can run as far as here
and is strong enough to kill off the one before him and
break a branch from the Tree, well, he becomes King
of the Wood until another comes along and repeats the
process. Don't ask me what it means, still less if it should
stop, for it is not my business to stop it. And no people
would do it, if there was anything else for them to do.
But I daresay the ritual explains why you all seemed to
feel the place what one might call common and unclean.'
We listened to this, then Charmian said:

"'A worn-out harlot for Diana's priestess. Is that

your Roman Faith?' Cæsar was annoyed. 'My dear child,' he said, 'have you then seen nothing in Rome of the order and decency of her Faith? I brought you here to see something curious, a survival. If you had not turned so fastidious, I'd have got the woman to amuse you. She's a character, and, as you may guess, an authority on the lives of the Kings of the Wood.' (It just crossed my mind that this was meant for Cleopatra, a wish to show her something, not pleasant. To put her down; and yet that he himself hardly knew what he was doing.) Then she, making as usual no effort to hide her feelings, said:

" 'How could one tolerate such a place? Would the Goddess, were she present?' He did not hide that he thought her silly, but Charmian interrupted again:

" 'It was no Goddess that you brought us to see, but a demon and two possessed of demons.'

" 'So you claim. I saw two amusing scoundrels.' (But not amused, we thought.) Then Charmian:

" 'Do you think that the Gods can be served by such as they?'

" 'Why not?' he said. 'One comes to kill. Kills. Picks a bough and reigns. Until he is killed and another bough picked. So long as there's no mistake. It all lies, if anything lies, in the continuity.'

" 'What has that bloody cutting and picking to do with Artemis? And what is this Diana of yours that she takes Her name?'

"Cæsar stroked his chin, considering her reflectively:

" 'It seems to me an excellent thing for the Romans

118

to re-name their original—shall we say rather shapeless—deities, after their clearer, more elegant equivalents in the greek mind. As they stood, I confess, they are hardly adequate for an imperial people. But merged in what even a philosopher would allow to be their originals—it has enlarged our ideas——'

"Charmian answered him soberly:

" 'A lot you, Cæsar, care about ideas of the Gods. All you want to do is to keep people in order.' He laughed. She went on:

" 'You will find in the end that it won't work. You will go all over the earth for your Gods instead of finding them at home. People have got to do that for themselves, find out the whole way to tell themselves the truth. Find out what the Gods really are. Which means in the end what God is. If you don't you may get God in a shape you don't like; one that may conquer you whether you will it or not——'

" 'What sort of a God, my child, would conquer the Roman State, whether it will or no?' She looked at him a long time before answering: 'One out of Egypt, perhaps.'

" 'Crocodile-worshipper,' said he, 'and ape and jackal and half the beasts in creation. And when you die, you'll have your insides taken out and be shut up in a box, dressed and painted for a party; and if anything happens to the box, out goes your little puff of a soul. That's your religion in Egypt.'

"Now Charmian is the gentlest of the gentle, gentle as Meleager's Heliodore; but now she stood, quivering, as the light shakes in the strong sun. A tear like dew caught on each lash as she faced him. Not to defend the Gods of Egypt, not even her Maiden. By Aphrodite! I don't know what in her heart she was defending.

" 'It is not for you, Cæsar, to speak of the Gods. Our Lady Artemis, who lives in these woods, has been driven out by a slave and a harlot. Slave and harlot, and both possessed, spilling their filth into the bath of heaven's Huntress——'

"Cleopatra broke in saying:

" '——Who draws her crystal bow on the hearts of maids like Charmian.'

" 'The Goddess forbid,' said Cæsar, taken aback, 'that any Roman should be found wanting in respect for Virginity. You can hardly accuse us of that. Surely our Vestals are unique. If you weren't a foreigner, Charmian, I'd try and get you in.'

" 'I need her too much,' said the Queen, 'and her pure prayers. Being a maid no longer. Your fault, Caius——' But Charmian went on:

" 'What is your roman faith but magic, when it isn't custom or ceremony? Magic and Luck? Magic and the Fortune you say goes with the City? Destiny for men like you. Luck for the common people. And you, who do not believe a word about the Gods, are pretending to join them, beginning to call yourself the Divine Julius, a something for the Romans to adore.'

" 'Taking a leaf,' said the Queen, 'out of *my* book. The one I am forbidden to read, here in Rome. And let me remind you, Caius, that I'm the real thing. I did not have to wait until I thought that people would stand it—till it was politic for me to become divine. Between Gods together, just when, my Cæsar, and why did you decide that the time had come for a cult and an altar to the Divine Julius?'

"You can often tease Cæsar, but this I saw was distasteful to him. As if, Philo, for once he had *not* reasoned about it, was about to do it for some secret satisfaction he did not quite approve—was even perhaps afraid of. He said: 'It's usual to do it now.' 'It isn't,' said the Queen, with about as much tact as you could put on an obol: 'No Roman has ever tried that in Rome.' His closed lips showed that this Roman would. I stopped myself from laughing. He must have counted seven more than once before he answered her, and then it was to say:

" 'Well, Cleopatra, suppose you tell us now what you make of it. What you have to say about being a deputy, at least, of the divine?' Seated on a fallen tree, she leaned over, her knuckles under her chin, clenched round a ring of green stone. A ring, they say, Alexander gave to the first Ptolemy.

" 'I don't think it's lucky,' she said. 'A divine queen like me has in some measure to play Providence to her people, which means bearing more than a share of their griefs, let alone their resentment when things go wrong. (Not that we look to do it. It has a way of happening like that.) While Iras here would say it was silly; and so unpropitious, because it simply is not true.'

"You see, Philo, how generous she can be, not

121

grudging me my share of the Hellene, whose blood, in that respect, is purer than hers. So I spoke up:

" 'I mean Alexander. What he did was an un-greek thing, and I don't see that it brought him any luck. It is different for the Queen. She has to rule a land where custom has made it necessary. But in the Palace, when we are together, it is our way to keep our greek memories bright.' She went on from that:

" 'Iras is right. In Egypt I must do what they want. What they need or think they do. And remember, in the Time before Time, so the priests teach and Charmian, Egypt inherited something. A knowledge of what is real, and the things their Pharaohs did and I do are a mime of this reality only the instructed can understand. An inner and an outer Mystery in one. I suppose if I wanted to find out more about it, I could. For them it is enough if I play my part. What is divine does the rest. Only it may not be a fortunate thing to have to do. Or, if you like, dangerous, because exactly of the truth in it as well as the lie. Remember it was only yesterday that the Greeks found out that man isn't God. Or only very rarely and you can't tell beforehand—and then not exactly God; and it's safer anyhow to wait till you are dead. Rather hard, though, for princes and people with an itch to rule, for it's useful, especially with men who are not Greeks. Then, just as men were beginning to do without that flattery, Alexander happened and started it all over again. It was Egypt who put it into his head. First because it was useful. Then because of what happened at Siwa. Then, like some final secret

122

between himself and his daimon, because a part of it *was* true. Then, in the end, because it went to his head —the part that was truth as much as the part that was a lie.' Cæsar nodded, tolerant of her account.

—" 'Then it all came back, and even greek princes, even Sotêr, followed him, and all the Epigonoi. First when we had done something to justify it; then when it looked as though we had done something; then when we wished to persuade. When we were crowned; then when we were in the nursery, in the cradle, in the womb. Lastly, when we had made of ourselves the very opposite of what is proper to a God. Most especially then. Remember Physkon, Aulêtês, my father, and his just-deceased brat.'

" 'Um,' said Cæsar—'then we are to take it that as deity incarnate you consider yourself a fraud?'

"I do not know if I was surprised or not when she shook her head.

" 'It is not quite like that. Not quite. Here is the difficult part, and where Iras is happy, whose mind has been made up for her, quite clear and nearly true——'

" (At this it was I who felt like a bird that has laid an egg. It is her truly royal gift, that of delighting people with themselves.)

" 'When I said that to-day such things are dangerous, I meant most dangerous of all to do from birth. I was born it, and so given less chance to become what I am by nature, and every chance to make that nature into a monster. As for what you are about to do, Caius, now you are old, and have done such things as astound men,

123

and have even learned what there is in your own soul—
that is different.

—" 'Still, all the same, what I would know is this.
Are you, Caius, doing it from policy, or because you
think that you are united to the Roman Genius in some
special way? Or both——?' Instead of answering her, he
asked another question.

" 'All this time, Cleopatra, you haven't yet told us
what you believe—or feel—about it in yourself. Come;
as you say, you were born to it, whether you think that
you should be or no . . .'

"She sat, drawing her rings up and down her hands,
until the collets hid the long nails we now lacquer green
to the despair of the Matrons, who have never got
beyond gold, or that dreadful animal-red. (What they
heard her call 'bloody finger-tips.' More trouble for
us.) I tell you this now to make the whole of it seem
less dull. Dull, in a way it is, but important. We are
not usually serious like this, Philo, and you'd better
know when we are, because you think we aren't, and
you can't say now in your next letter that we've forgotten what we came for and can only play the fool.
Besides—besides—I would show you if I could that there
are times when my mistress is moved to speak like a
divine woman.

"Where was I? The queen was saying:

" 'I was born to it, as you say, and all the time I was
a child I was taught to do certain things. Public things;
and to myself I put out my tongue at it, because of the
people who believed it and the people who did not

124

believe it. This for as long as I could. Then a time
came when they put me into the Sacred Robes and I
stood before the people, holding the sistrum, when I
did not think any longer, solemn or idle thoughts. It
was then that I gave myself—or was given—to the air
and the light and the earth, and to all those natures
palpitating before me; and offered myself—or was
offered—myself to myself. Then it is that I come out of
myself, and Something—call it the Goddess—becomes
me and I That. That which was August in time
had departed: that which is eternally August entered.
When it has done that, my body is as though it had been
in a different state, as though it were impregnated with
a life that is not the common run of the blood. I move,
distinct, elated, but not with myself. I do not want—
I am—power. I am filled to the lips though I do not
speak. I have seen the things of which our actions are
the translations. Only Harpocrates had laid his finger,
called Silence, on my mouth.

—" 'This is the best I can do. Now, Caius, it is your
turn. You have not told us yet why you are doing it,
and what it is you believe?'

"He looked down at his ringless hands. Not best
pleased; and if moved, most unwillingly. And it was
with a large naked lie that he answered her, neither
generously nor with grace.

" 'You can take it that my affair is nothing more than
simple politics. Done to give the Romans something
to talk about, and something more effective to adore
than—shall we say—Diana and this King of the Wood.

Whom you all seem to find, and quite reasonably, to be, for a sovereign people, an inadequate object for devotion.'

"There was a stupid little empty silence. Until Cleopatra said gently:

" 'That's good—good, I mean, that you will be their Agathos Daimon, Cæsar, to us and to the Roman People, and to men everywhere.'

"After that we rode away."

V

"Charmian, waiting-woman to the Divine Cleopatra, Born of Isis; To the Lord Osiris, Daughter and Spouse; To Horus, the Son, Mother-on-Earth; Eyes of the Upper and the Lower Land; Image of Khem; Crowned with the Double Crowns; Wearer of the Sun and Moon; Day-Star of the peoples, and of Egypt, Queen—to Nar-ti-râ, her kinswoman and friend.

"It is not easy to write this, even to you whom I call my sister; for I cannot, like Iras, make words written down sound like her voice talking; nor do I dare leave for long the king-child Cæsarion, until his next tooth is through.

"There is one good thing about this land, and that is the trees. Not shut up in courtyards, but growing by themselves, where there are no men. And they are better than men. They are better also than temple-pillars, because they are part of a temple, but to Gods we do not have in Egypt. Very blessed Gods. You can talk to them and each one has something different to say. In winter they strip and box one another. In spring they put on new clothes, and men come and dance under their green light. They say that a woman called a dryad lives in each one, but we think there is

127

a man too. For they look like men, not women. Yet men who do not harm women. I've married one and can stay a maid. So have the others. Only they haven't time to mean it.

"This land has its back up, arched everywhere like cats. So there is a great deal more room in it than in Egypt; and to get anywhere you have to climb up and down sides. In between and half-way up you find the best trees.

"This city is built on seven ups and downs. Little ones, with people in their houses stuck all over their backs.

"These people are perfectly glad to be nothing but themselves. But they hate us for being foreigners, and me for being most foreign and an egyptian magic-woman as well. Though some of them are very curious about egyptian magic, and think that I can do new spells. When spells are the same everywhere; and when the fury in their hearts would be quite enough to poison Cæsarion's milk, if milk could be turned to poison that way.

"The worst thing is that it could never enter their minds that we are here to make a great magic come true, make Cleopatra and Cæsar's daimon-power work properly, now that they have made Cæsarion between them. So that what they are can go on happening till it is perfected. It is Isis and Osiris and Horus all over again, ready to happen to the world, if only the world will let it. If we can make these people know. Only Cæsar doesn't quite know what he is. He began to in

128

Egypt, but here—perhaps a secret part of him is afraid; and anyhow he wants to do it all by himself, forgetting that his marriage with her was a marriage of Gods, Hieros Gamos, and even Iras knows something of what that means.

"The Queen knows that we have just got to go on. And that anyhow we have Cæsarion. (His teeth are coming fast.) He has a little sword of soft gold to make him brave. I rub him over with oil and let him crawl naked to make him hardy. He has balls and boxes of coloured wood that fit in to one another, so that he may know the shapes of things. We hide what he wants round a corner to make him curious; and hang it up to make him climb; or where he least expects it to make him think.

"There is glory about him. The Queen knows it. She has given him to me to show him how to begin, and she is not jealous. That is like her. Nor is Iras. That is like her also.

"It is most difficult to keep a magic working right. So that it does not turn into something else. Keep people thinking about it the right way; and not thinking too much. Too-much is worse than not-at-all.

"The Queen remembers in the right way. Leaves the remembrancing, the processes, the mind-shapings, to me. I only showed her one thing: to say to herself at the turn of the event: 'Cleopatra Lagos, it matters everything and it matters nothing.' To know that, that is truth; and whether you believe it or not matters nothing at all to truth. This is hard, I know, but by far the best way. When it gets too hard, I comfort her; telling her that in one way or another it will come true, and she and Cæsar become part of the heaven in men's minds for ever. This is true and more than this. Then she asks: 'What about him?' looking at Cæsarion's cradle. 'He too,' I say, only there I am not so sure. I do not know. Not about this world, I mean, that matters so much to his mother.

"Then she is content because she is so young. But I have less to do than she or Iras or even Cæsar in being old or young.

"It is no use to tell my Father or my Mother these things. They want other things too much: that Egypt should have a king again who is an Egyptian. But I know—as Isis bore Horus, the Saviour—that Egypt will never have a king who is an Egyptian again. For we in Egypt are not able to live as the world is living now, and not altogether because we do not want to. Nor are we strong enough to make it live our way. I mean the way we used to live. Nor can we go on living our own way without the rest of the world. We can only grumble, we can't alter things.

"Unless of course we use the Curses. If we warm what is cold. But that is the ancient evil; and anyhow I think they are forgotten. Only at Thebes you never know. A thing the Lagidæ have never even begun to find out.

"Now there is Cæsar. It is he whom we have to keep on remembering, and in the right way. Cæsar forgets. Forgets in the wrong way; loses himself in his own way.

He is making a God of himself now, because they haven't any Gods here.

"(Remember, my sister, that I have lived for a long time among Greeks. So that I can no longer see things only as an Egyptian. Only the first thing that such living took away from me was my Father and Mother, and I hope it will not do the same to you. But if it must, it must.)

"Think of all the images, in Egypt and in Hellas and all over the earth, that we have made to show what the Gods are like, and that here there are no Gods. Gods they have borrowed, and Gods they are beginning to make up out of themselves; but who really have no business to be called Gods. For the Gods they started with aren't Gods at all—little spring and wood and field and garden and in-and-out-of-door magics. With here and there an evil spirit, to placate with sorrow and human blood. We went to see one yesterday, and I asked Cæsar what he thought about it. He did not begin to see what I meant. It made me wretched to see how such a man could not even begin to understand. Cæsar forgets. He may forget us, and try to do by some other way what he can only do through us.

"He is never afraid because he is Cæsar. I asked him once how ordinary people got on without real Gods.

"'We have Rome, Roma Dea,' he said. Iras answered that Jupiter Capitolinus made a bad husband, but I saw what he meant. Rome, the people and the City, is like one huge, living, growing God to them. A God and a Goddess, so much married that they have only one body. It can do for them what each of them wants, and each part of them is what it wants; weaving service and served into one piece, the strongest weaving man has ever done. A piece of stuff that will last for ever, and build up the earth into a shape that will never pass away.

"That is what Cæsar is really High Priest of. But he is not so easy about this God he is making of himself. It is not all politics, though he says it is. He never gets drunk, but there is something that is not sober about it.

"(Men will say that he thought of it because of Cleopatra; and that is true, but not our fault. We did not mean him to do it, because he does not know what it is or how it is done. The Queen is enough. We need no copy of her. Her Goddess-hood and his manhood would be sufficient.)

"What the people in Rome do not like in me, why should they agree to in him?

"He thinks he can be a God because he has won battles. That is not the reason. Alexander could tell him that.

"Even to come near the Gods you must do the proper things which make the bridge between their life and our life. You and I are Priest-Women and were taught them. There are scents, sounds, objects, names. Ceremonies. Then there is yourself. You must be the same in your inside life as these holy things. Slowly you come to know the links between them. That is how a Pharaoh is made. I suppose that Father and Mother are right

when they say that Cleopatra is not a real Pharaoh.
While I know at least that she is trying to—having to—
be three things at once. Pharaoh and then a greek
prince, and now a kind of roman matron.

"All this she may be able to do. But only because
she is what she is herself. Not because the rules say
that it can be done.

"The rules say that you can do it, if you can. The
Gods do not object, if—. That is in every history. Look
at the Greeks.

"But I fear it will come out wrong. We have to see
what sort of a God Cæsar will make of himself, who has
no more than himself for God.

"All I care about in the world is my Lady and her
son. But I would like Father and Mother to understand
that if she gets her way, Egypt will be again the greatest
country in the world. It will have to be great from
Alexandria, but that would be enough. The East and
the West would become part of one another. Rome
swallowed if you like. And if we pure Egyptians are
any good, we shall come in for a great enough share.

"I don't suppose they will believe this, but this is
what they should believe, because it is the truth.

" (I think by now they know that it is useless, as it
always was useless, for them even to see it in their
sleep that I should give poison to Cleopatra and the
child. Do you remember the instructions they tried
to make me learn—how I was to do it? I found the bead
the other day with the poison in it for me to take
before the torturers took me. I shall not throw it away.

There may come a day when we shall need it. Only Cæsarion shall not have that one to suck.

"This from Cæsar's villa across the Tiber, in the gardens and orchards outside the gates of Rome. Charmian, your sister, now a Pharaoh's nurse, bids you farewell."

VI

". . . In Thebes the Curses are out. When your letter came, I saw it in the curl of the wax that sealed the parchment-cord, on which you had written in the ancient language the secret thing. And at the end, after your name, was the small sign not even a priest can write and live.

"So we know. But watch the sky for the Featherless Birds. How high they circle, on bone wings. And the Thing that was Cold is Warm now.

"Now it is for us to take the sacra. Those that will prick off those birds in air. Those they will find when they get to us here. In the bath and the cup. Under the stone, the fold of the linen, the fall of the hair. There is the Plumed Fish and the Egg with Eyes. The Fire and the Milk Bee.

"Take the Toad in the leaf, the Snail with pearl horns.

"Put the sand to the steel. Let it sing.

"Put the Wasp to the Oil, the Wine to the Salt, the Pebble in the Milk——

"Add the Bitter, the Sour: the Salt to the Tasteless: make Sweet.

"Thread the Ring on the wax. Kiss the flame. . . .

135

"Crown the Hawk: burn the Jesses.

". . . . You know the rest. Should you see the Lion, remember I too have heard Him roaring on the Capitol, three nights past; and the Divine Eagle also has lent me wings. These are not the Enemies of the Rose. . . .

"Tell me what comes out of the pearl. . . .

"It must be a blue stone. . . ."

VII

B.C. 44. *Spring.*

THE past winter had gone sweetly to the three girls from Africa. The winter of their second roman year, sharp nights and sun-spells, clouds whirling up to loose their snows on Mount Soracte, rolled out over the Mediterranean and vanished down the sky into the winter sea. The steady brilliance of a roman winter, varied by a knock-about wind that met them, tumbling round corners, tuning up their young strength and activity and delight.

All seemed to be going well. They had lately left the trans-tiberine villa for a house in the City. Once inside, it was the roman mob who saw them, and the mob liked them, as the people like all pretty things and young. Accepted them at least as an interesting adjunct to their Dictator's private life.

As Venus Genetrix, holding in her hands the apple of life, a statue was made of the Queen; set in a shrine, in a temple of its own, for the Romans to adore. Which they adored as they were ready to adore all egyptian things which had to do with religion and which the young queen had helped make popular. A Lover and

137

a Lover, a Sister and a Brother; a Sister and a Sister; a Father and a Mother and a Son—Isis and Osiris, Isis and Nephthys, Isis, Osiris and Horus. 'The child never spoke. The Wife wore the Moon.' Whatever old-fashioned people might say, it was all very exciting; and so was the new Julian College in Cæsar's honour with priests called the Luperci Julii; in whose temple stood his new statue, the cool, stern, witty face softened into the respectable benevolence of a being known as Jupiter-Julius.

Those were not proceedings to startle the queen. (Not, say, as Lady Haig might have been startled if, just after the War her husband had been allowed to build a small annexe to St. Paul's, to include a portrait of himself above the altar; while the Dean provided a new order of deacons for its service.) To Cleopatra it was matter for a smile or a shrug. What she may have doubted was its wisdom. And to see the Romans taking to foreign devotions with the enthusiasm of converts may have had its ridiculous side to the Lagid girl.

All the same, there were moments in those days when she knew herself for a woman standing under the Tree of Life, its apple her hand; her son beside her, no longer at the breast but on his feet. For Cæsar had not changed his mind, as they had feared he would a year and a half before in the woods at Nemi. He had tried to once with Queen Eunoë of Mauretania; given the Court in exile some anxious moments. Was it possible he would think that she would do as well, the moorish queen, whose brown body was all that the vulgar supposed Cleopatra's to be? (And, to judge from the temper of subsequent historians, still suppose.) The oriental lady of temperament incarnate, loaded with jewels, eyelashed 'like a panther's whiskers,' apt at torture, assassination and sex. The Romans were being shown something very different, a girl cool, sensitive, with the aloofness of one who knows what doom may be, yet one in whom the evil secrets of her race showed not at all. Only its glories, in her elegance, her energy, her wit. A passionate mother, and in her utter candour, her intelligence as well as her bearing, a creature truly royal. But with a royalty they could not reject as oriental with contempt. A majesty of the West, as was her training, her descent. To hold her kingdom she had won their Cæsar's heart. She had been the only woman to bear him a son. Married to him by roman law, she would bring him Egypt. King he would be in Egypt, and in Rome its First Citizen——

But, suppose, suppose the double titles would not mix?

Suppose the girl herself would not agree to be no more than first of the Matrons in Rome?

Suppose—which seemed only too probable—that Cæsar would find the quick change from Pharaoh to senator and back tiresome, unnecessary, inopportune?

Suppose it occurred to him that what was good enough for ancient Egypt was good enough for day before yesterday Rome?

Suppose all these—and other—considerations shaken together——

139

The conclusion was already painfully clear——

Cæsar, to whom it had been proposed that he should wear a crown in every place but Rome itself—Cæsar, whose golden throne was now a fixture in the Senate—Cæsar, whose bed of state now ornamented every temple —Cæsar, whose leaves of golden laurel were so woven as to look more and more like a crown—Cæsar, who had lately taken to saying that a thing was so because he said it—Cæsar, who was about to pass a law to allow him to have two wives at once—Cæsar, who was falling more and more into those fits of equivocal sickness, the sign of death or apotheosis—that this Cæsar would soon tire of the whole complication, would discard his lawful honours for what his countrymen hoped never to see again, the crown of the ancient Roman Kings.

Slowly the roman people were working themselves up into a frenzy about this very question—and were being worked.

To Cleopatra it must have seemed that the problem was nearly solved, her own and Rome's, Alexandria's and Egypt's. She was hardly twenty, yet in that time she had gained her first heritage, had mated herself to the greatest man on earth, who had once been known for a lover; and even in his fifties had not lost his power to delight. If that part of their alliance was over, what of it? She had borne him a son. A few months —weeks—would see her his roman wife, and the earth theirs—the earth for Cæsarion—the Return of the Lagidæ——?

In actual truth, it was at this instant that the real

difficulties, the things that prevent, were coming out of hiding; massing themselves behind the array of splendour, the speeches of Senators, the social triumphs, the crowds' roar of applause. Behind love and hope, ambition and determination, like vapours solidifying, first in the shape of clouds, then water, then ice; then by some final transformation, stone; the forces that deny the reasons why the purest, the most burning will has no effect, out of their hidden places of origin were moving upon Rome, to where the world's pulse beat.

For the last two years—ever since that little trip to Alexandria, and the boy-and-girl war whose victories he had magnified on his return into a Triumph—Cæsar had lived alone. (A Triumph that has a curiously common ring, as we are accustomed to imagine Triumphs. The *Veni, Vidi, Vici* displayed on posters; and people in chariots, haranguing about Cæsar's virtues and his dead enemies' vices; and bits displayed of the deceased, and the Princess Arsinoë in gilt chains, looking like a rather self-righteous martyr, before that personality had had time really to emerge. The description reads strangely.) Yet perhaps he was right to have one. On that visit the greatest of his ideas came to him; on that visit Cleopatra made her entrance on the world-stage; that visit gave him his last—if ever he had one—love-affair.

Yet one thing is clear, that two years later, he was alone, as even Cæsar had not been alone before.

Throughout his life he gives the impression of a man essentially alone, not by accident or any sorrow or

141

ineptitude separating him from other men, but with a solitude imposed by the conditions of his being—by his greatness, the quality we call 'Cæsarian,' by his sensibility, his intellectual splendour, his wit. By the egoism also that was the product of these. And it is at least possible that in Alexandria there were moments when he did not feel himself alone. Anyhow it seems clear that his final conception of his destiny, his own and his city's, took shape there. A destiny that was not to be realised by him. We know now what was about to happen, but he did not; unless the undoubted omens, in an omen-fearing society, made him uneasy. His was a heart's desire so nearly right that a little later it came off, only most bloodily; and sealed by a sacrifice of a most curious kind, the death of the two people its author had loved best.

From which follows one of the greatest of the historic 'Ifs.' It is not a familiar supposition. With Eliza Fay, mankind has usually preferred the picture of the queen 'revelling in luxury with her infatuated lover, Mark Antony, who for her sake lost all.'

Yet if those two had brought it off—. If Cæsarion had succeeded them—. If the seat of government had been transferred from Rome—. Then one can imagine that what *did* happen might have happened differently, with perhaps a grace added; that one 'being so nobly named' might have been the holy king the world could have recognised with its reason and served from its heart; that Christianity itself might have found a society to shape as brilliant and less brutal. Instead, in roman

142

society our Faith found an organism too far gone to save; its war against a state so exhausted, so tangled in economic problems it had failed to solve became inevitable; nor could the church find an ally in the ancient 'virtus' when it had ceased to exist.

So it seems that much depended on the fact that during those last years, in spite of Cleopatra and his son, in spite of Antony, in spite of the praise of all men, Cæsar found himself more and more a solitary man. A man on a throne, so high up that there are only the winds about it, the naked heavens' intolerable blaze. The voices of men borne up to that height are indistinguishable from the cry of storms; and if the words of adoration had turned to 'crucify him,' the airs would have lifted and carried them all on the same note.

Alone too in a place it was bad to be alone in. In Rome. Rome in the hour before the opening of the final phase of her history, a racked, agonising place, lately habituated to atrocious proscriptions and to civil war; to Sulla's suave horrors, the wild experiments of Cataline. Already capable of poetry, brimful, furious with destiny; and Cæsar was a God in it and to it; and not a soul, unless it were the Queen or Antony, to realise the human being out of which the God was made.

·   ·   ·   ·   ·

One or two *contretemps*, it is true, were anxiously discussed at the little court. The quarrel over Dola-

bella, who, according to Antony, would have been better
dead, and according to Cæsar should be the pet lamb of
the community. But the way Antony put an end to the
situation made the girls laugh; and eventually—as was
the way affairs had—brought the queen no good.

Antony was not the man, so they noticed with approval
and surprise, to submit himself on all occasions to his
chief. If Cæsar chose to encourage Dolabella and blame
Antony for the action he had taken to render the young
man harmless (it had been a proscription-list little
short of a massacre and so foreign to Antony's character as to seem to us likely to have been justified) Antony
would show him, and that without sulking or nursing
a grievance, that he could act even without the master
he adored. So he claimed as his share of the victory
of Pharsalia Pompey's house on the Palatine, with all
that was in it. In perpetual need of money—a chronic
affliction of the Romans of that period in spite of the
immense sums that passed through their hands: men
who had lost their antique simplicity to find a flood of
foreign luxuries suddenly necessary to them—he pro-
ceeded to sell the place. And to do this, he went to
live there, entertaining roman society with a classic
series of parties throughout the winter of 45–44 B.C.

It was Antony's delight to give presents, with a
generosity that was more than lavish, that was kind.
Founded on pleasure in the delight of others, even a
will to share their troubles. And the troubles that could
be lessened by the gift of a pretty slave or a gold dinner-
service were doubtless lessened; and the man's reputa-

tion stamped as a prince of good fellows, who gave what
he gave not out of calculation or to be rid of the needy,
but out of something like love.

Parties followed—parties that lasted in groups of days
and nights together. Parties—one knows that kind of
party—to which *everyone* went. 'Every salon a saloon
and every bedroom a brothel'—as Cicero, who was not
invited, said. The host appearing as Bacchus or as
Lupercus, in rehearsal for the spring-sport that would
open the year in February, the Lupercal Feast. Senator
or no Senator, he meant to run that course, naked and
laughing and bloodied, and half-daimon and half-man
and all splendid, and bring matters for old Cæsar to a
head. (Shortly after he had taken possession of the
house, the young and the old statesman had made it up:
and all winter long the parties had gone on, among
the apparently inexhaustible treasures of Pompey's
house.)

To these parties the queen must not go. These she
longed to attend. Charmian prevented her and Iras
tried to. Until one night neither queen nor Iras was
to be found. Or were found finally, by Charmian,
shrieking in a pillow-fight with Antony, in his bedroom,
leaping across Pompey's embroidered sheets. In a wine
cratêr someone was trying to have a bath: another to
support a wine-glass on his person, in the manner of the
Sileni on the Douris cup; Antony, dressed for the part
of Hercules in the lap of Omphalê, was trying to weave
Iras' hair. Cleopatra was showing them how to be three
Goddesses at once. 'Quack! Quack!' they said each time

145

a pillow burst; and that one of Leda's eggs had laid a duck, and they were 'all going to hatch—hatch—hatch out together.'

Into this Charmian strode, in egyptian dress, wrapped close in a mantle wound tight above her bare brown legs, stepping like a crane, her hair covered with a wig; and her grave young fury was sufficient to prevent her from being taken for something that she was not.

She knelt to the queen, who stamped her foot, lost her balance and tumbled sideways on the bed and bounced. Antony had the wits to see why the girl had come. Stepping out from his woman's dress, mother-naked, he called for the Queen's litter. But he was surprised when Charmian said to him through her teeth: 'Kill—kill—kill the slaves who have seen her here.' Beamed and scratched his head.

'Can't do that, you know. Old family servants. Know better than to talk. I know—I'll send 'em all down to the country.' He stooped towards the cratêr into which his friend had got most of his shoulders and his head; lifted it, tipping it up, so that the man staggered, the wine sluicing down his body, his head inside.

'That's all right. Now he can't see. Only having a romp. No harm done——' A slave drew a mantle round him. A minute later he was escorting the girls out of the house, and their litter sped away through the streets, now quickening with the dawn.

VIII

"THE spring has turned unkind, *frater carissime,* not like last year. We are troubled with the wind, dry as if it came off the desert and with icy fingers. Life seems like it suddenly—people, I mean, and Cæsarion's last tooth. Perhaps it's the Parthian war——

"The Queen weighs it all. I give it to you in her words:

" 'We are like people on tip-toe, stretching, stretching. Will our arms and toes reach any higher or even stand it any more? They advise Cæsar, they advise him: "Put it off until you return in triumph from Parthia." Meaning that after such a victory he will be the earth's absolute master, and there will be no more talk of what the people will stand and what they won't.

—" 'He came to me the other night and asked me what I thought. I told him I had left my kingdom for him: that it was hard to wait when one is young. I tried to speak lightly, but very skilfully. He seemed such an old man, as though he were not the same Cæsar who came burning into Alexandria like a torch brighter than Pharos' fire. He answered me unkindly:

—" 'You think I mayn't survive it, and then where will you be. You're safe enough in Egypt if you keep your

147

head.' I don't believe that and no more did he. What would happen to me now without his protection, I dare not think. Also I *am* afraid for him. Apart from the risks of battle, this falling sickness comes on him more often, and with it strange fancies. Calpurnia, I know, is distracted by them. Now, when we meet, she talks to me about them, quite simply, as though the Fates have given it to us two to share this man and his sicknesses. As though neither of us had ever been a lover of his.

—" 'No. If he is to go to Parthia before the child and I are acknowledged as consort and heir, I do not know what I shall do. Or if I can bear it at all. I have a kingdom of my own to see to, and all the housewife there is in woman makes it intolerable not to see with my own eyes what is going on there.

—" 'And I do not like my Caius Julius so well now he is a God.'

"So she said, discreetly smiling, not falling into one of her furies which, though they last no longer than a bird-scuffle, hurt her; and partly because afterwards she cannot forgive herself. Says it reminds her of her blood's evil, and the demon who lies in wait for the Lagidæ to destroy them.

"Indeed he is a strange mate for her, the man Cæsar has become. Once it was April, April with the end of March in it, wedded to July. (That's the new month they've named after him.) Now it is May, and not exactly to December. Something of that winter the pirates of the north talk about, that is to last three years and no spring ever comes again and is the beginning of the end of the Gods.

"Indeed, my brother, it is different with us now from what it was last spring. Early it went sweetly enough, but now it has altogether changed—and we cannot have grown old so soon. Or is it an omen, this wind that shrieks about the houses and curls, wraps them in its arms as though it were lulling, shrieks after and tears and screams and drums and throbs——? Is it the roman eagle, stabbing with its beak, beating with its wings—crying out a future so awful that it is no wonder men go about the streets their faces white as their gowns?

"And yesterday I went with Charmian to the shrine where our Mistress' statue stands. To see about the ordering of some rite that Charmian will not trust them here to do properly. We looked up to where she stands, smiling only with her eyes, the sanctity of Egypt the artist has caught; the grace of a Greek, the calm of the Mother, the Queen and the daimon of the Queen. It is all there, and the apple is not her reward but her gift. Only while I was still looking, Charmian went round behind the statue and I heard her cry out. There on the ground, as if it had struck the back of the statue and fallen, was a dead bird. Only not all of it. Not the feathers and the flesh, but plucked bloody bones, all of them, and with open eyes. A horrid thing to see. We called an attendant and he said he knew nothing about it. Told him to take it away and he didn't want to touch it. Charmian stood staring at it. She was like a person appalled, who would not explain. 'It is done. Then it is,' was all she would say; and when we got home tried to make the ceremonies and prayer only she knows. I am to say nothing to Cleopatra. Only later, I asked Aurelia Orestilla to take me to see one of the Augurs; pretending that our business was quite different, to do with the cult of Julius. But when I asked him what such a thing would mean, he said he didn't know. Then, when we were leaving, as though it had suddenly come into his mind, he told us that a slave, an Egyptian, belonging to one of her temple attendants, had gone suddenly utterly mad. 'As though a sponge had been passed over his face and burned away what was inside.' That was all. Oh—and that he can't shut his eyes. That was the last I heard.

"Charmian won't explain: because I should not understand: because I might tell: because it can't be told: because it must never be told: because if I knew, my eyes would never shut again. I tell her hers are as wide and dark as usual. I told her she had a bee in her bonnet. She only said 'So long as we have bees . . .'

"She has just left us for Cæsar's villa outside the City, with the child. Making anything, air, crowds, riots, sickness, separation from the cow she goes to see milked herself, her excuse.

"We are left alone. The streets here are dark and narrow, crawl up and down: and are often built so high they overhang, brow to brow, as though their foreheads would knock together. I crossed the other day from one house to another, on a plank, and a fellow from the street below called up 'Viva! a virgin.' So I would not

let the Queen follow. I remember because it was the last
time we laughed. That was the night the wind came,
the night before the Feast. I had better tell you about
it, though it is really a common feast, and we only
watched it because of Cæsar.

"Charmian wouldn't come. Said the Queen wasn't
barren, so it wasn't necessary, and we didn't need it anyhow. Two men run through the town, bloodied with
dogs' blood and goats', cracking whips made out of the
beasts' raw skins, and you get in their way if you want
a baby. A people's business really, though some of the
Elder Matrons pretend to be serious about it, tell you
about the triplets they had after, and frowned when
they heard Cleopatra meant to go. As though there
might be a new infant Cæsar when Calpurnia can't
manage even one.

"We watched though from the temple steps. Crowds.
The Crowd, as you say in a city like this, which has its
own crowd, like ours—only not *like* ours. Just as savage,
and neither so witty, nor so gay.

"It was strange. Do you remember when we used
to listen to the sea—if you listened to it long enough,
it seemed as though you heard voices in it and music?
Nearly a tune, nearly words? Since this wind came, it has
been like that; and this time it was the same with the
crowd. Before I saw them come crying from the Palatine,
from the cave of Lupercus—He-of-the-Feast—I heard
their sound, hurrying before them—a wordless music I
did not understand. Then they came pouring down
from the hill, and you heard what they were really

151

saying, their words for *'Evoë, Evoë, Paian, Paian;'* and there was Antony, bounding ahead, shaking the red whips they call *februa,* prancing and stepping high, with his huge shoulders back; and swinging them forward to hop on one leg after the other and bump his bottom into the man's dancing back to back with him. Though the air was cold to us who were standing still, cold and smelt sad, we thought we had never seen anyone so gay as that man; and thought how strange it was that we only felt like sighing, when there's no real reason to suppose that all's lost. It was just then we leaned forward and saw one of those arranged accidents, which tell you so much of affairs if you're in the know——

"There was Cæsar, with a lot of Senators, walking to meet Antony—Cæsar on foot, looking as respectable and as antique Roman as he knows how. Antony had on a sort of satchel; and as he bounded along, tossed away his whips and took out of it a golden crown. Like the ones that used to be worn when this place had a king. Up he danced, straight at Cæsar, holding it out; and we watched Cæsar pause before he waved it away and said 'No' in a loud voice for the people to hear. What happened then was really interesting. A few men shouted when Antony offered it, but that was nothing like the yell that went up when Cæsar wouldn't have it after all.

"Bad for us, though Antony carried it off with a wonderful actor's air that said: 'People will soon have enough of this modesty, Cæsar.' But you and I know something about crowds, Brother. It didn't come off.

They howled when they thought he didn't want to be a king.

"One thing more we heard. That old demon—for that's the sort of God he is, if he is a God—told Antony to be sure and strike Calpurnia; and that looks as though he's not past thinking of a child by his roman wife. Bad—very bad—for us. Nor was it allowed to escape us. They got nothing out of the Queen. She was perfect. But when we got home, it was as though the cold were inside us as well as without."

IX

"THE wind blows now as though it were trying to drown us, and we are sunk in it. Unless you stop to listen, you do not hear it; and if you listen long you hear voices speaking above it all the time. What is it they are saying? I have time for these thoughts because less people come to see us now. It is not so fashionable as it used to be to wait on the Queen. We are no longer exciting and new. That means, I suppose, that we are getting less important; may be dangerous; may be of no importance at all. You can take your choice.

"The Queen and I sat at a window and watched the wind blowing a piece of sacking up and down the street. It picked it up and filled it and drove it and dropped it. It lay in the gutter and sometimes it twitched, but the wind was tired of it. It went nowhere. Only here and there. It made me think of so many people going nowhere, only there and here. Wonder if any person really went anywhere, but here and there. We tried to remember the stately stories of our houses, until that too became a question which of us had gone really anywhere? And what were we? The descended of heroes and their successors, or rags torn off something else, wind-filled and raised and dropped? Cleopatra

lay, burying herself among the couch-wrappings, holding out her hands over the dish of hot stones on three
legs they move about here in the cold from room to
room. Until I had to stop us both from such thinking,
reminding her of the Lagidæ, shivering away under embroideries, lying about the palace in Alexandria, listening out for steps which, for good or bad, never came;
waiting for the wind to stop. Reminding her that that
way kingdoms slip through the fingers, and that we'd
do better to go out for a ride.

"I dragged her up; then we mounted quickly, with
next to no escort, and rode out beyond the walls. After
an hour, we left the plain, riding to the edge of the
great road to the north they call the Flaminian Way.
Ox-carts and a few people riding out of Rome. A grey
dust rising, and over us the grey sky that has spread with
this wind. Then, a long way off, far up the road, coming
towards the City, something in the air, that shone in
front of something that was grey and moved and a far-
off sound went with it. We waited to see what was
coming. A few minutes later we saw that what went
first and was bright were the Eagles: and behind the
Eagles, the Legions. One after another, marching on
Rome. To assemble outside Rome before marching
from Rome, across the earth, to Parthia.

"In step, in rank, in armour, in silence, in strict
rank. Ten abreast, in the stride, at the pace, that eats up
the miles. Fifty, a hundred, a thousand, two thousand,
ten thousand. So they passed. So we sat. On our horses,
watching them.

"Going always, going somewhere, getting there. Ready to turn from a mile-long serpent into a square; into any shape that will get them where they want to be. Broken only to make themselves back into their shape; across men's bodies, and over them, through them. We watched them, drooping in our saddles. Not one of them turned his head. We were watching Rome get ready, as Nature gets ready, when the cattle herd and the fish come together in the sea and the wolves gather in the woods. These were to be turned back by one woman, for a child.

"When we could endure that fear no more, we turned, and spurred away across the plain, and entered Rome by the southern gate. That night the wind dropped. . . .

"Since that day it has not been Spring, but sound-less cold and bright. Quiet in the City, but on the hills a snow-brightness and at night the stars shake. While we are all waiting for something to happen.

"Cæsar has not made up his mind. He is much troubled by dreams. He came here last night and sat, warming his hands over the brazier, and their veins stood out blue and hollow, brittle like the stalks of a dying plant. It was dull and he restless and the Queen near weeping. Then he spoke about certain Romans he disliked—that this one was a coward and that one un-just; this one ungrateful, and another, a Caius Cassius, wanted he knew not what.

" 'Knows it as well, Cæsar, as you do,' cried the Queen, at last: 'you speak as one tired of being Cæsar.'

" 'You are mistaken,' he answered coldly. 'Cæsar is

not. He is only weary with persons who hang on the edge of his mantle; who beg to have the lacings of his sandals, and slip a stone into them for him to tread.'

"She spoke with her chin in her hands:

" 'How often have you told me, Cæsar, that a workman must not quarrel with his tools. When you were teaching me to be a queen——'

" 'Oh you——' was all he said, and though he saw us both flush, he went on complaining. Of Cicero's vanity, of Octavian's greed, of Dolabella's taste for treason. Even of Antony's light-heart. Of this man's stupidity and that man's cunning. Of the ingratitude of one, the blindness of another, the faithlessness of all.

" 'Have women been so bad?' she asked, piteously.

" 'Oh women,' he said, and then—why had he no son?

" 'Cæsar!' she cried, and he muttered that he meant one he could train now. 'Brutus?' she said quietly. He paused, staring, and then replied:

" 'Yes, I could love him, but he would not be loved by me.' None of us can understand this. Brutus, even Charmian admits this now, is a philosopher-trained man, who wants philosophy to be the same as life, and 'ought' the same as 'is.' The kind of man who has grown angry because people are not the same as ideas. Until words about people get to be more important than persons. I wonder what he thinks of Cæsar or knows whose son he is.

"Cæsar sat on, like a man who has missed something. Missed what, you will want to know? It is a poor thing if to become Cæsar brings you no more joy.

157

And what is it that brought him so fretful that night to the Queen of Egypt's door; who has been his love; who waited on him then as a daughter might on a peevish father. What is it that men miss when they are old, and the greater the man, the greater the miss? Or is it that in the end they become afraid? If it is that, then it is partly fear of old age itself. We fear old age in Alexandria, but no man, nowhere on earth, more than those Romans do.

"*Life is a pure flame, and we live by an invisible sun within us.* So says Charmian that a priest said, repeating a dream; and that that is a thing no Roman but Cæsar knows.

"Then it was that I was seized with a desire for the Cæsar we knew before; when after the Palace-siege he ran up the water-steps with one of us in each arm, and brought us back to the Queen, saying: 'Braves to the brave. For the bravest,' liking us well. After that, for a time we treasured his every word. Not, as the Queen said, like dead bees drowned in honey, but storing a living comb. Then I heard the Queen ask: 'Do you, Cæsar, ever hear voices in the wind?' and his answer that he left such idiocies to Calpurnia and to us.

" (That is not true. I have heard from all sides that he pays attention to such things of late, sending messages to the Augurs for private news of the entrails, and brooding on the answers they bring back.)

"Philo, it is strange. After the wind, then the cold quiet. Now, in the March Kalends, as they reckon it, there are clouds, climbing over the rim of the earth and up the heavens, to sit like blown-out mountains and watch us; and then we get our ears boxed with peals and claps of thunder like a bronze bull roaring: then like bells. A spit of blue lightning, a crackle, a hiss of rain. Till out of a clear sky the clouds pile again, and you hear the storm returning with muffled grunts and thumps. .

"Perhaps it is that the Gods are sitting round on the cloud-tops, playing ball, and watching what is going to happen to Rome. Waiting, not as we wait—even for someone to come and wait on us. Though Aurelia Orestilla is faithful still, brings us the gossip. Waiting because they have set the stage; smiling because, before it is played, they know how the play will end.

"The Romans are frightened of omens. Not because they found out about them. A people who were here before them frightened them with that knowledge. Perhaps it was revenge.

"It is different with us. No doubt it is possible, as Charmian says, to go peering and picking into the future; and Egyptians are sometimes very clever at it. Only who cares? I suppose it is necessary for armies or when you found a city or do anything that will take a long time and give you a chance to catch the future up.

"But here it is always: 'Did the chickens eat this morning?' 'Was it six birds or seven you saw flying on your left?' 'The ox had one kidney black as a stone.' These are the only questions you hear asked lately. Philo, what does it all mean? What are we waiting for?

Philo, why am I afraid? Let us tell each other clearly the worst that can happen. Philo, it means that Cæsar will go to Parthia and leave us here. It means that he will not come back from Parthia; or if he comes back, he will have forgotten us. Or the marriage will be put off and put off and put off, until the meaning has been drained out of it; and at most the Queen will only be known as the last-hour fancy of a withered man; who, however many battles he has won, has lost his war with men when he lost the war with old age, and is only fit to huddle into his grave. As the wretched Old Year shuffles off into night with the pack of Young Years giving him a kick as he goes."

X

". . . It is much better that people who have no business to know the future should leave it alone. It is fitting only when it is done by people who are taught what can be known and what cannot be known: when to look for the signs without, and when for those that are inside one's body: under what ways it is possible to look round the corner of the earth-mirror and to translate rightly the things seen. When to keep silence and when to speak.

"It is not the business of private persons or of meddlers or of the no-more-than-curious. Only the man born a prophet will know what to tell and how much. Except in times of fear or great danger, men are agreed upon this and leave well alone. It is at the Turn of the Event—when the Signatures are out, and the air, the soil, the water, the fire cry aloud and make patterns— the voiceless speech of the earth-stuff—then it is that every man becomes his own prophet; and, as Iras says, argue about what is going to happen until it catches him up.

"Much good it does them as they are doing it now in Rome. The quiet is quickening on us. Bee-quiet, the stillness in the hive that comes before the swarm-roar;

161

when the queen soars out and all her people with her, until they find the hollow place and fill it, and the honey-making starts all over again.

"Here, in Rome, there is something waiting to break in, and no reason that it should be wise like bees. Senseless it may be, and awful and useless, and its aim poison, not honey, and its stuff not wax and flower-dew but the filth of dead bodies and blood. As likely one as the other, when the people have no man to guide them, trained as they are in Egypt to find out what is the will of the Gods. Or how to get what they want. Or even to know what it is.

"I told you the Signatures are out—plain for men to read. And each man reads and interprets according to his fancy—the man he saw who passed him in the street with his hand on fire; the men in shining armour these moonless nights, who say nothing and walk abreast; the little owl that sits crying all day from the ridge-tiles of their Senate House.

"There are all sorts of people up and out and about you should not meet. They should be on their backs, not walking. Instead you rub shoulders with them in the street, and on your flesh is the ice-burn where you touched. You cannot always tell which, except that some cast no shadow, and others leave no print in the dust. Or that one has come out of its place without an ear, or an eye, or a breast. Something they must leave behind to get back to their own place; whose bodies are not given to the fire or received, as ours are, in a place prepared.

162

"In the end of our garden-court I myself saw a man-dog, a cat-woman and a man-bird change shapes as one day changed to another. The last I could prevent, who have the bird-magic of Egypt. The rest are out in packs. Neither is there a full grave left by night in the city.

"On the high air has been thrown the image of a battle, men and horses fighting in the sky.

"The sky has distilled blood for dew. From a crucified slave ran water instead of blood. He called upon an Image, in whose image he hung. These eidola hang about the city and the air. Even in the garden across the river, by the fountain where Cæsarion plays. He runs to me where I sit under the trees, the pure child and the son of heroes. It was yesterday he told me: 'Who is the man in a cloak, leaning on a stick? He is always a little way off in the garden, looking——.' I said 'You tell me who it is?' 'He is a bad Hero,' he said. Already Cæsarion is very wise.

"Nor have I the place or the instruments to make the translations, the correspondences for these spectres. All I can do is to turn the mind of my Mistress and of Iras away from them.

"This morning the captain of the *Hirundo* came up from Ostia, said he had had her up and careened her after the winter, and that it was time the lord Cæsarion got his sea-legs. What were the Queen's orders?

"I saw that she was ready to go to sea."

XI

"PHILO, when will this reach you? You who have gone to Cyprus? You who have left Egypt and Alexandria, and are now in that island where nothing has ever happened. *'Would God I were the ceryl-bird, over the wave-flower with the kingfishers——'.* Almost I could throw myself from this window, out into the air; so that some God, lover of the love between brother and sister, would make me a bird. It was for such things surely that women were given wings. Birds to fly off from man into the air-world. All my life, girl or bird, I shall keep crying the things that have happened to-day—the ruin, the intolerable loss.

"I am Iras, the Alcmæonid, who have known but two loves—yours and the Queen's. I am a cat in a hot cage. I am a-crying. I am a bird, its feathers stripped. I am the voiceless dead. I am on a cross. I am a creature running as no creature ran, my hands out to meet the hands of my love, to the place where my love is. O love, my brother, who is not there.

"O Romans! *You have killed the nightingale. The winged bird of the Muses who sought no man's pain.* No, I mean what I have to tell you, I don't mean my Mistress—I mean——

164

"(I write as I wait, for Cordax, the *Hirundo's* captain, to send this by his friend, mate of a ship sailing at dawn for Cyprus. With the Queen's permission, whom Charmian is watching.) Know this first—that more than ever now our lives are more hers than our own; and listen, listen, listen as even you have never before listened, you whose ears are mine.

"Philo, when you open this letter, we shall be off Pharos again. If we are not dead. The Mother, the Child and their two Maidens returned. Not in state, not in triumph, with no spoils added and no crowns.

"Cæsar is dead. He was murdered this morning, in the Senate House. The day they call the Ides of March.

"So you see. There will be no marriage. No coronation in Rome or in Egypt. Nor is the will signed that declared Cæsarion his heir.

"What we have done has been to no purpose. What happened in the desert and on the sea, in the Palace and the Lagids' marriage-bed; before the nations and in her heart; with her body and in her mind. These things are no more thought of now than the amusement of an elderly general on campaign. A general who got too heavy for his horse, so that it fell under him and he cracked his head. A man the Romans grew tired of; so they showed him where he got off, he and the fancy-queen he'd had a child by. The Romans are a little out of breath to-day with the bump of this unhorsing; but that is what they will be saying by the next moon, and will go on saying for ever.

165

"Two years we have spent here, fooling ourselves. So many months, clutching at the purple stripe on Rome's mantle, like children after a toy. Trying to play with the wolf, make the eagle eat birdseed out of our hand. So many months we have made ourselves a public gaze, the Pharaoh of Egypt, Aphrodite-in-the-Body, the living Isis trotting round after her Roman, the bitch and her pup. The hellene noblewoman under tutelage of the roman matrons. The last of Alexander's set. (Yes, yes, I remember. She called Caius Julius his successor, Epigonos; and he is dead, more dead than Alexander, for it was his friends who turned on him, not nature; and now he's lying, an old man with twenty knife wounds in his lean carcase, his Senator's stripe blotted out with his own blood. For they would not have him for King.)

"The Last of the Lagidæ. He would not have her for wife. He forgot their love, the world-plan they made together. The son of their bodies can take his chance. Whether he could not or whether he would not, he cannot have her now. When her time comes it will not be Cæsar who will walk beside her among the asphodels. Or reign in the Islands of the Blest, who will be there with Helen and with Achilles, with the first Lagid and with his Master. I do not need to be a priestess like Charmian, to know my Mistress' place— as I know my own.

"It is midnight now. It happened this morning. Brother, I must try and tell you what happened on this thing called morning. Let me try and be very clear

166

while I remember each thing, as though it had not happened to *us*.

"I suppose everyone in Rome knew that something was going to happen. Was that the Gods, trying to break it gently? Or amusing themselves with us? Or its own awfulness, breaking through the nature of ordinary things? Aurelia Orestilla came across the Tiber early this morning. We had all gone back—Charmian persuaded us, and was going through lists with Cleopatra of our gear and the presents that had been made her. Valuable but mostly ugly things. Also she said that Cordax, who was coming up about the yacht, would get lost in the city; that Cæsarion had twenty new words for her and some swears. You know her way. Anyhow, she made us come. Then came Aurelia O—almost as if she had made up her mind to be an old woman at last. Kept saying that she felt like the morning Cicero made his last speech against her husband. Complained of everyone complaining of the ghosts; Charmian questioning her about them and getting them sorted; and Cleopatra asking what the Sibylline Books had to say—thinking of the dirty turn they did old Aulêtês. (You remember how they faked a text to say that the King of Egypt was to be helped, but not with arms?) Nobody in Rome, so it seemed, had had time or nerve for the Books; and we traced a lot of the stories back to Calpurnia, who has been in a state for a month past; and Cleopatra won't have it that it's jealousy of her.

" 'There's another woman,' said Aurelia O, 'who's going about upset—I had it from my maid. I could never stand the pious creature—Portia, young Brutus' wife, old Cato's daughter——.' 'I remember her,' said the Queen; while we were all thinking that she is one of those women who play the matron for all they're worth, and wouldn't have Aurelia across the door of their house.

"However, it seemed that Aurelia's woman's sister's husband's wife's niece is Portia's; and she said her mistress was hearing voices. Voices in the wind, and Cleopatra said something rude, and Aurelia said, 'If that's your alexandrian notion of wit,' and we babbled, until the Queen asked:

" 'What has Cicero been doing these days? You can always tell from him if there is anything afoot——'

" 'Making up his mind,' said Aurelia, 'which side of the fence he looks best on, most roman, most respectable, most well-bred.' We were enjoying ourselves. Then we stopped to think. Which of us *had* seen him? We all had, once or twice, here and there, but not marking him. A little more important perhaps than usual; and Aurelia O said that some one had said to someone else that the old man was in a blue funk about something, and a yellow rage because he hadn't been asked to be in it, whatever it was.

"Remember, Philo, that this was morning—early morning, and Cæsarion paddling in the dew. He went off with a scarf and came back with it, saying he had on his man's gown. Then lugging a grass-snake by the tail and asking if he'd have to wear it for a crown when he was king; and that he'd find another and strangle them both and be Heracles; and that he'd seen Heracles grown up, and he was that man Antony.

"It was then Artemidorus came. (You remember how he helped us before; and though we didn't keep him in the Household for fear of scandal, he followed us to Rome—to train with the Legions and run any messages of ours that needed wits and discretion. He said that some day the Queen would want a soldier and maybe a minister, and anyhow any service of hers was good enough for him. A bit too good to be true, you say— still, now and then, good things come true. Besides, some day he'll come for his pay like all the rest.

"Well, we heard his horse in the courtyard. He must have dashed in through the house, and he stood before the Queen, very pale, with the sweat running, saying to himself, 'I must. There's no time to be lost.' Then suddenly, though he's the image of respect—'Cleopatra, they have murdered Cæsar.' 'When?' said someone, as though it might be going to happen next month. She whispered: 'Tell me.' Then 'Tell me,' again, this time loud and clear. He answered: 'In the Senate: an hour ago or less: under Pompey's statue. Brutus, Cassius, Scribonius, Cinna: with their knives, like butchers.' Trying to be brief and roman till the Greek ran away with him.

—" 'It was the wild horse the asses kicked to death. It was the panther the cattle trod. It was the God the worshippers tore. Yet he died quietly. You see, he saw Brutus. They say he said *You too.*" Then hid his face like Pompey and fell at Pompey's feet.'

"It was rather like the word you have forgotten the moment it flashes into your mind. I think we were each saying to ourselves 'Of course. This is what it has all been about: this is what the Gods have been keeping hot for us. The old fool who has betrayed my Mistress had his suspicions, but not the right ones; the hero who left the stage too soon and not soon enough.'

"No, it was not a surprise. More like a question answered, a release. Philo, that is true. For us three, I mean. Aurelia Orestilla is different. She was dreadful to watch, to whom it hardly matters at all. The fountain went on playing and Cæsarion stumping round. She, Cataline's widow, she childless, sat still, her mouth and her eyes absolutely round. Staring, and her little old body fallen in over its sharp-pointed breasts. When she got up, she tottered, keeping on saying: 'Cata—Cata—Cat——' I do not know, but in her husband's life there must have been a moment when he changed from a man who might possibly be right into a monster; and that was Cicero's doing, who by his speeches showed him for a creature who would destroy Rome. Rome destroyed him all right. But he had just married Aurelia Orestilla for her beauty, whom Cicero hated; and they must have gone through some exceedingly strange things together. For her Cataline was a man made to die, a man offered up.

"I am telling you all this—why am I telling you all this? Because the night is long and who could sleep? Because now it has happened, I am quite outside it. See it now almost as Charmian sees it, only differently;

as part of a huge play, a tragedy and a comedy the Gods have set for their remote purposes. It is our achievement to know that. So that, whatever we may be, we are not their dupe. Only that is left to us.

"Can you possibly conceive, Philo, what happened next? Of all the unreasons, of all the perversities, of all the triumphs, of all the unspeakable gifts of the Gods —we were suddenly at peace. Inside I felt white. I looked at the Queen. She had risen. She seemed, who is a small woman, very tall. And I heard Artemidorus cry out: *'O Dea certe,'* and knew then that I served an Immortal. She was looking down the garden, south across the trees, where she would fly. Shaking off the Eagles, like a gold bird, desert-bred. That for Egypt. Then the meaning of the rest swept through me. I thought of a young moon, tip-toe above hills, a star in its arms. And the dreadful smile of Isis when they brought her Osiris' body with the manhood gone. I saw captivity captive. I saw Orpheus torn. I heard Harpocrates speak.

"These are words only. I do not possess what I saw. I am still too angry—that we have been tricked by Gods and men. This was not my mind, it was rapture or possession by some God. And out of it all there comes a sense that is almost joy. I have learned the quickening there is in times such as these, the danger, the glorious activity of the turn of the event. 'Tolmâ,' we called them once, and 'Zeus-of-the-Lost-Battle.' Found them sweet.

"To see the Queen move was to see Royalty more

royal than Plato's pattern. Artemidorus laughed and wept. Laughed again with us, because of this joy that came as if it streamed out of her to us—

'In the deep-feathered firs
That gift of joy is her's
In the least breath that stirs——'

Thus, and not for the first time, have I found what it is to serve a woman who is truly an Immortal. Could I have known it more if I had seen her crowned beside him . . . ?

"We were not left long to this, although time had stopped for us. There came a rush of our people to the garden, shouting and crying, Cleopatra had them in and stood them before her, telling them to be quiet; and they fell round her, some begging her to die like a Roman: like Dido of Carthage: to weep: to shriek: to faint. To poison someone. Cicero, half Rome, herself. I knocked sense into old Lousa, the housekeeper, who came from Cæsar's household; and we went off to pack and put under seal the presents in jewels and in gold he had made her; before any of the Romans came to claim them as left to them or as part of his estate. Or, anyhow, not hers. It was all quite light and easy to do, so long as I let myself remain in the joy. Charmian took Cæsarion straight down to the yacht. It might enter their heads to make a clean sweep of possible Cæsars. Left him there with the crew for nurses and none of the ornaments of a prince.

"It was then Antony came. We saw a huge creature

with torn clothes, that rushed in, weeping and awful, almost strangled with anger and grief. Violent as one could see, with resolution as well, the strength and the burden of a man on whom the whole state rests. That knocked a different part of the truth into us and some of the serenity out. He stood, speaking before the Queen in a loud voice, as he might to some unknown but quite important officer on a battle-field.

" 'You can see now how it happened——? Those brutes. No matter. They'll keep. Their turn is coming——' (He had told us no more really than Arte- midorus. Neither man had been there at the moment, and Antony was half crazed with his own grief.)

" 'What will you do?' the Queen asked.

" 'That'll keep too,' he said roughly. 'I came here to tell you to get out. As soon as you can. I'll send a troop here to-night to guard the house; but if those swine work up a riot, I cannot guarantee your personal safety—neither here nor in any part of Italy.'

" 'I know,' she answered, seating herself who had risen, thinking deeply, I knew, her head on her hand, and with the most elaborate quiet.

—" 'We will go, if only for the Prince Cæsarion.' That seemed to make him think, while I could see her still- ness surprised him. I suppose he had expected tears and wailings, scratched breasts and torn hair. Then he said:

" 'You'll be all right in Egypt if you keep your head.' Cæsar's words. What those two men had been planning we shall never know now. Comfortless too, not a word anywhere in memory of us.

173

—" 'You'll see the way the cat jumps from there.' If he were brutal, it was like Atlas, holding up the earth. And there was something about him that made you feel the cat would jump the way he kicked it. She thanked him.

—" 'Two widows on my hands,' he said grimly. 'And you, madame, for your own sake, go as fast as you can.'

" 'Go I must,' she answered, 'but not run. When you have a kingdom to run to, you don't. Remember, I am still a queen, with a king for a son. And that king Cæsar's son. And I thank you for this visit and this warning, and for such help as you can give. We may meet in better days——'

" 'Pity he's so young,' he said, still rough, his mind already back in Rome. In a city, dangerous after a fearful wound, now about to recover and strike back and strike blind. I liked him for coming, who had the town on his back; whose future he must direct instantly or follow the man for whom he had no time to weep. It is something that he should have found time, in that first incredible hour, to do something for us.

"Without so much as a salute he flung out of the room. I can still hear the fury of their horses as he and his escort charged back into Rome. Charmian and I went back to our packing and sealing. The Queen went to her bedroom and stayed alone. When we came to undress her, she had already fallen asleep. She had been crying. Only the sistrum she carries as Isis of the Egyptians, its rings quiet, lay beside her on the bed."

PART III

I

THREE years later. Alexandria sunning itself in a delicate light. A little autumn mist, the lightest conceivable of coloured veils, hung over the City; the sea running long fingers up the Pharos rocks. The air inclined its plume ever so slightly inland, across the city roofs, over the market-gardens to the desert. To the valley of the Nile, to Hundred-Gated Thebes, to the Cataracts; to Abyssinia, to the Mountains of the Moon. To Central Africa, where in their millions the tribes of the black hunters fought and flourished, as yet untouched by the white man's world. (What did the classic world, hazy as to the shape of the earth and where places went to, make of that teeming blackness and their relation to it? We do not know.) A continent that had fifteen hundred years of non-interference ahead of it; whose masters were as yet practising on one another, as steel on stone. Fifteen hundred years before the Portuguese and the Spaniards, the English and the Dutch. Early T'Chakas rose among them; unobserved they carved the faces of their mysteries; their demons and godlings of anguish and grief and the subtleties of fear. Naked and shining and not in the least like their gods, their spears and plumes making

177

them tall as trees, a few stood about as guards or as ornaments in the mediterranean palaces; in the cool corridors of pure stone, where the sea-breeze sifted, and in the courts where fountains raised crystal feathers and the sun poured, his fury caressed away by running water and the trees' lifted arms.

Three years later. The Queen sat in her cabinet, a woman near her middle twenties now, her beauty grown indeed, but a little starved; her bearing perfected; her reason, her intelligence now hardened for use. A little worn, wrapped in a reserve that was not natural to her, sometimes a little enervated, a little bored, showing the strain of long watchfulness, the damming-up of her energies as a person and as a woman. Not quite cynical, by no means perfect in patience, she sat; an egyptian secretary before her, cross-legged on the floor as his ancestors sat, writing on a scroll across his knees.

Details of administration, taxes and the relief of taxes; public works; irrigation; calculations of returns, of corn, cotton, peas, papyrus; yield of silver mines, of ivory, of rare beasts and plants and woods. Of elephants and plumes of ostriches from the evil coasts of the south, the old trading-stations of the macedonian ship-masters and the vast hinterland. Returns of spices from the islands that lie south of the Hadramaut, the ancient kingdom of the Sabæans; and pearls from the sea between India and Arabia. The wealth of the ancient world, pouring into Egypt. From the unknown into the known—treasure—into the land that has always been the border between the known and the unknown.

Donations to temples; her image to be set up here and there, with Cæsarion beside her, as joint gods. Appointment of officers, recall of officers, rewards and punishments—all the complex of government, which, in its final stages, passed through her hands.

It did not weary her. Ancient arithmetic, which, outside a few professionals, falls under the head of sums and usually came out wrong, was easy to her. She had even, it is said, some notion of mathematics, enough, in a sovereign at least, to warm the heart of old scholars working in the Museum on the elements of pure science. At least she knew what they were talking about, in this reviving the earlier traditions of her House.

Long ago Cæsar had put the economics of her position in a nut-shell: 'Think, my child, if your parent Aulêtês—one of nature's bankrupts—could not ruin this land, think what could be done with a little management—a little common honesty and common sense. Remember also that there is one thing man cannot do without, Roman or Egyptian, and that is corn. Corn is no longer grown in Italy. If ever we decide we have a moral right to take over the government of Egypt, it will be on account of your grain.'

So, on her return she had seen to it that the surplus of their harvests went to Italy—cheap.

(The records of her reign are actually very few. Octavian saw to that—forced by his own acts to destroy as well as defame the memory of her and of Antony. Yet it is possible, on negative evidence, to suppose her a better ruler, at least, than her immediate predecessors;

since we hear little of the egyptian nationalist conspiracies which filled previous reigns. Besides, it would
have been utter folly on her part not to have reversed
her father's policy, to have continued to treat Egypt as
no more than a milch-cow; and so encouraged it, as
a mere change of evils, to open the door on the Romans
behind her back. Good interior government was as
essential to her as the use of her power over men; and
in that respect it is reasonable to suppose her prudent
and even understanding. And in her position she
could afford a few parties . . . even the gift of a gold
dinner-service . . . the dissolution of a pearl. . . .)

She dismissed her secretary, left her chair for a
window-seat, and once again the exquisite, rather tired
head turned its eyes to the Pharos. The sea was up to
one of its hundred and one games. She had looked at
it all her life. Most of her life had been spent near the
great building her ancestors had called into being, saying: 'Let it be there,' and it had risen, the Eighth Wonder
of the world. And with it the City and the Palace, the
Museum and the Library. Now it was all to go, to this
Power risen in the west, stretching out and taking as
much of the earth as it wanted, with its heavy, beautiful, adaptable hands. She saw herself standing alone
between her kingdom and this Power, this Rome, a
Hellene against barbarians. This much of her own
mystery she must have known. That much of what she
stood for had to die to live again, is not one of the things
known in advance; nor how far it was necessary for
Alexandria to perish for the spiritual city to be born.

Indeed she was like a person seeking an essentially spiritual victory in terms of the body. That will not do. Not because she was a specially sensual woman, but because she knew no other way. A rare body, a quick mind, a high spirit, immense prestige, limitless wealth were all she had. All her life, until the end, they seemed to her enough, tempering them as she did with her gay cynicism, her brilliant understanding, her wit.

Standing by the window she remembered the look of Pharos from the sea, grey through a flying squall, the day of her return three years back. That return—in rough weather, in hideous sea-sickness, in fury and agony of mind. Beaten, fooled, discredited, with nothing to show for it but the yet undigested facts of experience and grief and pain, wisdom only in the making. With the wit to pull herself together and Charmian and Iras; insist on a royal entry, a display of splendour and unconquerable youth she had seized on the business of government. Mastered it, with the crude mastery of a ruler who is absolute, whose Privy Purse is the entire revenue; who, outside scruples of common decency and common sense, has only to please herself. Her housekeeping sense helped her, as it has helped many royal women, whose sex has made them able to assume, without the pain of discovery, that it does not do to kill the goose that lays the golden eggs. Of what we call patriotism, she had probably no conception. She was a greek princess who had inherited a large oriental property, in her case a royal one; a state she must placate with ceremonies in reality only proper

181

to its original rulers. A fact her ancestors had grasped when they had modified the local cults by the intro-duction—it was practically the invention—of Serapis. Loyalty to the City, to Alexandria, their creation, she may have felt. Anyhow pride, delight, a sense of kin-ship and unity. It seems too, from tradition, that the Museum was her friend, the great University which had worked hand-in-hand with Sotêr and Philadelphus. It was with these that her heart lay, with these and with her House. Re-born in Cæsarion, and so prevented from extinction. Yet there was only Cæsarion. For more than three years now, Aphrodite-on-Earth, in the flower of her youth, was without a mate.

II

So the years passed, and it is not impossible to imagine that there were times when heaviness of spirit descended on the Queen. Government-routine and palace-ceremony over, she would withdraw more and more into herself, her mind brooding on the north, deep in the european scene. She was older; Charmian and Iras were older. Cæsarion grew. For what? For what were their lives—these 'things for a prince to endure'? Three and a half years ago her life had fallen in ruins. Since then she had lived as a woman replacing a fallen structure, stone by stone. A house, but who to inhabit it? No one knew better than she that nothing had been determined, nothing was secure. She was holding Egypt, holding it together, but by threads that would snap at a touch. She had thought of an alliance with other powers, which seemed likely to mean with Herod, not only their king, but their man in power there; and outside the roman orbit, the most powerful politician alive. As yet he would have none of her, asserting loudly his contempt for her and his mistrust. So there was only Rome to which she could turn. Still there was only Rome. Rome, suddenly short, as the ancient world ran short to a degree inconceivable to us, not only of bullion but of corn.

So there was Rome, but a changed Rome and a changing. Terrible hours she had spent, gauging that change. Now she knew it was time for action, if ever again she was to act. And there seemed no possibility of action.

The comparative stability of life in Alexandria compared with the desperate chaos in the Peninsula must still have impressed her. To one in her position it must often have looked as though some God had given the Romans enough rope by which to hang themselves. The decay of the Senate, the rise of the workmen's clubs, the forced recruiting, not from the old recruiting grounds, but up north round the Po, or even—as with Cæsar's pet legion, the Lark—from Gaul; the abstention of the old governing gentry from politics—these at the time must have looked very like a breakdown of the whole concern. And being a woman with an eye for those changing details of existence we call fashion— so many feathers to show which way the wind of the world is blowing—she must have laughed at Italy and at the Romans. A race of peasant farmers, in its best days an aristocratic democracy, suddenly given more clothes than it could wear, more food than it could eat, more houses than it could live in—but not more money than it could spend. Never enough money, and borrowing it at terrifying interest—to obtain more things than it knew what to do with and yet refused utterly to do without.

Gilbert Murray says somewhere that it is ridiculous to talk as though there were more luxury in the ancient

184

world than there is to-day; that there was probably not a tenth part as much. But that it does, at certain periods, seem to have had a more demoralising effect upon people's souls. While Jung speaks of the unchained *libido* that roared through the streets of ancient cities. Yet Alexandria and the great hellenised towns were accustomed to their pleasures. They had long secured a state of society to guarantee them, and had sat down to their enjoyment as gentlemen should. It must have been an untiring joke to men long practised in the suave delicate indulgences their cynicism had kept sweet, to watch the Romans gorging themselves on the right things in the wrong way; stirring up all the fashions together in one melting-pot, without the sensibility to devise new forms of their own.

Gorged on the loot of the East, on Pompey's victories and on Lucullus'—that strange aristocrat who gave Europe the cherry-tree; who, at the banquets given in his old age, by which his name is remembered, remained tranquil and indifferent as a god.

What Lucullus did on a large scale, every Roman must do. It was not only a question of food and slaves, scents and jewels, of horses and wild beasts and strange faiths—the historians' stock-in-trade—that produced what is called, and what they called, their 'corruption.' It was a spirit, an intoxication, of which mere tangible objects and practices were the expression, the breath of a New Thought, breathed on them from without, the spirit by which the vanquished became even with their conquerors.

185

A version of this was passing through the Queen's mind, whose assumptions were those that no Roman shared. Unless it had been Cæsar, who had seen in his country's organisation the instrument through which the hellenic mind could continue its priestly task. She thought of the men who were succeeding him, and that to her mind there were few who could be called gentlemen—or, as she said it, civilised men. Until her smile changed, and she winced, as one does at the memory of a folly for which one has been punished. Indulging in a sense of humour had done her no good in Italy, nor the elegancies of one long-practised in the use of beautiful things. (As ever since it has done her no good with historians.) That never does a woman any good. It is 'le dossier accusateur de toute jolie femme'; and once brought a queen of France to the scaffold.

It was trying now to remember that if she had not laughed, worn more clothes or less, countered display with sobriety, grossness with wit, luxury with splendour; appearing in turn, and always unexpectedly, as a young athlete, goddess, lover, scholar, minx and queen, Cæsar might have married her. And even if that had not happened, she would have won hearts in Rome. Be remembered there for what she was. (Some thousand odd years later a queen of Scots came to the same grim conclusion; while both women would probably have admitted that there was something in them that would not retract that laugh.) Still the thought of Rome became intolerable, until she heard herself crying out:

186

"Common barbarians! They were not worthy of us. Nor of their Cæsar whom they murdered, nor of me they had not the wits to imitate." Poor comfort. It is always bitter to say: "My own intelligence betrayed me."

A wave of the old passion beat up her mind, for the Lagidæ, once the earth's princes, then breeding tired, breeding lazy, breeding ferocious, breeding odd. Slipping into follies, into disgraces, into crimes, sane and insane and all hideous. She thought of her amiable-comic father with his secret twists into the monstrous, his fires of butterfly wings and his possession by the God—being the rather rare type who likes his vices and his religion well-mixed. All he had done was to have the wit to see his title established, and for that pay and pay and leave the rest to his children. To her elder sister, who through hatred for her father had destroyed herself with her husband; to her two brothers, one who had wits and no luck, to the little one who had had neither luck nor wits.

She was whispering: "We have hated too much. There is Arsinoë, my sister. Hating me. Why? When our House was in its glory, we loved one another; and it was the delight of Euergêtês to see his wife's hair in the stars." Again the splendid names rolled down the path of her memory: Sotêr, Philadelphus, Berenice, Epiphanes—'The God-made-manifest.' 'What God have we shown forth the last hundred years?' Yet in the very word Epiphanes there is *hubris*—and the answer to *hubris* is known to every Greek. She wondered, as many

187

wondered in the antique world, whether Hubris in the end would catch her out; child of an age in which that lesson was read every year with the cycle of the sun.

Alone again in that long upper gallery of the Palace, where she had watched Pharos as a child, as a girl; where Cæsar had paced, waiting for news of Cæsarion's birth. Over its pavement:

'. . . *bright*
With serpentine and syenite'

she also walked to and fro. Over the pavement—dark marbles to represent the bottom of the sea. Green stone for rock and weed, coral-red for fish and shells. A wonder for little princes. Design from the cartoons of a famous artist, whom the Piper had ordered to make him a house under the sea. And had been distracted by the suggestion that, since Dionysos could turn the wicked sailors into dolphins, his Majesty of Egypt, when he assumed the God, ought at least to turn something into oysters, and make up for a bad season. Aulêtês had been tickled by the idea that he ought to be able to turn something into something else—several Palace-memories shook his daughter suddenly with mirth. How she and Arsinoë had stolen his mushroom omelette and put a very dead crayfish in its place. Assuring their father passionately that he had done it himself, in absence of mind, but his divinity had assured. And Aulêtês had believed them. Gone grey with terror and was heard begging Dionysos to forgive him and not to let it happen again.

Light memories of youth—innocent things. But not enough of them. Iras' memory was a store-house. She would call her, and for an hour they would laugh together, remembering old sports and devising new ones; give a party in the Palace or a water picnic off Pharos. Play practical jokes; until the dreadful sense of being an actor on a stage prepared, the future determined for her and the stars against her, passed away.

Cold, she drew her thin mantle tight over her arms, and hurried along the gallery, its windows full of ships.

Empty, its silk hangings stirred in the breeze. The sound of her feet passed and there was silence. Then, on her track across the marble, something fell with a light thud; and where her feet had been, there fell in as though from the skies and lay there a dead and rotted bird.

.   .   .   .   .

If it fell to Iras to keep her gay, on Charmian fell a very different task. There is a story told, about this time in her reign—a story that is part of the Cleopatra of legend—that another native rising was prepared in Egypt. With the eternal aim to set an Egyptian, a descendant of the true Pharaohs, on the throne. One of the leaders was a young man, their descendant, and a cousin of Charmian's. He came to Alexandria to kill the Queen; and Charmian, not knowing, received him at the Palace. Then asking him if he would care to see 'the rarest woman on earth,' asleep, drew aside curtains and showed him Cleopatra, sleeping in the midday heat.

Then it was, it is said, that he forgot all about his

189

conspiracy and the men he had involved in it, and crazed with magical passion, betrayed them, and only escaped himself through Charmian's aid.

A story that has its origin in the tradition of magic sex. Yet, if Cleopatra haunted others, she was herself a woman haunted; and who knows, in those still years after her first and before her second entry on to the stage of history, what dreams troubled her mind?

In Alexandria, in the Palace, which as much as Nero's House, or Babylon with its gardens, remains in men's memories as a supreme palace of antiquity—the Palace where royalty assembled science as it assembled art, the utmost refinements of living, elegance and wit, with high european statesmanship—the House, made for one House, by one House, was now actually ten years from its extinction. Its hour had struck, but one thing at least was given it, that its end should be worthy its beginning. Not petering out in the imbecile wit of an Aulêtês, but in war and death and splendour and eternal life; and the beginning of a new order for humanity.

For, out of the ruins of her last royalty, Alexandria was to build herself the spiritual city; in which our Faith, requickened in the fires of the greek mind, should make itself intelligible to the world.

'When beggars die there are no comets seen,
The heavens themselves blaze forth the death of
    princes.'

Such events are not so stealthy as men would like to believe. Presented to a prince in at least one dream, whose poisoned details only Charmian could, and dared not, interpret; image of the burden Cleopatra bore and had to bear; a series of pictures that entered her mind, sleeping or waking, a sequence she must follow, and in a state when sleeping was confused with not-asleep. It began with the sound as of a small poisoned mouse gnawing, or an empty seed-pod tapping on a wall. Tapping on the closed door of a room at the end of a passage. A room that led into a garden, a rank deserted place, that could not belong to the Palace with its fountained glories. Yet it was from the Palace that the Queen must start, every time—

Only from what part of the Palace ran the corridor that led to the garden, the Palace that she knew as a sailor knows his ship? She would find herself among the accustomed beauties—though she could never remember exactly where—beside a statue in a recess, whose face she could not see, nor liked to think about it, except that someone had laid an offering before it, and it wasn't flowers; and that there she must leave her shoes. After that, past pale green walls, but somewhere, half-way along, they changed colour, became scurfy in patches, with a plaster sweat like white fur. Then as she went along, before she came to the door of the room, the walls were full of holes, and behind the fallen plaster the woodwork showed through in a pattern like bones.

In the room there was a cupboard with its doors shut.

191

Inside it there was something that must not be let out, and as she passed, she heard it wake up and come thudding across and start working on the panels.

None of this varied ever, unless she paused for an instant, which was not allowed, and said like one with a heroic duty: 'Show me what I must find,' and 'I promise to look.' Then it was that whatever was inside the cupboard gave a nasty laugh.

Through these places she must go, the last Lagid, alone, unsandalled. To the tune of the tapping, the mouse-scrape, as though it were a dance. The door she opened, from the room out on to the garden, was stiff and spider-stuck, and the mouse ran across her foot, and a dead plant stood, stiff and set drunkenly across the threshold. On the stalk there were several snails, old and horny and climbed high up, clinging on asleep. On the path there was a slug, as long as a short black snake, and the plants in its way were slimed and withered with its climbing and its embrace.

Across these she must step, whose touch was death; and out into the place where there had been a garden. The garden of a long-past planting, and now gone back to savage weeds and the sense of uncleanness that appears when man has taken off the hand he had laid upon nature, and his works have not endured, nor have hers returned in the rough glory of the wilderness.

Out in the garden it was her misery that here was no Psyche's task. No sorting of wheat and millet, the clean grains fit for a goddess, but the choke of nettles round headless bodies of statues, patched with green; and always a place she must get to she could never find, because a voice somewhere up in air kept telling her that it did not exist.

Still she would go on, until it seemed she was about to find the place. And, here was the point of it all, the place once found, the whole would change back instantly into the clean glory of gardens, the room into a lover's bower, the thing shut in the cupboard to a most sacred cat, the passage into a royal corridor. When a smooth unpleasant old man came walking quickly out of nowhere, and tried to take her hand.

'Not that way, dear lady. Not that way——' and to avoid touching him, he somehow got her back along the way she had come. And when they came to the door of the room, he picked up the slug like a naughty boy, saying: 'It can run now,' and threw it at her. Then she knew she was swept back along the corridor at dream-speed; and reaching the end, she was just going to see the face of the statue, and if it meant one thing, it was consolation, and if it meant the other it was death. Then she was again where she was when it began, in her bedroom or wherever it was that the vision had fallen on her, with all earthly beauty around her, the cry 'Arsinoë' on her lips.

This was the magic thing that happened to her again and again since her return from Rome. Five or seven times in the year. As is the way of such things, it seemed as though most of it came from inside herself, a private bad-dream-magic of the Lagidæ. But that the old man who met her in the garden and what was in the cupboard were something that had got in from outside. The only person she told was Charmian, and she was not pleased to hear that Charmian put some of it down to what her sister might be doing with the help of the priests. It seemed to make all the care and ceremonies and sub-scriptions to temples such a waste. Charmian tried to comfort her, telling her that she had only to be greater than her sister's hate; and there was not much comfort in that. For generations Lagid had killed Lagid; by poison, by torture, by treachery, by cruelty of the mind: in vile calculation: in sheer insanity. Their hate had *worked.* Lagid had weakened Lagid. And since it had worked, suppose the last of them lay now under a super-natural curse? Cleopatra was not superstitious—no more so perhaps than a lady of the XVIII century—but she knew something about the priesthood at Thebes. More than we do, who have long escaped their grasp.

So, there were times when it became easy to impute all disasters to them; the roman failure, her difficult throne, even Cæsar's murder—let alone this haunting by a dream. Easy—and then too easy; until Cæsar's training asserted itself and the training of a Greek. At length Iras was told, and poured her vehement scorn on it, saying that no one knew better than the Queen that such a magic persecution would only be true so far as she allowed it to be truth. Deriding Charmian, who would only say that there was more to it than that, and would not explain how much, and said she could not in words that would mean anything to them; and that they must take her at her word.

194

But when the two young women spoke together in private, Charmian told her something that made her look grave.

"There are some who cannot be harmed, some who must and some who may——" she said. Iras had answered: "The Queen is among the third. What can we do?"

"Only fortify her will——"

"And if the Lady Arsinoë is the instrument——?"

From that time on they were at the subtlest pains to reassure the Queen; but as the years in Alexandria went by and the dream repeated itself, Charmian told her mistress that, when it came, she must make the search on which she set out. Find the place in the garden the old man prevented. This she tried. To come out, sleeping or waking, so sweat-drenched and terrified that Charmian ceased to urge it. Instead she spent long nights in places said to be haunted, alone, making the prayers and offerings of appeasement—to the dead Lagidæ, and to those whom they had made dead. To do this adequately for her own mind she found it necessary almost to invent a deity of her own. Elaborating at least the theology of Isis and Osiris. For their need was unspeakable, and no one form of the Divine seemed to include it. So, with stones chafing her thin knees, she prayed—to a God whose love for man should have power over crime and death, or—unthinkable blessedness—over the sum of man's egoism or will for destruction. And, from the other side, Iras fortified all that there was in Cleopatra of the greek mind.

195

III

So the name 'Arsinoë' came easily to the Queen's lips, the sister she had not seen since their roman days, who had walked in Cæsar's triumph, who had run away into the country to haunt temples, and especially the temples of Artemis.

Cleopatra had been there, seen her sister, perfectly safe, thanks to her; but there in gilt chains on foot. Why should she have stayed away from a triumph that was partly her triumph, fruit of her diplomacy, to spare the sister who had always hated her, as only a Lagid could hate? Hated her largely because of Cæsarion. Hence Artemis. And now the priests were using her to work spells with. The late-Lagid solution would be to send someone to poison her, and get her out of that sort of harm's way. If it would. See what Artemis would do about it. Iras laughed. Nothing finally had been done.

Yet something must be done to end this life of vision-haunted suspense, the presence of a sister who would never forgive. Never forgive under any circumstances, which makes the practice of virtue difficult. Oh, Cleopatra knew what she was up to! Visited in secret, by priests and by her own courtiers; to plan her murder and Cæsarion's. So that she herself could mount the throne—a plan as silly as it was vicious. If Rome did not find it too difficult to brush away Cleopatra and their Cæsar's son, what would they make of a fly like Arsinoë? No, count her out, go on governing as best she could. Keep a weather-eye open for alliances. Make friends if she could, and with Herod, Galilee's governor —the man with the future; collect news of Rome. Digest it. Surely even those pitiless men would realise the strength of her position—the cards she held—not up her sleeve, but displayed triumphantly? Mother of Cæsarion, of Cæsar's body the only living heir. How could they forget that? Yet it seemed they could. Or, what was worse, ignore it with filth and with sneers.

'In Alexandria it's a wise man who knows who his father is.' Things like that.

.   .   .   .   .

It is difficult for us, with the conclusions of number-less historians before us, to follow with anything like detailed comprehension what happened in Rome after the Ides of March. To the best-instructed, it looks like a madhouse. While the colour, the atmsophere, the cross-currents that flowed in men's minds, the mysterious meaning of it, is all but lost.

Mark Antony, wild but not crazed with grief, seized the direction of affairs before anyone else had had time to think at all. The party led by the assassins was too powerful at first for him to think of revenge. And, between that party and his own small faction, there was the vast body of the citizens, pro-Cæsar, in point of admiration, but nervous of his late ambition; part horrified, part relieved at his end. They did not know which party to back, were not certain if they wanted to back any party, and would take some persuading to come out on Antony's side. It was all too clear. The roman world was in for one of its phases of civil war. (It was to be the last before the great peace of the Empire descended, but no one knew that.) A situation in which any man less sanguine than Antony might well have despaired.

The reaction in Cæsar's favour did not go far enough. There was trouble in Gaul. There was always trouble in Gaul. Cæsar had done the essential work, but left his successors with plenty on their hands; and they were inclined to contrast his conquests with Pompey's, which needed no fresh sending of troops every other year.

But the truth was that Pompey had had the easier job. Human energy, the *mana* out of which great nations are born, was passing over to the West. Millions of men and women, rising up from the green breast of the earth; their roots running deep, meeting the springs in the cool soil; the earth's kiss still on them. Pompey's conquered made no great name in after history. Ancient folk, already getting tired. In Cæsar's stubborn battles and narrow victories the Western world was brought to birth.

The situation in Rome remained of hair-raising complexity. A series of reactions, in Cæsar's favour; in his murderers': crime and counter crime. In favour

of the Republic: a Dictatorship: the 'will of the people.'
Demands for vengeance, peace and quiet, miracles. On
the night of the 18th day of March Antony asked Cassius
to dine with him, and, after what must have been a
dreadful meal, asked: "Cassius, have you still a knife
up your sleeve?' To be answered: 'Yes, and a long one
for you, Antony, if you should come the tyrant over us.'

Yet Antony at first managed very well. He persuaded
the Senate to send Brutus and Cassius to remote
governorships, biding his time for the production of the
will and the great oration over the body of his lord. The
universe, we are told, is full of the murmur of our
speech, passing in ever widening circles into outer
space; and that somewhere beyond the stars that speech
is ringing yet. It is an old faith that the poet
alone has the faculty to recapture those sounds; that,
as our ancestors said, the Muses whisper them in his
ear, and only in his. Anyhow, Shakespeare has given
us the essence of that speech, not only what Antony
said—that was given him—but how he said it.

The Senate was exceedingly grateful to Antony. It
seemed for the moment that he had discredited the anti-
Cæsar party and averted civil war. Then the fun began.
They buried Cæsar; and all day long the actors per-
formed scenes from heroic plays, with special stress laid
on ingratitude and on treachery. He, who had always
been amused by lovely things, lay on an ivory bed,
covered with purple and with cloth of gold; under a gilt
catafalque, a miniature temple of that Venus whose
representative was now preparing for flight across the

199

high seas, the corpse's son in her arms. Then came Antony's speech: 'in every way beautiful and brilliant,' as even Cicero said, who was not there. The text quoted by classical writers, though it keeps to Shakespeare's matter, is completely depressing. But there were no shorthand writers there, only a crowd in hysterics. Beauty of phrase has been given back to us, without loss of matter; we can be content with that.

Then followed riots Antony did his best to stop. The natural reactions of the body of a people who realise that they have come to a dead end. That there is a wall in front of them they must break down, in order to arrive at a more convenient form of society. A people whose chosen leader has perished, and who have no notion at the time how this is to be done. The assassins either flew to the country or found themselves besieged in their roman houses. A sacred column set up over Cæsar's grave became a kind of Hyde Park, where every man who had a grievance mounted its base and explained his quarrel. Some exceedingly odd theories and desires were aired there; communist theory, and a cult of all-round castration, due to the influence of the Phrygian Atys and the Great Mother, a religion newly-arrived in Rome.

For Antony in this state of unstable triumph it was a question of money, money, money. 'There was nothing in the world,' says Cicero, 'which anyone wanted to buy that he was not prepared to sell.' No doubt he took from Cleopatra as much as she wanted to give; who, as she packed up to go, must have thought of it as a rather desperate insurance against the future.

Meanwhile Cicero was writing: 'I fear me the Ides of March have given us nothing but the pleasure and satisfaction of our hate.'

It was then Antony left Rome, to do a little recruiting and take the pulse of the country. His wife, the terrible Fulvia, was left in charge at home. In south Italy he was successful, calling up Cæsar's old troops; and on the way he rested himself—Antony's notion of rest—at a house-party in Marcus Varro's villa. There he invited all those blessed people who care not two pins for politics; and the day after, on his official entrance into Aquinum, all the inhabitants heard from behind the curtains of his litter, were the snores of their general, fast asleep. (Weigall tells all this with point and wit, showing how, before his marriage to Fulvia, people expected no more of Antony; how it was she who made him take himself seriously, and that he was the kind of man whose need is for a clear-headed wife to see that he makes the best of himself.)

His next difficulty, his next fence was the one he never cleared; before which eventually he fell. Like the 'little cloud,' the lightest feather in the sky, it must have seemed to him, glorious in the flush of manhood, the heroic shouldering of a great burden, the direction of the western earth, when he heard that the young Octavian had arrived in Rome to see about his uncle's will.

'Go home, boy, and play,' was the sum of his advice. 'Your money is safe. Come back when you're older.'

Instead, Octavian left Antony's house and went round the corner to call on Cicero.

He makes a curious impression, this Octavian, on his first entry onto the Roman stage. Spotty, delicate, athletic, and a martyr to hay-fever; like a girl, but untidy, with flowing hair. Quick on his feet, a footballer, a dilettante of the arts, and careful to speak, in contrast with Antony's romantic and coloured eloquence, in the clipped slang that was then the last elegance of fashion. This might have been well enough, the samples out of which a man is afterwards made. From which, as all history knows, a man *was* afterwards made. Only, in his youth at least, there went with it an egoism which made even the men of that age uncomfortable, a cold, bisexual sensuality and a turn for cruelty, which earned him from the start neither love nor admiration, but a slow dislike followed by unwilling respect.

From the first he disconcerted Antony; and it is possible to discern from the text of ancient writers that men felt at the time that there was something uncanny about this. Antony, a man so different in nature and capacity as to keep him eternally a stranger to Octavian; while giving both men every chance to hate each other. He tried at first to bluff him out of the way. The young man's answer was a quiet persistence over the matter of his heir-ship and his uncle's will—a counter-move of a most embarrassing kind. With Cicero's help he turned to the extreme conservatives, the men who disliked Antony as much as Cæsar; whereupon the conspirators came to him, suggesting that they should all make common cause against Antony. This extraordinary young man did not say 'no.' That was not his way. He was not yet twenty, and Antony, his uncle's executor, had treated him as a child. That was the sort of thing he minded—not sitting up at nights with the men who had just killed the man to whom he owed name, fortune, prospects—all that he had.

If Antony had received him otherwise—it is another of the historic 'Ifs.' But there began that strange division which was to end in one of the tragic contests of history. A contest between two kinds of nature—almost between two principles in life. That is all. Useless to ask—'Why did not Octavian strike a bargain with the man Cæsar loved, and together avenge his death and afterwards share, as peaceably as possible, the earth between them? With Lepidus or some such financier for a useful third? At his age, how could Octavian be aware of his own potential ability, let alone what destiny had in store? Was Octavian aware? Did he know he was to become lord of the world, carry Europe through to the next phase of its development? Suppose he did, could it not have been done in alliance with Antony, a man, one feels, whom sheer good nature would have kept loyal?'

'Why not? Why not? Why not?' says the voice of good heart and good sense. As it asks perpetually. And there is no answer. Only the dreadful things man has to watch, and among them those meetings between men, each representing one of the orders of power, when one is prepared for destruction by the other.

The religion of the west, now soon to be born—and
not before it was needed—set out to give man a spiritual
training which would bring these contests and torments
under control of his spirit. Show them in relation to a
divine will. Yet one doubts whether, if a Fénélon
had stood beside Octavian, bidding him with the com-
fortable words of holiness to get on with the work of the
world in peace with Antony, he would have listened.
The soldiers—Cæsar's old legionaries—tried it once,
marching on both men's houses. Whereon Octavian hid,
thinking, with a fear that is part of the price paid by
such men, that they had come to kill him. Antony did
not hide, but was, it seems, no less alarmed. Both men
were finally persuaded. Both found the men who had followed Cæsar hard to resist. Both found it difficult to cut
Common Sense when she stared them in the face. Both
agreed publicly to work together. One at least knew
that he neither could nor intended to.

Both were like men entering separate boats on the
back of a great stream. Both knew there were rapids
ahead. Both that at one point lay a giant cataract it was
possible to avoid. Each intended that the other should
take that way. Each knew that one was doomed. Did
either know which?

It was only then that the conspirators made up their
minds to accept their various governorships and leave
Italy. Previously they had hung about Rome or near
it, making every variety of trouble. All but Cicero, who
had gone off to Greece earlier to have one of his nervous
breakdowns in peace, finish the *De Senectute* and be in

time for the Olympic Games. Now that Octavian had made it up with Antony, there seemed nothing further to do. Just before their reconciliation, the mother of Octavian had one of those inspired dreams which play so equivocal a part in ancient history. It was one of those dreams when a god appears, incognito, this time as a snake; and after the usual sequel, 'caused her procreative organs to be taken up to heaven to be blessed.' At the same time, her husband had a dream too. He saw his wife—the affair throws a sidelight on her appearance —lying in bed and reminding him of a range of mountains 'out of whose centre came a great light.' A story that gave general satisfaction, 'much to the annoyance of Antony, who felt . . . that the objectionable young man was stealing his thunder.'

Lightened by such relief—of which roman history, little as you would gather it from historians, has its full share—the fatal situation was preparing. Grimly it began to shape. Antony won hearts. Octavian turned men's minds cold. Antony thought of his dead master; of what an old soldier wanted of him, a freedman, or a slave. What Fulvia would like. What was best for the roman people. Octavian thought—we do not know of what Octavian thought. Yet it was he who brought the Roman State through its troubles into the Empire's peace, finished Cæsar's work. Not Antony, not Cleopatra, the man, the woman he had loved. Him he destroyed and the woman with him. In such a way that, dead, he found it necessary to cover their names with infamy.

From which Antony's reputation has more or less

recovered. Not the Queen's. That is natural. Natural but cruel, while only poets have suspected the truth. And it seems to the writer that the undisputed facts do not make the Queen out a harlot or Antony besotted. Read without prejudice, with some psychology and some common sense, it can be seen that when Antony's judgment failed him, it was not necessarily by any fault of hers. And Antony's judgment did fail. If we knew less than we do of his diplomacy, it is only necessary to look at his profile as given on the coins. Profile of a Hercules, a humorist, a child. Profile of a man who, down the ages, is mastered by such men as Octavianus Cæsar, afterwards the Father of his people, the Emperor Cæsar Augustus.

Yet the decision seems throughout to have hung by a hair—or rather a series of hairs, one snapping after the other. Posterity has blamed the Queen, but it is not quite so simple as that. Was it under her influence that Antony degenerated, if he did degenerate, until he became unfit for command? Think of the long periods they spent separated from one another. The more one reads this story, the more one feels that some all-important knowledge has been lost—some detail, sign of a fatality inherent in the whole situation, that brought it to the conclusion we know.

.   .   .   .   .

The Queen was still in Alexandria, still in the Palace, when the courier arrived with the news of the battle of Philippi.

She ordered the lord Cæsarion to be brought to her.
He was six years old. Her hands on his shoulders as
he stood on the window-ledge, mother and son looked
out together at the Pharos, which, wherever you stood
in Alexandria, focused the eyes. Alexandria, still the
chief city on earth, still royal and all hers and all his.

She told him about the battle, how it had happened
at last; and when he asked about the men who had
killed his father, answered:

"They are dead. They are dead. The lord Antony
has killed them all."

Then to herself she began to tell the story again, the
story of Rome, stretched on the rack of her yet un-
adapted greatness. A scene her mind never left for an
hour, with its twists and convulsions and lightning shifts
of fortune—one bout of agony succeeding the other;
while the ring of outer kings looked on in fear and hope,
but none who had more to gain or to lose than she.

Long ago she had sensed the uneasy relations between
Octavian and Mark Antony. A slight matter—she had
seen little of either of them. Enough perhaps to observe
a grown man put out by a schoolboy. To her Octavian's
position was an infuriating accident. It had been discussed before Cæsarion's birth, when Cæsar had not expected to become a father or to be murdered. No one
in Rome, except Atia, his mother and one of those
women the Queen had done nothing to propitiate, had
attached the least importance to the lad with the
ridiculous legs. Except perhaps the general agreement
to dislike him. After his uncle's murder, he had got

in the way. Everyone had pushed him aside—to find him round the next corner, unpleasing, satirical, sometimes hysterical; not apparently formidable, a source of annoyance and at the same time of dis-ease.

Only one thing about him seemed certain—he would ally himself with either or any party or with all at once. The one man with whom he would come to no lasting terms was Antony. What—supposing the question worth asking of such an unpleasing youngster—was his game? A generation of men had seen Antony, whirled round and round like a man crucified on Fortune's wheel, but each time spun off on to his feet. 'The best man we've got, and, by the dear Gods, a man——' The whole roman world was saying that, and the Queen agreed. And plain men agreed also that since this young man insisted on playing a part in affairs when nobody wanted him and every other man he met was ready to murder him, the least he could do was to make himself the humble ally of Cæsar's friend and successor. Yet he would not. Then Decimus Brutus, the man who had gone that day to Cæsar's house to persuade him to come to the Senate, had gone off to Gaul with an army and re-opened the civil war there. (An act which to spectators like the Queen must have looked like the final disintegration of roman life.) Then, before anyone knew, Octavian had joined him, persuading, by what seemed like enchantment, Cæsar's old legionaries that he, fighting side by side with his assassins, more nearly represented their great lord than Antony. It was stupefying. And above the tramp of armies, meeting in the passes under the stupendous walls of those mountains that divide Europe from Italy, a song was audible. Music of a kind, a solo, a single voice, cadenced phrases of the purest latin, the little old man, Cicero. Day after day in the Senate, talking, talking, sentiments given immortality by a pure choice of words. Oh! he knew his business, the little old snob with the grey straggling hair, the master, not of ideas, but of their expression. Of the most admired art of the rhetor, to which the ancient world was suggestible in a manner inconceivable to us. To the ancients any excuse seemed to serve, to whom it was one of the great arts, and as detached from morality as music.

The Queen detested Cicero enough; but even to her the reason was plain why men so long tolerated him, the two-faced man, who had helped talk them into killing Cæsar and talked himself out of having had a hand in it; talked Octavian from Antony, and Cæsar's soldiers from their master's friend. Talked himself into two places at once; father of his country and its sacrificed lamb; talked himself onto both sides of the fence—as Demosthenes had talked—but he could not talk himself into being a gentleman. Selling his daughter to one after another of their debauched aristocrats—that hadn't taught him how to wear his toga. 'Borrowed books of me—as though I'd done him a favour, and I never got them back——' A meditation followed on her unfelicitous relations with the orator, and of more than one terrible little sentence, lashing her memories and her hopes.

As when he spoke of 'the magnificent banquet of the Ides of March' or asked—'if men could not tolerate Cæsar, does Antony think that they will tolerate him? . . . when I, a child of peace, have no wish for peace with Antony.' 'What is rotten in the body of the Republic should be cut out, that the whole may be saved.' Then, anticipating Talleyrand: 'It is nothing to me to be called either victor or vanquished, who can be neither without the victory of the Senate, or its defeat.'

It was after her departure he had risen again to speak, like a wind, measured and furious, lashing the Senate, to destroy the work and the memory of Cæsar and of Antony, his friend. A gale, she reflected, that behaved as such storms are wont to behave, carrying all before it, but round in a circle. So that bruised and dishevelled men found themselves, the storm spent, much where they were before.

Which was, finally, the exact result of the Philippics, whose real future lay ahead in the stormless æther of the arts.

For, in spite of them, what had Antony done? Defeated, he had managed to cross the Alps; and then Cicero, triumphant, had sent after him Octavian and kind old Lepidus. The Queen stood swaying, rapt in it, her lips parted, making the scene come to life in her mind.

Antony had shaved off the hair of the wild hero, beaten and starving and mighty, driven off into the high places of the mountains, above the world of men. He had washed the glorious body, like a marble column, veined, transparent, warmed and lit from a fire within. Had come down to meet them in the scarlet of a roman general, Cæsar's scarlet, in brilliant armour, the hands jewelled and the hair curled.

Met them on an island in a river, to win them over—surely this time for ever—to him, to Rome's future, to Cæsar's ghost.

They had come for his submission, to offer him in exchange security. They had returned, the three rulers of Rome together, and Antony their chief. Or two dogs, an ill-bred puppy and a wise old watch-dog, on his lead. How had he done it? By what mixture of deep laughter and passionate urgency and manly counsel?—and Cicero, the old goose, cooked in his own fat. What there was of it? Not enough to baste him properly, when he stuck his skinny head like a fowl out of the litter and begged them to cut it off clean. Stuck him with a sword for basting-pin! (I shall never get my books back now.)

After that, what had Antony done? Marched on Rome again. Now his turn for the killing. Here she paused. Proscriptions that decimate a ruling aristocracy had never appealed to her. Those Romans killed each other off like beasts. Yet was it wise to destroy your enemy wholesale, so that you have no one left to fight? You must have someone to fight, and there are only your friends left. Though no doubt reports had exaggerated. There must still be some senators left. Dead or alive, they had shown themselves Romans. Stories crossed her mind—of one who, hearing that Octavian and Lepidus had joined Antony, fell before them, in the name of the ancient Republic, on his sword. In Rome, of Pedius, a consul, going at night from house to house bearing the sentence and instruments of death, falling down at dawn in the streets, his heart stopped dead. Of a senator who stripped his house, throwing all he had out of the window to the mob, so that it should not fall into the new master's hands. Of what was done to the slave, who had shown the officers the direction of Cicero's litter, when he came to claim his reward. Of the quiet roman death of many a man and wife. ('If I had such citizens, I should promote them to honour. . . . If I had men of such quality, I should not fear Rome.')

Of Octavian's cruelty, of Antony's mercy. Then of the battle at the place called Philippi. There had been the final victory, the final killing. And talk of Cæsar's ghost. A ghost that had given them the victory against now desperate men, taking from Brutus (the parricide —my step-son?) the desire for victory with the desire for life.

After it the same story of cruelty and compassion, of lives taken and lives spared. Then the captains had parted. Octavian to go to Rome, and wait for the daggers no man doubted would find him. And that man, Antony, had gone east, into Asia Minor, to look for money and take the pulse of affairs from court to court.

Just then another messenger was announced. A messenger the Queen may have known as big with the future as any fate-bearer in the ancient tragedy. A chamberlain announced an officer, Quintus Dellius, bearing a summons from Marcus Antonius, Consul of Rome, to the Queen of Egypt, to proceed at once to Tarsus and give him an audience there on high business of state.

IV

"MARCUS ANTONIUS to his friend, Lucius Torquatus, sharer of the pleasures of his youth, the designs of his manhood—By the memory of our first adventures, by our lives before we knew ambition, by Cytheris' pearl-twisted hair—Greetings!

"Since ambition led me to the field and to the Senate, and you, for want of it, back to the Umbrian estate you have made illustrious by your genius as fruitful by your industry, we have known our separation to be no more than that of brothers, who part on the morning's business, content that at evening they will meet, the work of each day done.

"So it has been with us. I in the Forum and the camp: you at Pomona Sylvestris, among your fields and orchards and from the library-terrace I know so well, surveying all that is yours, and all that has increased a hundred-fold since it became yours.

"Fine Ciceronian opening—what? There are people about who call our speech a dead language now he is gone. Well, the use he made of it cost him his head. The golden tongue betrayed by the head that wagged it, as the poets might say. That's about the only thing for which no one has blamed me yet. Not even Octavian,

214

with his backside warm from sitting in the old man's lap. Though, between ourselves, I'd rather not have done it. Rather have spared the old man. It's the sort of thing I leave to my respected colleague and boy-friend. It is not often that a young man of his sort goes about asking to be murdered and in a world that asks no better than to murder him; and yet it is not Octavian's death you hear of, but instead that of men Rome can ill spare. It beats me, Lucius, it beats me. Somehow he manages to wriggle his worm's length through it all, and I have to go behind his back. I, Mark Antony, toddle off unbeknown to undo what I can. So we'd still have a Senate left. There are times when I say 'it isn't natural.' The Gods must have put him up their sleeve for some immortal piece of dirty work. Someone is in for it. Let's hope it isn't me.

"Yet this time I fancy all may be for the best. When we separated after Philippi, and I made this round of Near-Asia, looking for money and a holiday—two things which don't usually go together—Octavian returned to Rome. Where my respected wife, Fulvia, is waiting for him. A woman, as you know, on whom I rely more than I care to admit, but not often to my disadvantage. I've had no more wives than any other Roman, since the custom came in to try over as many as possible; and though I may have had about enough of her, I am, as you know, sensible of some gratitude——.

"What I am trying to say is, that if she should think it necessary in my interests to finish off Octavian, I should be the most thankful husband in Rome. She may, old friend, she may. And I believe she's about the only person who could. She can do the things in cold blood I can only do when I'm worked up. Some things I would rather not do, hot or cold. It was her I saw when the Martians mutinied and we sent their heads spinning on the floor, screaming out 'Murderers!' as they bounced. When, if you come to think of it, it was we who were doing the killing; and Fulvia squeezing their blood out of her black plaits. I couldn't get that out of my sight, and I haven't touched her since. Which always makes for trouble, women being what they are. Besides, she's getting too old for children.

"Yet I am still confident that she knows what to do in my affairs. A woman, as the old wives say, who should have been a man. Pulled me out when I was sticking in the mud and set me climbing, and I ought to be grateful. So I am. But you know how it is—one doesn't like to see a woman, one of one's own women, howling after blood, even if it is that of her husband's enemies. I'd have got them round without all that killing. The business was critical I admit, but she lost her temper. I wish I could forget her squealing and that red wet floor.

"So you can see things are not what they were between us. I am here on holiday, and by Hercules! not before I needed it. My affairs in Rome are in her hands, and she would sooner see Octavian dead than I. But, if you see what I mean, she is keen on seeing people dead, and that is no woman's business.

I've nothing to say against Julius' barbarians and their priestesses, consecrated women, putting heart into their men and sharing the danger and declaring the will of their Gods—or even giving the wounded the once-over. That's another affair. But our kind of woman ought to see to it that we don't go too far. You know what a man, even a man like me whom you were good enough to call the most amiable ass in Italy, is like when his blood's up. All my life I've felt what a lot conciliation does, let alone what it could do. One of the results, Lucius, of your friendship; and what I am trying to say is that our women ought to remind us, and they don't.

"There—you will say I am inconsistent, who have left my woman behind to do my murdering for me. My friend, I tell you that I would not—it is not my way, as you should know, if it were a question of anyone but this Octavian. With him I am like a cat-hater when he knows there's one under the bed; and this for reasons that neither reason, nor omen, nor enquiry of the Gods makes clear to me. He is sickly, and is lately grown sicklier; and I, who send all my colleagues that clever greek doctor I bought and gave his freedom—well, by Aesculapius, why do I not send him to Octavian with instructions to give him something to take him off the sick list for ever?

"He is a stink you cannot smell, a poison you cannot taste, a disease for which there is no cure. I, Marcus, of the great house of the Antonines, have put out my full strength against this weasel with the mange. Each time I have mastered him, to feel the marrow sucked

out of my bones. I have seen him turn tail at a
look from me and run; but like a dog so pleased it
hardly bothers to lower its tail. As though it were all
going to plan, *his* plan. It is intolerable. It has followed
me here. I leave it to Fulvia. Yet we are so made that
I shall find it hard to forgive her, either way.

"Forgive these musings, Lucius. Still better, understand them. For a man whose business is the governing
of men must have one friend to whom to open his heart.
I come to you for a woman's counsel and a man's. Do
you still fancy yourself as a wife? You'll admit, I've
known worse. Or you a better husband? But, Lucius,
what would you say if I turned up this time with a new
one, a real one?

"But that comes later. You will want to hear what
has happened in its order, and not the rumour but the
event. Here it is:

"Cæsar is avenged. We can say that at last. (With
Octavian and without him. Curse him—Octavian, I
mean.) I have avenged you, Cæsar. You are now become one with the Planets and the Kosmocratores and
the Immortal Elements. Where we send our ghosts. It is
'*all Ares, all Aphrodite*' with you now. Or as I, for one,
say with more certainty: '*Deus est mortali invare
mortalem et haec ad acternam gloriam via.*' For, Cæsar,
you remembered that.

"You would have had your peers remember it, the
Senate and the Roman People. What you got was every
scoundrel in Rome, out for the rich man's loot. Or
Clodius and Dolabella out against their caste. I was one

of them when you picked me out—the half joy-boy, half man-at-arms you made into a statesman. You taught me to use the goodwill I felt for my kind. For their use and my own. Not like the philosophers say you ought— it came naturally. I wish we'd a name for the divinity whose essence is good-will. Not the fact of peace, but the spirit of it. What even makes it worth fighting for.

"I am writing you this from Tarsus, and here it is the Gods have sent me one of my Good Ideas. Or my Daimon—by Hercules! it was him—the kind of thing he would think of; and by the way, we're in Asia now where it's politic for us to assume the God, and you can think of yourself raising your arms to Hercules Antonius.

"I rather like this new fashion of putting on the divinity, like a pretty woman with a new dress. While as to pretty women—I'm coming to it—now at last. The Idea was—to send off to Alexandria and ask the Egyptian Cleopatra for an audience here on urgent public affairs.

"You remember her in Rome—before the Ides of March? How our lives are cut in half by that date. When I saw her last—and what it meant to her doesn't bear thinking about—I saw only this, that she was a brave woman. Before, I had not known her well. Cæsar did not allow you to poach on his preserves. (Though there was a party once—but she came out of it immaculate— thanks mostly to me.) Well, I did what I could for her, put her away at the back of my mind for the pretty carved knuckle-bone that might yet throw us up six.

"If she'd been popular in Rome, I'd not have let her

go. Kept her there for Cæsar's half-widow and consort-to-be. Above all, as mother of his son. I'd often urged him not to let the old will stand, assure this boy of theirs, Cæsarion, his place. You know what happens when you put off changing a will. The wrong one stands until something happens, and a great injustice is done and endless trouble ensured. As it was, all she could do was to skip before someone remembered about her, and killed her. It was, in spite of what Fulvia says, only half her fault that we didn't like her. Young enough to be silly and amuse herself with us. But a royal baggage in the making; with so much behind her, that we'd be bound to seem a bit unfinished.

"Now I'll say it, and you can have your laugh out. One result of the Idea is that I've discovered that she and I are the same sort of person. Natural allies. We like the same sports; make fools of ourselves in the same ways. Quick work, but I'm a quick worker. So is she——.

"I tell you she is everything I like and haven't been allowed since Fulvia set my feet on the path of Fame; got rid of the snakes in the bed and in the wine-cup that were strangling the offspring of Hercules. Put it into poetry. I rather feel like that myself——.

"Mind you, there's a lot more in this queen than I've said. Besides, she's changed greatly since Julius died. Become a ruler from her brow to the arch of her foot. Our meeting was something I'm not likely to forget.

"It was evening. I'd waited for her since noon in the Governor of Tarsus' house; and when she didn't come, I got tired and took a nap. When I woke, it was

to find the slave I'd told to attend me craning his head
out of the window, trying to get a look at the harbour;
and if you'll believe it, the whole main street below us
was empty. Every soul in the place, let alone in the
house, down on the water-front; been there all day in
the sun, waiting for her.

" 'What's up?' I said, and he explained, if you please,
how the whole city was determined to see the Queen
of Egypt, who was arriving by the water-gate, on her
barge, in her ritual get-up as Our Lady of Alexandria,
Isis of the Egyptians, Aphrodite-on-Earth, and the Gods
know how many other Goddesses besides.

" 'Aphrodite,' said I, and it went through my head—
by Hecate, sender-of-unclean-dreams, it went through
my head, and I saw again Octavian's pimpled mug and
pursed mouth, speaking the way he does about 'oriental
insolence,' mincing and snuffling and calling me to
order when I spoke once of her boy Cæsarion, as
Cæsar's son. 'Son of her bath-slave,' he said; and how
she cleared out of Rome to get back to the royal stews
in Alexandria—three men at a time in three different
positions and a dozen a night. I asked him how he
knew. He said 'he had every reason to suppose——'
'Out with your reasons,' said I. 'Cicero,' said he. 'Cicero,'
said I; and there we were at our usual deadlock. This
was some time ago. But she does not look as if she
were that kind of woman. I'll say more—I'll swear she
is not.

"But to return to the quay-side at Tarsus.

" (I hadn't heard her then on Royal Impersonations,

and I swear I all but raised my arms in the salute we think only proper to an Immortal.) Aphrodite Pandemos, as the Greeks say? Neither that, nor Our Lady of the Heavens, and certainly not Love-at-home; but a divinity; and no egyptian mystery-beast, but, as the Hellenes say, an Olympian. The divinity of herself at least, and I'll swear she has enough——.

"She lay on the harbour-waters of the Cydnus, on her ship. Very blue and green water along the quay which is of white stone. The boat had the neck of a bird for prow and its wood was gilt. Round the mast they'd raised a dais for her to lie on; and there she was, alone but for two of her girls, those two we saw in Rome, who are always with her. One fair and one dark, and she neither dark nor fair, but with points from each, which in her go perfectly well together. Robe girt high under her breasts, shown as a Goddess shows them; and a thin open mantle to cover her shoulders and arms—I remember because somehow it insured her modesty; fastened under her chin by the largest emerald I've ever seen. Like a green egg burning in a white shadow.

"As I've said, she carried her breasts like the Goddess, like Isis, the Mother. It's her dress, and though it's transparent and hides nothing, the wearer was her own modesty and her own pride. Oh! she knows how sacred dress is worn.

"She'd the arms and feet you'd expect. A little head; and under a crown like a tower with a snake, almost to the tip of her ears, a wave of hair. Eyes that look straight ahead, straight out and straight through one.

222

"The whole town had been waiting for hours. She was just entering when I got there. You never heard such quiet. There was a priest astern and at the bows, a priestly-priest, one of those shaved men in a leopard-skin and a stiff skirt, who look as if they meant their business. Also braziers with incense. The barge moved slowly, there was no wind, and a blue cloud of it drew softly down the ship. Like a scarf drawn between our hot eyes and her.

"I tell you it was well done. Hardly a movement on board. Or on shore for that matter. I hopped out of my litter on the quay, as fast as I could so as not to miss anything, with my gown and my mantle flung on any-how. As I've said the Palace was empty and I'd no one to get me into armour. Told the slave to cut and run—hadn't the heart to keep him.

"Well, there I was, trying to get the wreath I wore straight. I'd worn it at lunch and gone to sleep in it after, and couldn't imagine what I was looking like, and only too well the things Fulvia would say—then, after I'd nearly tripped over a hawser, I stood up to salute.

"Once I'd been seen, things changed. The rowers below deck struck the water. Softly. In time. Then a breeze struck up, enough just to fill the purple sails.

"They moved on. Then my ears told my eyes what I'd been blind to before, for a song started. One of those clear remote songs in greek, and I saw that at the ropes and in the rigging there were girls, a choir. Singing the song of old Theocritus about Adonis. You know how it goes? *'Mistress that loves the heights of Golgi and*

223

Idalium and the high peak of Eryx, Aphrodite-who-plays-with-gold.'

"I tell you, it rang sweetly, as the rowers beat time and the smoke-cloud blew away, leaving only the scent of it, and the ship drew past, and the Queen lay upright, looking steadily beyond us; and her women—their names—I remember now—are Charmian and Iras—stood behind her, their fans crossed to frame her head.

"I cannot get it out of my sight, and 'I've seen a lot in me time,' as the sergeant said.

"And if you say 'amateur theatricals,' next time we dine together at Pomona Sylvestris, I'll choke you with your own snails. No. Though it might have been; and *we* know what professionals can do. Moving and glorious it was, and to the common people, a mystery. I thought my men's eyes would pop out.

"Well, I was presented. Mars, I suppose, to Venus. And do you know she gave me the wickedest little smile. Saw through it herself, bless her. (Not that she's not pious, as a woman should be. Or a man. I'm pious.) Only it took just that to make her perfect.

"It's coming out now. I'm head over heels in love; asking myself how I stood all those years with Fulvia. How I ever loved Cytheris even. Or anyone else for that matter. And yet I feel like holding a thanksgiving to all the women I ever loved who got me into training for this.

"Next day she asked me to dine. That was a real party. No wonder she thought us Romans gross brutes. And I'll tell you one thing—I've been soldiering so long.

224

Got rather into camp ways. Made a joke that would have gone down all right with Cytheris. Did she pull me up—stand on her dignity? Not a bit. Began to talk the same way, but funnier, ten times funnier. Same sense in delicate, wicked little words. I haven't had such a laugh since the old days with Julius—and she was sober as a priestess. And I drunk on better than wine. And what wine it was. And what a lass. And it's a gracious thing to see the way Charmian and Iras attend her.

"All the same, I'm sorry I spoke like that. Mustn't let her think we're barbarians, and I a kind of virile beast, without an idea beyond the camp and the rowdy party and the rough stuff of politics. Mustn't let Julius' training down. And if Alexandria is like its mistress, I don't wonder he wouldn't leave. I want to see their boy. He's left behind with his tutor. No eunuchs and palace-pets, but a brother of Iras, it seems. I hope he's all a son ought to be to a mother like that.

"Then we came to business. She made no difficulties. Had it straight out with me—candid as a boy. Said she was glad to see me for myself and for what I had come to represent; and that we both had affairs to discuss.

" 'Between drinks?' said I. 'Before them,' said she, *dulce ridens.* That's her laugh, but she's no Lesbia. That I'll swear, but a Queen and a mother, and by my great ancestor, as much a lover as I can make her.

" 'Quiet now, Marcus,' I hear you say; but it is not the hour for that. Nor the moment to turn round three times like a dog before he sleeps. Not the time, when,

for the first hour since the Ides of March, time itself
and the hours of the night and day are turned music.

"Now's the hour, when the bell is striking that rings
Mark Antony a man again. Not the soldier, not the
senator, not the play-boy even or the sweating bearded
captain, dried stiff with the sweat of armies and the
blood of Rome's battles. Mark Antony's a man again,
and more of a man than ever he was before.

"That's the wonder of her, that wherever she is there
is life. Not just life, the up and down, in and out business we know. An hour's fighting, an hour's planning,
an hour's eating, an hour's sleeping; an hour in a hurry,
an hour in a dream, an hour in the dark, an hour up
in air; an hour getting on with what has to be done;
an hour finding it was not worth the doing.

"Now I am riding the lot, see each in its necessity,
its rightness and its wrongness—as though I had the
secret of the source from which all action springs.

"My friend, I do not know what is to happen, but I
see before me a joy as great as a man may have. And
when we two come to drink the drop of trembling the
Gods keep at the bottom of each cup—well, that will be
an essence too; and ours will be no common grief when
we hear the black drums beating, see on the horizon
the red spears.

"Haven't we seen, my friend, with our own eyes how
things come at their right time? Now if I hadn't done
with Fulvia I should not be feeling quite such a God.
That's what my Lady of Egypt puts into you. Not one
God only. I swear to you that never before, not in the

winter passes with the innards of a frozen mule for banquet, not when Cæsar first called me friend, nor when I stood over his body and knew that death and what was meant by that death, have I been so filled with the knowledge of the Gods.

"What am I saying?—but, Lucius, you know. It is those moments that show a man what he is and what his life means. Your Marcus is now more than Hercules' son, he has desired with Adonis and charmed with Orpheus—even as he is charmed. And, like an initiate, has looked into mysteries; become the Purifier and the Purified. Become a woman even; and for the first time known my manhood, who once knew nothing beyond that on all this earth.

"I am a man who asked for a drink and has been given the wine of life. And its cup-bearer spoke of us both, saying: 'pages to our Cæsar.' And that we might call what has happened to us a gift from the dead. For with her divine directness, I know where I stand. I shall follow her to Alexandria, play Adonis to Aphrodite there.

" 'Then be careful of wild boars,' she said. 'I will,' said I, who have no need to be; whom the Gods have preserved alive and a master of men for this.

"I shall follow her to Alexandria. When I suggested that scandal might touch her there, she said:

" 'But I make the laws. I shall make a new one, as I did with Cæsar, to make it plain to my people that the divine Pharaoh has chosen a second Consort, so that there may be further children to reign in the holy land

227

of Khem. . . .' (You will say that it looks like bigamy and so it does and so it can.) It will look like—perhaps I had better not start thinking what it will look like to Fulvia. Rome——? Rome can take it or leave it. Octavian—? —Hecate-of-the-night-horrors, have you sent that face of him again, speechless but smiling at me? His smile is fouler than another man's excrement. What does he mean now? Octavian—if by your filthy power you should send us down side by side to the Capitol pits, our wounds would smile at you.

"On whom no woman will ever look as the lady Cleopatra Lagos looks on Mark Antony the Roman, her friend and her servant, these three and a half years past the Ides of March, these six hundred years from the foundation of our City.

"Cæsar, is this your benediction, the benediction of a God?"

V

Quiet in the Palace. Mid-winter dawn breaking, winter
of the same year, the sun up in a whirl of gold storm-
clouds. Like a lion roaring, with the east wind in its
throat, the gale tore at the cordage, drummed in the
sails, as from the Royal Harbour the roman fleet put
out to sea.

The roman war-galleys, sailing that morning for
Ostia, and taking with them the Triumvir, Marcus
Antonius, away from Cleopatra the Queen.

.　　　.　　　.　　　.　　　.

There was a room in the Palace that held only a bed.
A room shaped like a perfect sphere, like the inside of a
pearl. Of the Palace honeycomb of apartments, the in-
most cell, and there Antony and Cleopatra slept, fast in
each other's arms. The Queen almost lost in the hollow
of his great shoulder, her face hidden, her hair flowing
over the pillows and over his breast. Naked he lay,
the huge torso relaxed in sleep as profound and perfect
as ever Ares' in Aphrodite's arms. Not as Bronzino
painted it, in some land of the Immortals, in sunshine,
on the grass; a rabbit watching, a butterfly lit trembling
on the Queen's thigh to perfect her bliss. It was not
that delight. A short sleep, a snatched sleep, a last

moment's oblivion. The God of War must wake, and wake the trumpets. Blaze his way across Europe, across Asia, leaving the Queen of Love. Not in any earthly Paradise, but high on the world's stage, swept by all the storms of danger and of power.

Sleep—it was waste of time for them, who had so little time. Sleep—they took it in a hasty draught, at the last hour, whose pleasure in the other was the pleasure of Paradise. Paradise they must leave—if ever they hoped to call Paradise their own again.

It was the Queen who had made this plain, urging him to go, saying: 'Antony, you are not as safe as you think. What is Octavian doing behind your back? Remember what you have to lose. What you may win. What is a little kingdom like Egypt in comparison with the world? Why, it is too small a throne for me——' He saw the sense of it, whose ambition had not lessened. Yet it was almost as unbearable to leave Alexandria as it was to leave her. The City had captured him as it had captured Cæsar, making roman entertainment a debauch, and life there, for all its vigour and splendour, by comparison a poor affair. After years of the harsh realities of politics, the fury and fatigues of war, he had come to a haven. This city, of which, centuries later and in its last decline, an Arab poet said:

'There have I borne a garment of perfect pleasure among my friends, a garment adorned with the memory of beloved companions . . . and saw my friends like stars.'

There the roman Antony had found more even than

a lover's satisfaction. Found friends, the last descendants of Alexander's set. The exchange was not simply from the camp and the Senate, but from the blood and tears of empire-building to life in a kingdom long ago built. He knew what he had to do. He must continue the work which would unite Rome and Alexandria under one power. For that he must go away. That way only lay the possibility of return.

This conclusion they had arrived at before they slept. When he woke, he sprang from the bed, and a moment later the Queen, as she buckled on his armour, a second time played Helen to Paris.

.   .   .   .   .

Into the dining-room of the royal apartments servants were hurrying. There had been a great rejoicing on the last night of the general's visit and magnificent tips. Well pleased they came to their duties, in the long room abandoned after the feast.

There is no lesson in mortality like such rooms. On the day before, in the early night, they are set. Lit and empty and perfect. They wait until they are filled and become an instrument for pleasure, and in the delicate light of ancient lamps show all that there is of delight.

In the cold light of next morning they appear like something stripped and broken, something done with and left about, which must be hurried out of sight. The couches' embroideries hung askew or dragged across the floor. The flowers were dead. On the low tables, the crystal glasses stood, stained with the dregs of wine. A motionless disarray where, a few hours before, there had been order and brilliance; and grease on the jade-blue plates of royal ware, which was one of the prides of Alexandria. Bones and crumbs and crusts; what was left of exquisite food. A wine cratêr, tipped-up and left askew, leaned drunkenly. Things that had been set for laughter and pleasure and the hearts of friends; exquisite words had been spoken over them. In a clearing between the couches, where a girl had danced, lay a sandal, its pearl strap broken.

It was over, and it could never happen again. Not like that. There would be other parties, but this gathering, this party had peeled off into the past, as though Time were an onion stripping its own skins.

In the Queen's seat the end of a scarf soaked up a wine-puddle; melon pips lay slimy in a plate.

The butler entered at the head of a procession with trays; and stood, checking the glasses. Then the plates, a series painted with birds. Then the great centre-pieces for fruit, made of crystal and black onyx; then the flat silver dishes for almonds and sugared flower-petals and cherries in pistachio and oysters in jam; and rinds from the East, preserved in syrup, and the insides of sea-urchins on sea-lettuces, and breasts of blackbirds stuck with hawthorn-buds, and dandelion-leaves, a salad brought with great difficulty, to wrap round a paste of yolk of egg.

The rhythm of work caught them as they piled and sorted; while the old servant looked anxiously, precious piece by precious piece, for chips.

"Thank the Gods," he said at last, "the lord Antony did not see fit to make any of his friends a present of these. He can be as generous with other people's things as his own——"

"Our Lady is generous, too," said a footman.

"As she's the right to be, with her own—not that we've any cause for complaint, remembered most handsomely as is only fitting, but I couldn't have borne it if these had left the family." 'These' were the bird pledging-cups of the Lagidæ. They were made of jade in an abstract of the types of birds; a falcon, a crane, a gull, a swan, a singing bird, a peacock. Tradition said that Sotêr had brought them from India, after the Hydaspes; but that they had travelled a long way already before they reached the Punjab.

It pleased the old servant to see them in use, while he dreaded lest some guest should take a fancy to them. For their mistress loved the cups, but she loved Antony more; and he was one of those men who give away their possessions, shields or horses, sweetheart or sword or slave; not without counting the cost, but without learning there is a cost to count. And expected each person he liked to be the same sort of person as he; and forced to acknowledge the difference, fretted. A man who could only see the best that there is in any man. Such a man is easily destroyed by the difference between himself and another sort of man.

Already there had been vast inroads on the royal plate. Though the Queen sometimes and Iras often would send down orders to the pantries that the gold vessels promised to so-and-so in the heat of the moment were to be changed—since such gifts often represented gifts of hard cash—for something of equal weight and worse workmanship. For one of the pieces of presentation plate under which royalty groans.

This comforted the old servants, while leaving the Lagid treasures intact. Otherwise she found it hard to get the best pieces out, who herself had a woman's sense of possessions—a woman in love with a man who had no sense of possessions at all.

In this easiness of Antony's may be found a part-origin of what happened to him. For a man who will give anything away, may part with himself too easily; who cannot say 'no' to a friend, may not be able to say it to an enemy; may finally so weaken his sense of reality as to feel ashamed not to gratify even the man who would take away his life from him.

.　　.　　.　　.　　.

Up and down the servants went, stripping the table and the couches, shaking out of the embroideries crumbs, prawn-shells, peel, pips, little bones, limp petals, cracked nuts.

"We shan't be giving any more of these now he's gone."

"Worse luck," said the young footman—"I like to see her Majesty look ten years younger. If it's her Roman that's done it, good luck to him, says I."

"There's one thing," said the butler, "we've our reputation to keep up and this time we've taught them something. They don't have such entertainments where he comes from, I'll be bound. Drink themselves under the table, and throw knives at their servants by way of amusement, so I've heard. At Alexandria no gentleman comes to his meals armed. And I wouldn't serve in one of their roman houses—not if you made a free man born of me." The service cleared, the old servant led the procession away to a cool pantry of the inner Palace, and spoke again, polishing the jade birds with a soft cloth:

"The time I crossed the water, when Cæsar, their last great man before this one was still alive, to wait on her Majesty, it was my business to engage any extra service we might require. Send out to the slave-market for good, plain, local domestic help. I didn't want any of those fancy foreigners flooding the market just then— the sort of bastard who knows a sight too much and better than his masters, and the Syrian who knows all there is to know about poisons, and thinks there's a spell for cleaning plate, or the Gaul who knows nothing out-side the farmyard and won't learn. And do you suppose I found it easy? Couldn't make it out at first when I found what we'd got cowering in a corner of the kitchen, jabbering prayers to some image they'd hung round their necks on a string—because, if you please, they said it was the Alexandrians' custom to carve a little piece off the serving men and women, day by day, and eat it raw for an appetiser—all this by magic, until there was only a skeleton left to hand round the dishes.

—"Look at me," I used to say to them. "I had my freedom from the Queen's own father's hands, and do I look like a skeleton? We are Greeks, I'd say, though my Lady may have dominion over a lot of heathen Egyptians and lucky they are to have her; and then I told them how the Greeks were the first people to treat slaves as if they were men.

—"If that's what they thought of us in her service, can you wonder that they didn't know what to make of her Majesty's self, with her high laughing ways?

—"Yes, and they put them up to dirty work. Sometimes I think it wasn't the Romans, but through them, if you understand. That they didn't properly know what they were doing. To each sort his own dirty work; and they're the kind of people who have to have some sorts of devilry explained to them.

—"I had to kill a man and his wife once. A fellow and his woman we didn't buy, but who came from good service in Rome before, when I found they were taking money from a family in the city I'd rather not name, to spread evil reports of my Lady. He was a groom and she worked in the laundry; and one day in the sewing-room my wife caught her working a thread into the Queen's shift. My wife pulled it out and it stung her skin. 'Poison,' she thought and of the dreadful poison-threads of Egypt that open the skin; and it never closes and a sore comes, and spreads till the body is eaten up. She thought of our Lady's young breasts, and being a quiet woman, brought the thing to me.

—"We had them both up, and after a few turns in the punishment-room, some of it came out. They'd been

sent to spy, and when there was nothing worth report-
ing, given the thread to sew, which they were told was
a spell. It was they too, I suspect, who poisoned the
young Lord Ptolemy, seeing that my Mistress—to say
nothing of the Lady Charmian—did nothing but cherish
him as a sister should. I tell you when I heard their talk
it felt like some foul sewer, or a pit where snakes breed.
The woman spying on the natural functions of my Lady
as a means to their filthy magic; and at the same time
trying to make her out—whose life is as clean and as
open as the Goddess Pallas'—a secret witch.

—"It was then I cut their throats with my own hand,
and had their bodies thrown into the sewer as was fit.
But seeing our Lady had just become a mother, my wife
it was who gave their child to another woman to nurse.

—"They called on their roman masters to save them,
and afterwards we made some enquiries there among the
upper servants. Not that we ever got the rights of it,
but there had been a woman in the service of the Lady
Arsinoë, and a man, a stranger, neither a Roman nor an
Egyptian nor a Greek, but what they call an Etruscan,
one of the people, it seems, who ruled the land before
the Romans were; who live now, what's left of them, in
empty cities, speak a forgotten speech. And it is they
who have the secrets of the land. Much as you might
say the Egyptians have the secrets of Egypt, save only
in Alexandria; where, as they say, the Lord Sotêr said,
and had it written up, that he came to do away with
mystery-mongering and spells, and leave in their places
the Blessed Twins, the help of sailors, and Serapis, who

237

is the egyptian Gods made pure. Building a great house where man should look into the nature of things; so that, like Athens, Alexandria should become a city of wisdom and light.

—"I don't say it's all worked out like that, but that's what the Lord Sotêr meant. Howsoever, this woman of the Lady Arsinoë's, this Etruscan, and I don't doubt the Lady Arsinoë herself, were all part of some sort of a plot, and that plot led back to Egypt. Back into the ideas of men who remember Italy before there were Romans, and Egypt before Greeks came to rule in Alexandria. We tapped a hating there, my wife and I. A hating by a very ancient people, which is always dangerous. The Lady Arsinoë counted for little or nothing in it. That was strange. And when you come to think of it, far the most fearful. One could understand a plan to put her on the throne. But this was something that went behind time. Pushed out into the future—it was the Lady Charmian who said that. For we told her. She thanked us for our faithfulness and went away with that set look of hers. But we could see that it wasn't the Romans who troubled her. They were as much used as their slaves.

—"But there's one thing I'm as sure of as I stand here polishing these glasses, it isn't by spells and witchcraft that they'll turn those Romans out of their lands; any more than the Greeks out of Alexandria, whoever it is who goes on ruling there.

—"Which won't prevent stories of the entertainment of the Lord Antony by alexandrian witchcraft giving

the roman ladies the creeps. They'll say our scented
linen is corpse-rank, and so woven as to steal men's
valour and give them crazy dreams; that at our banquets
we take the egyptian mummies out of their wrappings
and set them to wait at table. That's what they'll say.
It's jealousy—that's what it is. Jealousy and ignorance,
by people who were no better than savages the day
before yesterday.

—"Yet it's lucky for us the Lord Antony is a man
other men believe. For they do no good to our Lady,
these stories, and it's a world of pities he's gone. Now
there's a word come from the Lady Iras that the room is
not to be used again until he returns."

.   .   .   .   .

The room lay cleared. One after another the servants
had gone out, the wide trays balanced on their heads.
The brooms swept the marble. The litter vanished out
of a door, a wave of broken bits and dead flowers. The
marble floor, flooded with water, took on deeper
colours; then began to dry in patches. On the couches,
drawn back stiffly against the walls, fresh embroideries
were folded, not displayed; and the long room took on
the aspect of something tidily dead. Neat and awaiting
resurrection.

VI

Quiet in the Palace. The pearl-room as much in order as the hall below. In another room, her maiden-room, Cleopatra lay. Lay and wept, with no eyes for Pharos or for Cæsarion. Charmian and Iras, sent away, talked in the little library, an octagon this time, whose eight panels held the rolls of the Queen's books. Silver knobs and scarlet cords, and a frame to hold them, a reading-desk.

Charmian picked up a roll, twiddled its knobs one way and the other, found the passage she wanted and stood at the desk, her long hands holding the place. Iras picked up a lute and sat busy with its strings. The sound of tuning squeaked in the quiet, in the immense house, filled for long weeks with voices and music, and the trumpets of the entry and the departure of princes and of kings.

Quiet in the Palace of the Lagidæ. So quiet it seemed they could hear everywhere the sobs and wild crying of their mistress so suddenly, so quickly, left alone.

Suddenly she had been given the utmost measure of laughter and love. Suddenly it had been taken away. The tears—as Charmian tried to show her—were no more than her body protesting—the Cleopatra-in-time.

240

They tried to believe it, Iras and the Queen,
creatures of the world; believe like children the woman
who was their priestess, their messenger between the
seen and the unseen. 'I am well served,' she had said,
'with Iras who is never wrong about a person, and
Charmian who is never wrong about the Gods.'

Iras looked up from her lute: "Is it well then,
Charmian? No—what I suppose I mean is—will it be
well?"

"It is happening as it should happen," Charmian
answered slowly: "He will return to her and us, if that
is what you mean." Iras drew a long breath:

"Then it *is* well. Surely, if he returns nothing can
go wrong—surely, surely—. Oh, I know what you will say
to that—that we do not know what the Gods will do for
our enemies: that they have earned their justice,
too——"

"So long as you remember that. But we do not
know on which side the balance will fall."

"Do you still think that your priests can spoil it
by their spells? Isn't the love between them a greater
magic? What magic is ever greater——?"

"I mean that we have been given power. A great
quick blast of it. But we do not know what power has
been given to others. Nor have I great faith in one
man's hot desire."

"But matched with hers?"

"Hers matches his. But, Iras, she is a light, fierce
thing, like one of Plato's bees. She needs a cooler wind
to blow her to her haven than this Antony. And

remember that there are many haters, and hate blows more steadily than love. And, this Antony apart, she has the Roman Will against her."

"This Antony *is* Rome; and if it comes to changing, it would be well if the Lady Arsinoë were changed off the earth. He has told me a thing or two about her——"

"She will be changed," said Charmian. "My sister, if it comes to telling, told me that the priests had withdrawn their protection; having now no further use for her. You say this Antony is Rome. I say, if he is, it is because he has made himself an image of their will. Let that cease, and they will spit him out. He cannot carry what broke Cæsar's back."

An uncomfortable silence followed. "I do not like you, Charmian," said Iras, "when you interpret men. It is for you to interpret the heavens. Me the earth."

"I cannot help it. This time they are too mixed."

Iras shrugged her shoulders: "I shall cheer myself up with the Lady Arsinoë's near end. . . ."

Silence in the library of the Palace. The scroll turned on its frame. Charmian said:

"Listen to this."

"What is it?"

"The voice of a King. On what few kings understand. If they did, their thrones would be safe for ever; but perhaps they would not want to be kings."

"What is it, and what king?"

"One of the Jews who live here, and whom they call a Master in Israel did it into the Greek for Cleopatra——"

"I know. One of those she asked to the Palace to find out how she could be friends with Herod Antipater. He told her she would never be, and she liked him for his frankness. I was there, and could not be sure if he was lying or not. Or, if so, why he should."

"I think he was trying to get her to see that this Herod hates her. It is another hatred."

"Another—I am sick of them. And you count them as if they were a chaplet. Why should she be hated? If she is, it is jealousy. But you, Charmian, set store by it."

"If I set store, it is because there are some persons to whom hatred is fatal. Some can endure it very well. Not Cleopatra. She is too wild and too candid, too gentle and too fierce. Too innocent, and yet not wholly innocent. Her boldness is like a boy's; yet she depends on being a woman too much."

"You always make me afraid when you talk like that. It is as if you saw, now, when our triumph looks like beginning, some dreadful thing waiting for her. I see it is possible, but you talk as though it were here already, as though it had always been here. And will not say what it is——"

"This much," said Charmian, "I know, though I may interpret wrong. I see her—I have always seen her— as something offered up. A sacrifice—

> *Beauty, truth and rarity,*
> *Grace in all simplicity—*

Offered up to the powers of this world. By an unknown

243

God. Her wit, her courage, her love as it were dedicated. A sacrificed bird. An image will be made of her. Not even a true image. Oh, she will have enduring fame, but of pride and insolence and lust. What Roman can endure to see a woman stand up against them? This is how Antipater sees her. That is why he will not meet her, lest this false image the world has already put in his mind be destroyed."

"This is horrible and I don't believe it."

"Perhaps in the end people will understand, but listen to what this king said: *'I have seen the travail which God hath given to the sons of men, to be exercised in it. He has made everything beautiful in his time, also he hath set the world in their hearts, so that no man can find the work that God maketh from the beginning to the end.'*

—"In another way it is as I said: she has touched the secret of the Roman Will. Run counter to it. They know it is possible that she may make them afraid. These are very secret things. But I have heard the last cry of the Hellene fall from her lips."

"Too secret for me," said Iras, shortly. At that moment a servant entered. They were wanted instantly by the Queen.

.   .   .   .   .

Exhausted with crying, Cleopatra lay by the bed, her knees on the floor, her torn hair streaming. A bed as neat as a grave. Pillows in the centre and for one only.

She flung herself round, choked with the weeping that disfigures, the racked sobs of despair; her eyes blazing inside scarlet circles, the lashes clotted to points.

"Bring him back to me, Charmian. Bring him back. You have the wisdom of the Egyptians; and what is wisdom if it will not bring back the lover to the lover? Two lovers, to the other. Wisdom is nature's, and nature is torn when lovers are torn. Torn. Torn." She tore her dress open, dragging her nails at the skin between her breasts.

—"Bring him back, Charmian, bring him back. If your priests can kill me, turn, oh turn, their magic the other way round. Turn it that he may return. Restore me what has been taken from me——

—"Charmian, I love you. Charmian, I entreat you——

—"You are to do it, I am your mistress. I have never yet commanded you, but I can have you killed. I will have you killed, I will have you killed slowly, if you do not do this——"

The passionate words ran on. Charmian stooped, and, strong as any Nile girl, lifted her mistress. Not on to the bed, but on to the window-couch, where she could see the City and Pharos, the blue of the racing sea. Like an old nurse she held her, relaxing her, murmuring the ritual: *'Let it go, my beauty, let it go';* until the taut spine began to sink and the wild eyes closed. To open again with a look of pain and trust.

"He is coming back," said Iras. "She has asked the God. He has answered. She has told me so."

The Queen said in a low voice:

"I wasn't at my best even when he left. I thought I had better try to be like a roman wife, and I didn't do it well. So I was only stupid. But he knows, he knows——"

Quiet again. After a time she got up, walked up and down the room, then turned and faced her women.

—"Charmian, Iras, listen to me. Look at me——" She was tranquil now, light-stepping as a cat, a watchful look in her eyes.

—"You have seen me, weeping for him. But there is something else I could weep for if it were possible to cry about such things. Because I, Cleopatra the Queen, as well as Cleopatra the lover, with my love, in spite of my love, must play the harlot with this man, Antony."

"Do you?" said Iras.

"I do," she said. "This love I feel; this separation which tears all of me in two, is what I must pretend to feel, for his benefit. Whether I did or not."

"I shouldn't worry," said Iras.

"I don't," she said. "Yet there is an inner hurt, more subtle and more lasting than the rest. I am a woman of some quality and this is my great love. The one time the winged Erôs opens the breast, the one time the Cyprian appears as a Bee. That does not happen twice. Not that. Yet at the same time I am the Cleopatra who must make my passion and his passion serve my turn."

"I can't see that it much matters," said Iras.—"Praise the Gods, they do."

"I praise," said the Queen, "I also wonder. I am a woman given a double thread. Which will break, and breaking, strain the other till it breaks? Or hold firm, so that the other is useless? Which is going to save me, my love or my imitation of it? Which is going to destroy me, my passion or my judgment? Which is going to keep me my kingdom, my love for Mark Antony? Or the use I must make of his love for me? Which is going to lose me my kingdom, my prostitution or my honour?"

"To me," said Iras, "this is over-nice. Besides, have you thought of the use he is making of his love for you?"

"No," said the Queen. "If only because he never thinks of it himself. However much he did it, it would never enter his head. I am afraid for myself, lest the harlot may spoil the lover, and the lover, the states- man, and the statesman, the mother; and so on, round and round. Weaving an infernal net in which we shall both be caught—and Charmian thinks this to be only too possible."

"I hold also," said Charmian, "that there will be a fitting end; and this song of Cleopatra's one to set be- side Troy's Helen, and any queen of that kind who may be born hereafter." The Queen looked thoughtfully at her.

"That is all very well for you, Charmian, to whom this life is nothing but a rehearsal of a play that is to be. Or that has been. Or that is going on all the time some- where else. Part of a mystery I do not at all understand. Sometimes I believe you, but always I am sure that what I have to deal with is this life. While Iras does not believe you at all. What can I do between two such counsellors but try and make all that I can of this world

247

and hope that Charmian's may have pity of me?''

"How took the Lord Antony this parting?" said Charmian, bluntly.

"As such men take such things—with a furious impatience that he cannot have everything at once; while already he is cursing his ship that it does not sail faster. It is a good thing that he will find waiting for him a wife he is tired of. He will be less ready to hear his people call me wanton——

—"Oh, it sticks, my women, it sticks in my throat—what men will say of me—that I am leading the greatest man on earth, through his senses, to make a eunuch of him; and all for the sake of a brat I have chosen to call their Cæsar's. Before our course is run I will make something else of Antony. The world has chosen to forget I was a maid when I came to Cæsar's bed."

Said Charmian: "Lies die."

"It is not," said the Queen, "all a lie. That is the core of my grief. Let us speak the truth between us while we may. With my love there goes something that was nothing to do with love, that praises the Gods that my body and his, my affection and his affection will serve a little private itch that belongs to the Queen Cleopatra, to show the white teeth of the Lagidæ, blood-pointed and grinning at the Roman Wolf."

"We are all like that," said Iras: "the thing is to know it and conceal it and make it serve our turn."

"I know," said the Queen, "but there are times when I would spit it in men's faces——"

"Let it go," said Iras, anxiously: "weep for him.

Think of that beauty and the glory of that strength. That you may make a fair highway between you yet——"

"Also," added Charmian, "that if he knew it, he would forgive you this."

"Forgive me—yes. But then he is single-minded. That is partly why I love him. There might come a time when he would count the world well lost for me. Not I for him."

"He," said Iras, simply, "is not Cæsarion's father."

"Yes," said the Queen, with a little hard smile—"you are thinking: 'what, after all, is an Antonine?' Yet it hurts that I should say that very thing to myself." Then softly, her eyes grown wild: "Antony, Antony. Oh love, love, love, my love, my love—what have I done to my true love?"

That cry brought Charmian and Iras to her, to hold her in their arms, glancing over her head, seeking right and left for consolation. Reminding her of what had gone, of what would come back, of what could never be lost. Until Cleopatra drew away from them, and into the wildness of her eyes there came something stern.

"There is one thing he has done for me. My sister, Arsinoë, will trouble us no more."

They knew what that meant, who lived in an age familiar with the death of the inconvenient and untroubled by it.

"You asked him for that?" said Iras.

"It is the kind of thing I have to ask. Though I would not seek her death, if she had not first sought mine. I could have had it from Cæsar. Love is often sealed in blood. Cæsar cost me two brothers; and you will remember how Berenice, for hatred of us all, ran on the knife?

—"As I said, it is a custom of our House to seal love with blood. Preferably our own. And do not forget, it may some day be my blood.

—"Besides, besides, it may be that I am going to pay Antony back in another way——"

"You mean," said Iras, "that you are again with child?"

"Yes. I think so. And, as Charmian would say: 'Everything will be altered by it. And nothing': what she learned up at Delphi, when she went to the Oracle for us. Do you remember?—it was to know if our cat would get well. We were little girls, but she stayed a long time, and came back with what we called her Pythia's poses. Until one day she really prophesied—do you remember—that Charkon, the black door-keeper, would find the jewel I lost? And one day we found him saying his prayers to it, and were too excited to have him punished. It was then we knew she was a priestess, our priestess, given us to interpret the will of the Gods.

—"And if I am with child again, it means another Lagid born. And another hold on the man whose hold is on me——" Her tears had dried away like dew, leaving her fresh as a plant recovered after a storm.

—"Even while he is still in my body, he alters the play. And I—I shall have paid, and paying is a purification.

—"As Iras says: we must not be over-nice."

VII

EPHESUS, which had fallen to Rome, made no attempt to imitate her mistress. Serene in her superb past, she offered civilities to her new garrison and went on her way. High as Chartres over La Beauce, her Temple roofs spread, ruling the city. Temple of the Goddess the Ephesians called Artemis, as little like the roman Diana as the hellene Korê, Apollo's holy sister, the Defender of Maids. At Ephesus she was our Lady, '*la Très Belle, la Très Amoureuse, La Mère de Toutes Choses.*' Like the Black Madonna at Chartres, Notre Dame de Sous-Terre, she was hardly represented as human, but as a head on a body with a hundred breasts, each with a bee for a nipple; and was served by men and women with rites that were full of bees and doves and flutes. Also her enormous temple was a sanctuary, for all sorts of men in difficulties, from the outlaw to the runaway politician. While she reigned at Ephesus, all men might come to her, and she hid them in her house, and they stayed in her cool halls till times were better; and many curious conversations must have echoed in the porticoes and up and down the high pillar-shafts.

Here, a kind of Iphigenia, with no brother to seek her, and less creditable hopes to sustain her, had come

the princess Arsinoë, the only other survivor of Aulêtês'
five children. A princess who had walked in a roman
triumph, and seen her sister watching it. Visiting that
sister, nursing the triumphator's son, received from her
her safety, her liberty, her means of life. Unforgivable
gifts.

Such treatment does not make for love, but for fury,
revenge, and sometimes chastity thrown in. Five years
before she had left Rome, to follow the Goddess from
shrine to shrine—the Goddess of the Electras of this life.

She must often have told herself that story, with Cleopatra for Clytemnæstra, and for Orestes, a dead child.
If Aulêtês made a strange Agamemnon, her sister was
more satisfactory; 'I might have been Queen of Egypt
if the bitch hadn't jumped into Cæsar's bed. Instead she
saw to it that I marched the roman streets. Took the
Capitol walk that morning, and I wore chains, though
they were made of gold.

—'Told me one of us had to do it, and that Cæsar
couldn't make her because of Cæsarion. Cried, the hell-
cat, when it was over, and said it was the best she could
do; and asked me to take what I wanted and wait for
better times and she'd give me Cyprus, and wasn't
Cæsarion beautiful and anyhow we Lagids had held on
to Egypt——'

A tale that ran like that in her mind. Memory of one
nightmare morning when she had walked the nightmare,
awake, on stones, a boiling crowd, howling unknown
words, pointing, jeering, spitting, with gestures lewd
enough. She had believed that at the end she would

252

be given to the soldiers, not hurried away in a litter with drawn curtains to a house where she had lain, unconscious, for days. To wake and not be able to remember if there had been the soldiers or not. Anyhow, on that walk, she had endured a hundred defilements. There had been a drawing on a cart, from which a man bawled—.

As she had passed the balcony where Cleopatra sat—it was always then that a black patch slid across the memory-screen. For it did not fit what she had actually seen—her sister's young face, solemn with destiny. Instead she made a design to fit the patch, a mask of triumphant, leering hate. And because she had invented this, she hated the real face more. When they were children, she remembered, it was Cleopatra who had spoken against the hate of Lagid for Lagid. Saying that the House was destroying itself: that they must find a way to do differently.

This had been Cleopatra's notion of doing differently. An adolescent girl, Arsinoë had received a frightful shock; a caste-ridden young egoist had been turned into a devil that morning in the streets of Rome; and Cleopatra, against Charmian's and Iras' advice, had been infinitely silly afterwards in trying to comfort her. Console without understanding—a problem that was beyond her age. Better if she had shouted at her:

'Now you see which of us is Queen.' Instead, she had tried to pacify a girl crazy with humiliation and terror, asking her for tolerance, pardon. With the result that Arsinoë had instantly become a bait for every

Egyptian who wanted to put an end to the ruling house. Men who fell into several classes. Idealists who imagined that, the Lagidæ gone, they could keep the Romans out. Men obsessed by hatred, who would swallow even the Romans to satisfy their hate; and realistic optimists who decided that these new masters, their attention divided, would provide an ideal world in which to hatch their own eggs.

So Arsinoë went to her life, a life of prayers seasoned with conspiracy. A maid's life, when unmarried princesses were rarer even than common women. A life of virginity, with treason for relish, mitigated at Ephesus by the affectionate interest of the High Priest of the Temple. With him came the general Serapion, an Egyptian, and a hater of the royal house. Their joint feelings they toned down to a commonplace plot. Cleopatra was to be assassinated, and Arsinoë, placed by him on the throne, was to take Serapion in marriage. A foolish business, whose only reality lay in the chance of the Queen's death. To whom Mark Antony had said simply: 'You had better leave it to me.'

News travelled slowly round the Mediterranean in winter, when the land routes were half impassable and letters went by ship; and the ships did not sail or found themselves in another port or sunk. Or were taken by pirates, as the young Cæsar had once been. Which profession Pompey's son, Sextus, had adopted, holding up the seas, keeping the corn of Egypt out of Rome. All in the name of his dead father and in honour of the

Republican Party; a source of endless trouble to the Triumvirate.

So, when news came, a great deal of it was liable to arrive together; and to Arsinoë, serving an altar in a court open to the sky, among a stir of doves and bee-murmur from the sacred hives, a number of letters were handed.

One described poisons prepared: the name of a cup-bearer: of a man who could handle a knife. Or by another means, poison for Cleopatra's bed-linen: her finger-nails: her hair. She stood beside a pillar, reading these; and the next, telling of Mark Antony's arrival in Alexandria and his life there as Consort; reading which left her walking round and round the column. Round and round and round the great drum on which Eurydice is carved, in high relief, walking between Hermes and Death. Round went the lovely figures, walking with the grace of Hellas. Round them and round them and round hurried the graceless woman, reading and reading again about the sister who had been given grace. Given it now for the second time—grace in the sight of the chief man living. First in privacy and quiet, then in open splendour, a double serving of the favour of Gods and men. First Cæsar; then Antony. First the Master; then the Successor. First a son; now rumour of another.

Sister and sister. One on foot; one on a throne. One in chains; one crowned. One a queen; one an exile. One a lover; one a maid. One a mother; one barren. The three-word-tune cut across her step. To fit it in,

Arsinoë would have to dance. Dance on hot stone. She would have to dance to that tune—— Arsinoë's face was pale. Drops distilled on her forehead. From heavy-pale, it turned yellow; from yellow, almost a green, like wax, as the daimon of the Lagid hate entered into her and took possession. Stopped her short and sent her walking round the column the other way, against the course of the sun; passing now on her left side Death, Hermes and Eurydice, brandishing the letter as one of the Furies her snake; as her hair began to knot, escape from its fillet and slip; and the blood suffused her eyes, making red in the one place where red must not be.

At the same instant, led by a hard-faced centurion, a squad of soldiers climbed the temple stair. At the peristyle they halted, wheeled to the left and made off to the back of the huge building, where were the cella of the Treasury and the Priests' offices.

The letter damp and twisted in her fist, she went on walking. Until she found herself at the little altar she served, and a woman waiting there with an offering of doves, Aphrodite's birds, as the greek Arsinoë remembered. Birds that are proper to love and to love only; that the common people offered to this Artemis, whom they imagined Lover and Mother of every living thing.

Then, to the woman's terror, she began to deface the ritual; with a pin pricking out the birds' eyes, breaking off their coral feet, tearing out their tongues, before she slowly wrung their pearl throats; stamping her foot and with unspeakable words summoning, not the great

Goddess, but the Chthonian Gods. The woman gasped and would have screamed, until she saw that a Possession had entered this priestess; and fell down in panic and horror of what her stamping was bringing up out of the ground.

At that instant a temple servant came out to say that the High Priest would have a word with the Lady Arsinoë.

Leaving the blood and the feathers and the offering unconsummated, she followed him.

She did not find him in the little cell off the Treasury, used as a convent parlour might be for visitors who had business with the temple-ministers. She looked for him impatiently, to whom also letters must have come. Instead she saw a man in armour, a roman officer, and beside him two soldiers. He had a paper in his hand.

"You are the Lady Arsinoë Lagos?" he said. "Daughter of the Ptolemy called Aulêtês and by the grace of the Senate and the Roman People one-time Pharaoh of the Egyptians?" Then she knew. Opened her mouth and did not shut it again. He began to read. A list of treacheries—crimes and meditated crimes. Some false. Others true. Ending with the formula many persons who have failed to get what they want or keep what is their own have finally had to hear:

". . . *Conspiracy against the government of the land, the maintenance of public order, the peace of the present sovereign, the Lady Cleopatra, her crown and dignity. . . . The punishment whereof is death—to be*

257

*executed at my instant order: by my officer: the
centurion, Quintus Valerius Palla. . . .*

"I, *Marcus Antonius. . . . Autocrator. . . .*

"*Given at Alexandria. . . .*"

She spat at him; and the soldiers not having closed
behind her as she entered, she ran out backwards. Then
turned and fled, something like a hen running, with
long strides down the corridor, holding up her robe. For
all its youth, her body had never been quick like Cleopatra's and apt for each change of use. Just as her skin,
though fair and white, was thick, as though the blood
behind did not heat it to transparency. So, when she
ran, you would have thought a much older woman
was escaping, nor might even have noticed that she was
running for her life.

The centurion shouted: "Catch her!"

Then, since there could be no escape and the thing
was to be done as quietly as possible, he marched out.
The soldiers fell in behind him, and tramped after her
at the Legion's pace.

At the end of the corridor, she glanced back. There
were three men coming after her, bright with metal.
That meant death. A moment after they had reached
her, she would be dead. It would hurt, a hideous hurt
first. Then she would be gone, thrust out into the grey.
Out of the house of her body. A bloody shell, dripping
on the stones. The warm body she walked about in.
Lived in: lived *inside.* She was not ready for it to happen: 'Maiden, Maiden, Artemis——' Then she remembered that would not do. This was not the place of the

Maiden, but the Mother; the Mother who liked men-things like those soldiers tramping. Tramp. Tramp. She could hear them coming, though they were round a corner, just out of sight. She must stay out of their sight one second more. Hide, of course, she must hide. She ran out, out of the shadow of the high walls into the courtyard again. Out of dim light into full sun. Ran across, back to the altar where the birds were still bleeding. The woman had gone away. There was no one about. She yelled: "They cannot kill me. This place is sanctuary!" The whole vast place, with its colonnades, was empty. She realised they had closed the Temple. The place was no more sanctuary. Rome had put out her hand and stopped sanctuary.

She was alone, in the Temple of Artemis at Ephesus, alone, with three roman soldiers after her. There was no High Priest any more. The place was turned into a cage—a box to put her inside to be killed. As the three men swung round the corner she started to run again, cut across the open space and ran on into the vast shrine itself. Up the half-dark, to where, at the end, stood the great figure of the Hundred Breasts. The Earth-Mother, her huge eyes staring out of her round curls, the Holy Bee shining on the tip of each breast.

She tore on and up the altar steps, scrambling on to the altar itself, kicking down the gold ornaments, reaching up to the waist of the image, tearing at the gold cross-work over the age-blackened wood, snatching at the breast-cluster thrust out over it. They were strong, the Earth-Mother's breasts. She threw herself at them

259

as though at a rock. But a rock is of stone, and stone is strong, and takes no notice. You cannot hide yourself in stone.

It was then that the sound of their coming made her glance back. They were half-way up the hall, and noisy in the half-dark. Tramp. Tramp. Jingle. Jingle. Their harness and their strong legs moving so easily. One of them had legs thick as a tree. "Sacrilege," she turned and yelled again. "This is Sanctuary." "Catch her," said the centurion again, spat on his hands and loosened his sword. All three men sprang up the steps. On top, their chests stood level with the altar. She was beating her forehead till it bled against the bees on the lower rank of breasts.

At their touch on her skirts and ankles, she let go. Turned full round and glared at them, her hair falling, foam round her mouth mixed with trickling blood. Stooped to wrench her skirts tight, her nails ripping the backs of their hands.

"This place is holy! Worms will eat you!" (It had not been easy to find an officer who had any wish to do this business. A killing of a royal woman in other men's Sanctuary. The centurion might have flinched, until he remembered that a Roman has only to obey his proper orders, however difficult, and the Gods are satisfied.) She had managed to get her foot onto one of their hands and was grinding it in. Then as she saw that they would be ordered to spring up and drag her down, she released it. Drew herself up and said quietly: "I will come down;" her voice echoing down the bare stones; and its sound had now changed, to a quality which made them instantly let go of her.

There for an instant she stood, free of them, standing high up on the altar; the bee-points shining behind her head.

"I will come down." She sat down quietly, her feet swinging in air, her dress pulled down to her ankles; and the officer felt an impulse to give her his hand to alight. She let herself down gently onto the top of the steps.

"Now," she said, opening her tunic, "in the presence of the Goddess, strike! Her servant, Arsinoë of Egypt, born and anointed of the Gods. Last of the Companions of the Greek Alexander—His body!—" She leaned back, her hands gripping the altar's edge, her throat straining as though arched against a knife, her dress open to the waist. The centurion, looking hard at her left breast, drew his sword.

VIII

"SAID the Queen to the Triumvir——"

"Said the Triumvir to the Queen——"

On either side of a table sat Antony and Cleopatra, one opposite the other, in a very private cabinet of another Palace, at Pelusium, near the eastern frontier of Egypt. Autumn 37 B.C. Their second meeting. A year after the birth of their first child.

It was night. The table was covered with memoranda and writing materials. It was nearly two years since they had seen one another, who had come now, unknowing, to the meeting after which there is no parting any more.

"Said the Queen to the Triumvir——"

"Said the Triumvir to the Queen—— It is her turn to say something. He is dumb. Fear and shame have struck speech from his lips."

"Fear and shame only?"

"Wonder and admiration, gratitude and delight; with a very great joy the Gods have given us no name for. Everything that ever has or ever will make up love. Such love as no man before has ever had for any woman, the innumerable loves—Erôs on foot and with

262

wings. Aphrodite-at-home, in a shrine. Or sitting on the moon. Holding a star or snatching a rose or raising a child. In her Bath or her Bed. Out of an egg. Out of the sea.

—"Though every man says this, Sweet, yet it is true. True for him and for her, for all and each. Since there is no measure to such love. Each is different; each is the same. Each may be greater than the other and yet no less.

—"You *do* understand what I mean? You're laughing. Let me guess why. Where did I learn all this? Your doing. Ask another——"

"Said the Queen to the Triumvir——"

"Said Cleopatra to Antony——"

"Said Cleopatra of Egypt to a Consul of Rome: How many times *have* you been married, Antony?"

He scratched his great curled head.

"Must I go into that? Let's see. There was Antonia, and Fulvia and Octavia. Then you. Mistress, sweet friend, now there is only you——" Though the table stood between them, she drew herself a little away, into herself.

"Antony, it won't do. Why have you just married that roman woman?" She was surprised when he answered her steadily:

"Whether you believe it or not, the answer is—that I might not return to you with empty hands. That, through her, I might get her brother where I want him, and keep him there."

"Fool! what is a sister to him?"

"To either of us, nothing. To my intention, a screen."

She shook her head. "I know those screens. Pushed aside, they still lie about for men to stumble over." But Antony leaned suddenly across the table, with a gesture so hungry as to check her withdrawal, send a rose to her cheek. It was now as though they had only certain formal things to do, certain words to repeat, before their conclusion was certain. Certain and dangerous and lovely and fated for them. Centuries before, or before time was reckoned, and it all went to music and immortal beings watched. Yet for good manners' sake and the ritual necessary at such moments, they must tell each other certain things and be told. Question and answer— before going through the door which once passed can never be opened again.

> *'Our ballast is a rose,*
> *Our way lies where God knows,*
> *And Love knows where—*
> *We are in Love's hand to-day——'*

A rose indeed! Our ballast is towns and towers, ships and palaces, lands and peoples and empire over the earth and men. If you forget that, Cleopatra Lagos, you are a woman who has jumped on to a throne when she was only fit for a man's lap. She heard Antony speaking, his voice husky as hers, and as she knew from a rapture like her own. On with it then. He said:

"Then let the Queen tell the Triumvir what has happened since they parted, that has brought them here

264

together again to this place." He spoke with authority. In the formal opening again she read his mind and its knowledge, matching with hers. She drew her wide-winged chair a little closer to the table and put her elbows on it, her chin in her cupped hands. Rolled papers, tied with cords and some sealed, lay all about. She nodded at them.

"Hints for kings. Men who make history do well to stop sometimes and listen to the history they have made. Let me see. 'Triumvir' is a new word. I shall call this man I am about to speak of 'the Roman.' And this last of all his wives—if she is a wife—shall be called the Greek Woman.

—"To begin with, when he first left her, no one could blame him. Octavian, his dear colleague, was paying his troops with the estates of such of the Roman's friends as remained alive. Saying it was Cæsar's wish.

—"Of course the Roman saw that he must stop that. But did he see that what Octavian intended—whether he allowed or disallowed it—was to make the Roman equally hated? While Fulvia, the Roman's roman wife, and his brother Lucius, left behind in charge of his interests, showed their care by making a war of their own against Octavian. Fulvia got into armour. It must have suited her. (What sort of a woman looks well in war-gear?)—and out broke your civil war again. Both sides called each other the same names by proclamation. Both sides said at once they had no quarrel with the Roman. Both sides called him back to judge between them. (Which side meant to abide by that judgment?)

—"Have I got it right?" Antony nodded.

—"So back went the Roman to Rome, with as much money for ballast as the Greek Woman could give him. Whether he likes to remember it or not, it was she who sent him, when their child was unquickened and their love just lit. If her imitation of a roman wife was a failure, if she ran round ten times after her tail like a distracted cat, yet she got him on board his ships. Not only because he wanted to see his roman wife in armour, or save what he could of his friends' estates, or kick Octavian's backside, or save his country; but also because a certain general Labienus had made up *his* mind—a mind made up of three hates, of Octavian, the Roman and the dead Cæsar—and was coming in from Asia at the head of the Parthian Horse, to put an end to all three. (Only it is easier sometimes to put an end to the living than to the memory of the dead.)

—"So the Roman went up north, soldiering; and at Tyre he found a siege, and at Stratonica he found a siege, and at Mylassa he found another siege, and at Alabanda and at Ephesus.

—"At Ephesus he heard of Octavian, at Perusia, of the taking of *that* city, and of the pardon given to his brother, Lucius, and the exile of his mother and Fulvia to Sicyon. Understanding that Octavian in showing mercy did it to tie his hands." Antony nodded again.

—"It was not mercy. It never is mercy. It can never be mercy. He was showing his dexterity, playing on the mercy that is in the Roman. Once they were gone, he showed no more. Who has not heard the name by which he is now known throughout Italy, after the dinner where the Matrons appeared as the Immortals, and he, the feast-giver, wore Apollo's dress. That Apollo for whose propitiation men scourge themselves in his temples—Apollo the Destroyer. He is young, this Octavian, for the part of Apollo Omêstês.

—"As he is young to share the earth with such a man as this Roman, whom people take for Dionysos, the Preserver, Dionysos-of-the-Flower. He whom men ask for life and he gives them a long life, as the Orphics say. But I hold that what he gives is immortality in pinches. He can spare it. Just now and then. As now to us."

"*Salve, regina*," she heard him murmur, his eyes on her, the great head unhelmeted, the hair sprung back in tight curls, the shoulders above his corselet showing like the bones of Hercules, his ancestor. But that night his desiring eyes were full also of a benevolence, like the God who sends the rain down and the flowers up; who is sometimes a tree. Cleopatra went on:

"So to translate from the heavens to the earth (which happens more often than we think, and is probably happening all the time), the earth is now divided between these two men, Eidola of the Immortals, this Apollo and this Dionysos, the death-bringer and the life: between Octavianus Cæsar and Marcus Antonius, between two Romans. Two Gods need a third—a Goddess. Two men, a woman. The strife that is behind the strife of armies is their strife; the war between life and death. This is what we are watching; a war that does not end

267

when the peoples fall exhausted into quiet. So speaks the Goddess——"

"And the woman——?"

"Agrees. Meanwhile, and still in the terms of war in heaven, it is possible for us to reckon up our forces. The Roman-Preserver-Dionysos has one—a War Goddess, on his side, as Fulvia-in-armour shows. Or should one say one of the Furies, an Erinys? Only at the same time, Aphrodite is watching as before Troy. Nor will she desert the Hero she loves best."

It was then that, for the first time, she looked into his eyes; and he sprang up as if to knock over the table and its papers, lift her up and bear her away—out of the palace at Pelusium, onto a ship; to carry them further than Colchis or any Kronos-isle. Away from the last bloodied agony of the Roman Republic. Take there and then their immortal nature on them, their doings in eternity; walk out into it, one beside the other; find the crew waiting and the ship. Or else a little boat, no bigger than Hercules' gold dish he paddled in to the Gates of Ocean. A dish that turned out to be the sun.

Like a young mother holding her child he saw her now, her arms folded across her breast, and all her bearing that of a woman, accepting what has been laid upon her; not only as a lover, or as a mother, but as a queen and a ruler of men. A drawn sword could not have held him from her. Now, as he trembled, his own clattered at his side. She began to speak again, her voice hard and quick and low-pitched.

"After Perusia, the Destroyer ate. Three hundred

268

of the citizens. 'So thin,' he said, 'it takes fifty to make a bite.' So they were slaughtered. And to Cæsar's *manes*. Since when have the Immortals added men-eaters to their number?"

"It wasn't as bad as that," Mark Antony said simply.

"It was worse. If this is your roman government, you will soon have no people left to govern. It was Cæsar who said: 'You kill in order to rule, not rule to kill.' For result there was one prayer to be heard throughout Italy, and that for the Roman's return. The men who had killed Cæsar and the men who had avenged him were united in this; against this Octavian with his butcheries, his pandering to the legions in his dead uncle's name, his stripping of the high citizens in his name again, but for his own ends. Which are—" she spoke shrewdly—"to buy himself an army for use against the Roman. So that one man, not two—for your Lepidus counts for nothing in this—shall have the rule of the earth."

He nodded again, but reluctantly, as at a thought which, however obvious to others and to his statesman's mind, he was loath to face. Cleopatra went on:

"He did more. He sent the Roman no help against the Parthians, ordering his gallic legions back to Rome. Against this, your pirate chief, great Pompey's son, whose ships kept the Greek Woman's corn-fleet out of Ostia, joined with the Roman. Then Octavian was frightened. Then the Roman saw his chance and crossed the Hellespont; met him in Italy, where the two scuffled bloodily for power. Putting off Dionysos and putting on Hercules. Until—" the quick voice broke into a laugh—"there was trouble in heaven again; when the war goddess, Fulvia, changed her clothes and died like any mortal woman in Sicyon."

She looked at him to see if he was grieved. Saw that he did not care, and a lovely lightness came into her voice, one of the changes that made him compare it to all the sounds of air and water that fly and flow and run. In anger the storm-shout of the Apennines. In joy, the pure crystal that rises through the sand-bubbles winking at the mouth of the spring. In sorrow, the storm lulling itself to itself. In high conversation, the strong breeze that bends the corn. In passion, the harp-tune that runs down from the crest of pine-trees and a thousand miles inland repeats the sea. In motherhood, holding her children in the hollow of each arm, as the wave-touch on gold beaches, the kiss of the pure.

"And then," she was saying, "the earth was allowed to laugh again. Everyone on earth, except perhaps the Greek Woman, and she had just had a baby which was the Roman's, and found it difficult to explain to her subjects why he should choose this moment to say he was about to take a new concubine elsewhere and call her his wife. The Greek Woman put it that way. Her people differently. She had made a new law to make the Roman her consort. Now she had to make another, to explain when a wife in Egypt is not a wife in Italy; and how the Queen of Egypt was a wife in one place and a concubine somewhere else, and in most places a harlot.

—"But I am telling you this story the wrong way. Listen to what it is possible to do under your roman laws.

—"It was just at this time Octavian took a wife also, Clodia, the Roman's step-daughter, child of his wife Fulvia by another of her husbands, the beautiful Clodius, who was Cæsar's lover once. (The first man who has a child will die, not in labour, but the women will laugh him to death.)

—"For reasons we are both guessing, and guessing right, Octavian sent her back, a maid, to her mother. But when Pompey's son made friends with the Roman, he tried again, the pirate's wife's twice-widowed sister, Scribonia."

—"Shall I wait while you say that after me, so as to be sure you have it right?"

—"When the Roman returned, it was Octavian who persuaded him to—marry, I suppose he would call it— Octavia, his sister. But Octavia was married already and six months gone with child. So, to oblige them both, her husband divorced her, and the Roman took her to his house to have another man's child, and when it was born, sent it back with his greetings; at the same moment as the Greek Woman was having *her* baby by the same Roman, who had only one husband and only a share in him.

—"Are you sure you have this right? Remember it, for it's important.

—"But, just as the Roman, having got what he wanted in the City or thinking he had, was off once more round

271

the earth, the news came, just as it did to Alexandria, that the day Scribonia had borne Octavian his first daughter, he found out what her other husband had found out about her temper and sent *her* away. Divorcing the wife this time and keeping the baby. Or rather, exchanging her for the Lady Livia, also six months gone. Only this time I've heard it was Octavian's baby—' Antony shook his head—'and again the husband handed her over, this time to Octavian, for keeps. Only calling the child after the husband who was *not* its father, Claudius Drusus Nero; and when the Goddess Virtue heard about it, she fell off her pedestal; and when they took her image down to the sea to purify it, it sank."

Antony broke into a roar of laughter. The Queen went on serenely:

"That was why I asked how often you had been married. If you call it marriage. This with your talk of the Roman Household and of Roman Law.

—"How am I to understand? For what reason have you sent for me, here at Pelusium? How am I to know what it is you want of me? Or of the world——?"

Rhetorical questions. Part of the formal things to be said, the mockery he had earned. Stuff of a thousand jests between them in their future, who were hurrying to a marriage faster than lovers ever went before.

Antony spoke quietly:

"There is only one thing that you have not understood, Lady Cleopatra, that in all this I have had no desire, ultimately, save in you, nor hope in any future but in our own and in Cæsarion's——" (There's Cæsar in his eyes. Mine in my new son. Like Hercules I've sewn the earth with brats, but never before by a Queen. She gets sons. And by a woman, in herself, by her office, a Goddess manifest.)

—"What use were I to you, a man whose authority was threatened every hour? To insure it, I had to return—to make sure that in this Triumvirate there should be one leader. Not three wild horses to part Rome's chariot between them. Now matters are set. Under the Gods they must keep the shape I have given them." (True enough. It would be all true if I knew Octavian's mind. Have I known it? Do I dare know it?)

—"So I have come at last. To bring you my work. To show you what I have had the mind to do, and now the power. What only we can do together." (That's true; whatever else is a lie, this is truth. If it can be done, only we can do it. If we can do it, it can be done.)

—"Look at those papers I have put out before you. They are Cæsar's memoranda. His ideas, his wishes, his last plans. Study them well." (Come away, girl. Let's be off. We will rule in another place. Come away, come away.)

—"You can sum them up in a sentence. If they are carried out, the world will be governed not from Rome but from Alexandria." (Come away, lass, come away. Or our boat will be gone. The ship I saw, standing in from the north, that's lying now down in the harbour, in the dark waters. I knew her by the thing she had shown on her mast. They'd hung up the Fleece to

273

show who she is, and we know the Crew. It's shining still and the Heroes are sitting at the oars, the Heroes of her house and mine, of the Roman and the Greek. Ready for the Roman Antony and the Greek Cleopatra, wiser than Medea, and fairer and with purer hands——)

—"What are you thinking of, girl? Cleopatra, listen. Isn't it our luck that the sum of what we want brings us straight into each other's arms? Since first I saw you I have wanted only this, to make you the earth's mistress, in a City that has surpassed Rome, and your son Cæsar's successor. While you and I reign together, and our children, a confederacy of kings.

—"This Cæsar saw. He died before he could do this. Tell me—do you want to see his work in yourself, in your son, through me, perfected?"

"I am a woman," she said. "If my man says 'play for power with me,' I will play."

"You are a queen also."

"That doubles it." (I wish, I wish this one thing were different. If I hated him, I could not say 'no.' Without him, were he Octavian, I should be lost. Don't think like that. One day I shall punish him for the truth of it. Not more than I shall myself, O Roman, I shall never leave. What is he saying?)

"The Republic is at its death. No more already than a corpse twitching. It is our turn now." (*Our time now*. Words like bells. Bells tell the hours on ships and the Argo is waiting. Great Hercules, you were on that sailing. Be with Antony now. Steer our ship.)

—"Sweet, what more? You have agreed. What more is

there? Only to send for wine, send for Charmian and Iras. No woman was ever better served. Tell them, and let us drink to our luck. What pair ever began such an adventure with so grave a face?"

(Did she look out of the window? Has she seen that ship?) After a little silence she answered:

"I will send for Charmian and Iras. You are right, Antony. They will stand by us to the end and after——" (They will, they will. When I would be alone, Iras can have him. I mean in years ahead. The door is open. I can walk through to him now. Into my joy. Then it will be shut and there will be no opening it. I will leave it open one last hour, and though I am his, I will be my own; and before I enter his house, I will make him face our fear.)

—"I thought I heard them come. Only it was not the step of a girl. Antony, a moment past, did you hear a step outside? Like a man's with a great tread but light? Almost to the door and then it turned. One of your officers, perhaps? I mean we must not be disturbed. It is gone—why go to the window, Antony? Antony— there is nothing below but the harbour and the sea."

(The light has gone out. The Hero came to our door to fetch us and went away. Why did he come so far and then go back?) Antony let fall the curtain, blue as the deep outside, and came back slowly to his seat, pushing back from his forehead curls that were damp. This time the Queen was leaning across the table, smiling at him.

"Antony, husband, lord—it is as you say. All is well,

and all is well, and one way or another all shall be well. That is the Goddess' marriage prophecy. The best she can do for us.

—"But before we start, you and I will look our fear in the face. We will begin this great game for power, and the governorship of the earth shall pass into the hands of the Antonines and the Lagidæ. This will happen. Or—it may be that Octavian will have what he wants in this life, even of us. Antony! Do not toss your great chin and snort when I say the name 'Octavian.' How many times already has he worsted you?" (You without me.) "At twenty-four this knock-kneed boy, who, on his third marriage shaved himself for the first time, has fooled the hero, Mark Antony. I should have him murdered. Why don't you? And do not answer me that 'it isn't done.' After the men you yourself have proscribed. Nor did you hesitate over Cicero. What do the Roman People care for the foreign woman, palming off her bastard as their Cæsar's?

—"Antony, do not wince. I will have my say before I come to you for ever. Let no man say that two heroes went into battle with their eyes shut——"

The superb man opposite her sat with downcast eyes. The image of the Argo, the steps of Hercules faded. This woman was showing him their way to the heavens. A long way round, but the right one. And he wouldn't have Octavian murdered, but meet him as a man should. Dead, his ghost would daunt him more. Yet he *was* daunted. Cleopatra heard him mutter: "It's as though he could steal my manhood." She nodded: "It is

276

what the priest in Egypt said: *'When you are away, your spirit stands up. When you meet him, it sinks.'*

—"Antony, it won't do. You are not to miscalculate or under-estimate Octavian. For your aims are one. But he has no Greek Woman and her son to be for him and against him at once. He can get what he wants without change in the seat of power and all the shattered pride that goes with it. The people loathe him. Yes. You they love. I know that. But he will ask no benefit from them to forward his love-affairs."

Mark Antony gave the thrust of his shoulders that a man makes breasting a wave.

"Let him be. I am not likely to forget him. But, O woman of cool judgment, our children are *my* heirs, and a man like me fights well for his beloved woman and the child of his body. What has Octavian got to put against that? Answer me. . . ."

She raised her head, laughing coolly up at him.

"Only remember this—that if it had not been for you, I would have made him mine. Yes and by the Gods' mercy it was not. It was this and not that. I may never have to go that way, and now I will set out on this. The Queen enters. And where the Queen goes, the woman goes too; and only the Goddess knows the end. Up Lagos. This ends my oracle——"

Across the table he looked at her with a troubled face, as though indeed he feared she would go, go to Octavian. Vanish with the Fleece and the ship and the eidôlon of Hercules. Go and leave him with an Octavian equally terrible as man or spirit. Instead he saw her rise, walk

277

round the table, brushing as she passed a roll of Cæsar's memoranda, so that it fell on the floor. Then, before he realised her meaning, he saw her take off the small snake coronet that signed her Egyptian, and hold it out to him, saying:

"Call Charmian, call Iras for a witness of this."

But what he remembered for ever, as if his gilt corselet had been stripped off him, was her breast against his. As though the touch of her body had turned its gold to air.

APPENDIX

Taking the historic and the traditional evidence together, the following note may help to clarify our notions as to what manner of woman Cleopatra really was. It is important here to understand that to the unprejudiced mind there is not a shred of evidence to show that she had amorous dealings with any on earth other than Cæsar and Mark Antony. In the first instance, she (who was theoretically the source of Law) could not help herself. There is a dim tradition extant that, for her protection and the people's also, the priests spoke certain Words of Association over them. There is no need to make such a fuss; to repeat the historian's stock phrase about 'sixteen-year-old harlots.' She was a girl, in a desperate situation, whose actions were *ipso facto* legal. What else could she do? Walk beside her sister in Cæsar's triumph or watch it as a reigning sovereign? Her own wishes apart, which would have served best to enhance her country's prestige?

Then there is Antony, to whom she bore three children; in an age when abortion was well enough known for a debauched woman, supposing her fertile, to avail herself of it. To him she was married, by every egyptian rite; and on his divorce from Octavia, some suppose, though the question is most complicated, by roman law as well.

In truth the legend of her as a crowned courtesan has its historic origin in scandals circulated before and after her death, by Octavian, anxious and indeed obliged to justify the annexation of Egypt, her death and Antony's. A sentence in the Liber de Viris Illustribus says: "Haec tantae libidinis fuit, ut saepe prostiterit, tantae pulchritudinis ut multi noctem illius morte emeruit." For not all men whose opinion counted approved of his campaign against their great general and Cæsar's beloved friend. There were many who, apart from the Queen—if Antony had not mismanaged his affairs, and, which was even more important, not gone about in a kind of paralysed fear of Octavian— would have accepted his leadership. Both men were trying to do the same thing, and one was Cæsar's friend and spiritual son. The other at the time of his murder no more than a boy with a reputation, just or unjust, already sinister, for cruelty and corruption. (A man who became later one of the first rulers in history; and the powerful benevolence, 'the calm government and mighty toil' of his maturity, a mystery of character no one has ever yet explained.)

For the Octavian of that period and his party no story was too vile; and with grim political ability they pursued the dead, defaming their memory and their honour, destroying their statues with the records of their reign. A legend was fabricated and took root, the kind of legend the vulgar mind loves, based on the phrase 'nameless orgies.' A tale stimulating to the lower orders of the human imagination; and in the case of a royal woman, a mother and a lover, a slaughtered man and a triple suicide, kindling it to the vilest possible interpretation. A revenge of the obscure and the base on the high-fated and the high-born; insults of the enemies of the rose.

As for documents, there is a tradition of memoirs, used by subsequent writers, of a court-doctor, once the Queen's body-physician, then dismissed her service for 'infamous professional conduct'—possibly something to do with indiscretion over a poisoning. This is hardly the testimony to take seriously. It was just such a book as Octavian might have paid him to write. Yet this tradition of the lost MS. of a disgraced man seems to persist for truth.

Yet what woman ever lived, conspicuous, gifted, attractive and alone, who is not a common target for such talk? Gossip too that served an arch-enemy's turn? One thing is certain. Antony was not a man to whom the esoterics of sex or the vagaries of oriental vice would have appealed. They would have given him a headache, made him sick, sent him to sleep. It was not by such arts that she won him and held him and bore him three children. A roman gentleman, he would not have had such a woman mother his child.

Most royal children they were, and perfectly legitimate. The girl, Cleopatra Selênê, Cleopatra the Moon, had an after-history one would gladly know more about. Her brother Alexander Helios—they were twins—survived also, Alexander the Sun. To Antony their mother was quickly married, and with all the rites of Egypt. If later by those of Rome she must have smiled at the repetition; as a woman married by a Cardinal in Notre Dame, might repeat the ceremony, to please her husband, in the chapel of some dissenting sect.

A historian may be a man with a miraculous gift for discovering lost facts, and an equal inability to interpret them. From a broken length of pipe, he will reconstruct the drains of a city, from an altar-brick a cult. Yet hardly making the inference that these were the work of a people with a use for drains; still less that the altar implied a faith, a faith a passion based on an experience. To such the Queen is a wanton; and each baby she had an additional proof of it. Forgetting that men —historians or not—do not like to think, and so refuse to believe, in an active woman, alone, enjoying the use of · power. It is a thing that does not often happen. We are not accustomed to it. There is a void in that situation, a natural void, with space in it for fantasies about the eunuch, the woman lover, the secret lover; then, since unfortunately he remains anonymous, the exterminated lover; then, since still no one can put a name to him and the personnel of a court changes—any number of exterminated lovers. Until, for good and evil, the Arts take a hand; and the Russian Ballet sets its enchanted seal upon a myth—not upon the woman who did not, but upon the woman who could not, exist.

A plain is not necessarily less interesting than a mountain. Though, to the common mind, anything is more exciting than the flat truth that, in reality, such

women may shrug their shoulders, endure their lone-
liness and busy themselves with affairs.

Again, in the growth of the myth of the Cleopatra sex-
appeal there lies a curious contradiction, a division in
men's minds, not realised but felt. Three times the
great writer has taken hold of it to shape it in words,
Chaucer, Shakespeare, and Bernard Shaw. In Chaucer,
in the *Legend of Good Women,* she appears adorably,
love's tender, gallant martyr. What were *his* sources?
Some early french romance? A tradition now lost that
gave her honour? (It is honour of any kind that our
tradition denies her.) Then, Shakespeare; and here it
took Mr. Shaw to point out a confusion in the mind of
the greatest of poets. He shows how, for a brutal and
glorious and highly realistic three and a half acts, Shakespeare gives us a crowned wanton and the typical ruin
by such a woman of a gross soldier of ability. How then,
mounting to the full height of his genius, he wrote such
a finale as even he never surpassed, to show 'the world
well lost by such a pair.' Mr. Shaw points out that it
will not do. He has reason in this. People who have
lived the life of the first three acts of *Antony and Cleopatra* do not die with the heavens opened. There is a
dichotomy in the play's fundamental structure. But
which part is nearest history, to the disconcerting thing
that actually occurred? Is it not possible that Shakespeare's intuition was right; that abandoning the scraps
of history he knew and throwing consistency to the
winds, something mounted in him like the wine of God,
and he sat down to his finale, saying: 'This was how it

ended. This was what they were really like. They died like that, being more right than those that made them die?'

'Shall we go mourn for that, my dear——
The cold moon shines by night,
And when we wander there and here
We then do go most right.'

Only those two were no lost ghosts, comforting one another by moonlight. Shakespeare did better by them, by the woman who said of her lover, remembering their sports——

'Even his bounty,
There was no winter in't; an autumn 'twas
That grew the more by reaping. Whose delights
Were dolphin-like, they showed above his back
The element they lived in——'

Who said of his wife, smiling, as the woman of a larger world speaks:

'Your wife, Octavia, with her modest eyes
And still conclusion, shall acquire no honour
Demurring upon me.'

Who, explaining herself before the end, cries out:

'Husband, I come
Now to that name my courage prove my title . . .
And welcome, welcome! die where thou hast lived;
Quicken with kissing . . .

284

Poor venomous fool,
Be angry and dispatch. O couldst thou speak!
That I might hear thee call great Cæsar ass
Unpolicied!'

This is not the same woman as the storming, alluring, crowned strumpet of the beginning; but the more her story is scrutinised with the imagination, as well as with such facts as remain, the more it looks as though Shakespeare were right, that the intuition of his genius hit on the essential truth.

Mr. Shaw himself follows tradition, a maddening, and what is worse, a vulgar version of it. It is one of his worst plays. His queen is a merry hussy, the kind of mindless, conscienceless woman he most dislikes. Ignoring history, he even has her ill-educated, a very young Aunt Sally for his crusade against sex-romance.

In truth this canonical form of her legend as a strumpet rests on very little but a tragic story misunderstood and slander repeated. Like the pictures one knows so well. Who has not seen the Academy painting of the last century, the huge canvas which shows a large black gipsy-woman, half-naked, lolling with an air of insincere despair between crouching slaves; a small snake held firmly to a melon of a breast. And there is a bed and palm-trees and perhaps a view of the Sphinx.

A tale only men have told, and the greatest of them seems to have changed his mind at the last. (Though one has heard of a french play, played, it seems, in Paris at the end of the last century. One does not know its value, but it was written by a woman, and allows for the Queen's interest in the things of the mind. Shows her in relation to other things than power and parties and passion.)

Yet historians are unanimous. Dear old Mahaffy pointing out in parentheses that it is rather troublesome to be forced to admit that she was an excellent mother.

Only Mr. Weigall has taken a stand. A 'gossip-column historian,' but entirely readable; and in his *Life and Times of Mark Antony* something more. There something of the age is evoked that is missing from the great classic accounts, the tremendous names are used to help us to identify human beings, not as labels in an exercise on political history, or as charms or 'words of power.' The result is surprising. One wonders at the points that have been missed. Above all, he shows the Queen, taken out of her setting in a false Arabian Night, and moving in a world completely intelligible to us, a world with a touch of Regency vitality to it; and in other respects only too like our own.